SECOND HELPINGS

DYLAN MORRISON

Storm
PUBLISHING

Ebook ISBN: 978-1-83700-436-2
Paperback ISBN: 978-1-83700-437-9

Cover design: My Lan Khuc
Cover images: My Lan Khuc

Published by Storm Publishing.
For further information, visit:
www.stormpublishing.co

PROLOGUE

On particularly busy mornings, Silverman's Deli sings.

Not literally, of course. The old building has its share of secrets, but Sam Adelson's pretty sure no one's ever come across a set of vocal cords. He'd know: it's his aunt Deb's place, so Sam's been visiting since he was a kid. He's also worked here and lived in the apartment upstairs since he was in high school, and after a decade of observation, he knows all of Silverman's noises. They're so familiar that they've become part of him: every creak of the stairs, every piece of equipment's associated thump or hum, every hiss and sizzle of each well-loved dish off a menu unchanged since his grandmother's time. No, the deli doesn't *really* sing. Nobody but Sam could listen to the cacophony of a slammed Saturday and hear anything close to music.

Sam does, though. It might even be his favorite song.

He dances through his most chaotic days at Silverman's on light feet, comforted and carried by the old rhythms. This Saturday is no different. Marty at the counter ordering his sixth corned beef sandwich of the week; Eileen in the back hollering at the temperamental oven; Al Fiskar knocking on the street-facing door with the 11 a.m. pickle delivery, like clockwork. When Sam picks out a wrong note in the symphony, a hiss from the deep fryer that doesn't sound quite like it should, he calls, "Somebody forget dropping an order of fries or what?" without even turning around. He grins as Alphonse calls after him, "Ugh, me, thanks. It's spooky how you do that, though, I swear to God!"

Sam takes over for Joey at the register so they can go on break. He cheerfully rings orders for a while, slapping together the occasional sandwich or pulling a container of potato salad out of the deli case, bouncing on the balls of his feet. Sam *never* feels so good as he does on mornings like this. The pressure of the long line, the clamor of the kitchen through the serving window behind his head, has always thrummed through Sam like a metronome, keeping him steadily on beat in the present. That's where he's safest, and where he belongs.

But today, as Sam glances up, his eyes catch on a head of brown hair outside, disappearing past the edge of the front window. Instantly a scare chord crashes through the pleasant hum of his morning. It's so stupid—it was just the back of someone's *head*, for crying out loud! But for a second, there had been something familiar about it, and Sam had almost expected to see—

"Sam!" Jerking back to himself, Sam realizes the speaker is Joey, back from their break, who rolls their eyes and says, "I think that one's good, boss. Very secure."

Looking down at the paper-wrapped sandwich in his hands, Sam realizes he's used enough masking tape on it to seal off roughly seventy additional Reubens, and has mummified this one. He swallows and hands it over to the customer—she raises her eyebrows but thankfully doesn't comment—and retreats to the kitchen, trying to sink back into the day's rhythm.

Sam loves his work, his staff, this deli. He's skilled at what he does, and it feels worth doing. He reminds himself as he hacks onions and celery apart that it's good, this life he's built. He has his health, his family and friends, a great place to live, a dog with so much personality that he sometimes wants to accuse her of being a

Muppet. He's happy, more or less, and Sam knows better than anyone that it's more than he deserves.

So what if sometimes, when his guard's down, Sam finds himself wandering the old, worn mental paths, and chasing rabbits he should have let run long ago? It's nothing, that's what it is. Sam's sure it's nothing at all.

ONE

NOW: MARCH (THREE MONTHS LATER)

Near the end of West Ninth Street, a few blocks from Lake Erie, there sits a little brick building clearly marked as Silverman's Deli. The sign is old and out of date, a mixture of hand painting and neon signage that was probably gorgeous when it was put up in the sixties. Now the once-white plastic surface is yellowed, and the sparkling metallic silver paint of the lettering has faded to an anemic gray. It doesn't light up anymore, either; the neon's been badly in need of replacement since roughly the Great Blizzard of '78. It looks out of place surrounded by the Cleveland of today—this part of downtown is mostly night clubs, boutique office buildings, and high-end restaurants. Silverman's stands alone as the last sentinel of another time, and so it sticks out like a sore thumb.

Sam's always liked that about it. When he was a child, he'd loved a picture book called *The Little House*, about a house that watched a whole city get built around it. Even then it had made him think of the deli, and his aunt's warm, practical presence within. He's glad the place can't help but stand out. It allows Silverman's to distinguish itself from its surroundings as something worth noticing.

Currently it's distinguishing itself by way of the cacophony coming from the little break patio around the back of the building, but Sam doesn't imagine that's doing much for their marketing.

"It's character assassination, that's what it is. For restaurants. Restaurant assassination. Not to mention *libel*." Alphonse, who was the Head Chef when Sam took over as General Manager, has been both the Kitchen Manager *and* the Head Chef for the last few years. The man insists, very fairly, that it's two jobs and he can't possibly keep doing both, but is equally insistent in refusing to give either of them up. He keeps saying things like "I'll fight any challengers to the death!" Sam thinks he's spending too much time at work, and it's made him a little hysterical.

Then again, he might not have any right to judge, because:

"I know! I know! And do you know what else? I've been through *every* ticket and I've double checked *every* order and *no* one, I mean *no one*, who dined in has ordered that combination of things in the last *year*. So how many rats, I ask you, could Mr. Norman Endicott possibly have seen? None! That's how many! He never came in! It's all a conspiracy!" Sam, realizing he's beginning to sound like someone you might see on the news for bad reasons, takes a breath and tries to calm down. Alphonse, next to him, does the same, and they slump together for a moment against the brick.

They're talking about the Kiss of Death review. How could they not be talking about the Kiss of Death review? Since it was published two months ago in *Hearth Magazine*, and splashed across their website and social channels, it's all anyone at Silverman's has been talking about. Even when they try not to—even when they resolve, very firmly, to stop bringing it up—the conversation drifts inexorably back towards it. It's as though they can't quite resist the temptation, the way the pain of pushing a stretch too far can feel almost good, right up until the moment you tear something.

Also, the whole topic has the added air of an unsolved mystery, due to the sheer volume of unanswered questions associated with it. Questions like:

- Why would *Hearth*, an incredibly famous publication that punches in the same weight class as *The New Yorker* or *Harper's Bazaar*, run a vicious hit piece on a deli in Cleveland, Ohio?

- For that matter, why would Kiss of Death, the equally-if-not-more-famous review column that *Hearth* occasionally publishes, go after Silverman's? Sam's been reading it for *years*. He'd been a huge fan until two months ago. But he'd liked it because it always punched up, targeting high-end places in much bigger cities, restaurants that were cheating their clientele or mistreating their staff. Norman Endicott didn't take down local mom-and-pop shops in the Midwest! His whole brand was attacking celebrity chefs who were selling people bad Camembert or moldy squash blossoms!

- Speaking of Norman Endicott: Who the hell did he think he was? Had he lost his mind? The whole article was full of lies, one thing after another that Sam knew couldn't possibly be true. That Sam has spent many, many years of his life ensuring would never be true! The man had suggested seeing both roaches *and* rats, although in a sneaky, tongue-in-cheek way that didn't actually go so far as to constitute libel. Apparently. Sam had checked that one with a lawyer, who was both condescending and deeply unhelpful, and Sam was sorry he'd bothered.

- Speaking of lies, who were the mysterious unnamed sources who claimed they'd gotten multiple rounds of food poisoning from Sam's kitchen? Why didn't any of them call in and *say* something? To the state, even, if not to the deli itself? What, exactly, had poisoned them? Sam's fairly certain that on a batch-wide level, nothing has left his kitchen without his at least tasting it in months, and he's a stickler on the food-safety rules to the point that his staff tease him about it. But nothing's impossible—a tainted batch of something straight from a supplier, a one-off bad piece of chicken, things happen. Sam would just have liked to be *told*, if it was true, although he suspects very strongly that it wasn't.

- And, somehow worst of all, Endicott had hated the food. How could he have hated the food? Obviously, deep in his heart, Sam knows that not everyone likes his food. He can even admit that the menu is a little dated, to put it a lot more mildly than the article did. But the article talked about the flavors and the textures being wrong, the temperatures being off. He'd even suggested there was a whiff of rancidity to some of his dishes, which is just impossible. Silverman's food is good! It has been good for seventy-five years! Sam would sooner die than serve a rancid batch of anything!

Mostly to himself, he mutters, "It must have been one of those delivery apps."

"I *said* we shouldn't do the delivery services," Eileen puts in, sharply, from the back. Silverman's Head Baker for as long as Sam can remember, she had been a ferocious, graying terror of a woman even when he was a child. The only thing that's really changed since then is her hair; the "ing" in "graying" has long since left the building.

Sam groans, but his voice is good-natured as he says, "I know you did, Eileen. We all know you did, because you remind us every time we get slammed."

"Well! Just because I think you should listen to me sometime, that's all!" She sniffs, clearly offended in spite of Sam's best efforts, and disappears back into her half of the kitchen. That's Eileen all over—she loves to dish it out but can't even begin to think of taking it. Sam sighs, wrestles down the urge to go make peace. He'd tried that with Eileen for years, with inevitably frustrating and terrible results, until Deb had gently pulled him aside and told him that with some people it was best to leave things alone and let moments of discomfort flow away without further discussion.

So instead of giving in to his desire to smooth things over and make it all fine, Sam turns back to Alphonse and says, "I tried to call the magazine, you know. Have them retract it."

Alphonse blinks at him, surprised. "Wait, really? I didn't know that. You called *Hearth*? When?"

"Last month." Sam rubs the palm of his hand briefly against his forehead, as though trying to force his growing tension headache up and out through the top of his skull. "I called to see if I could talk to Endicott and ask him what the hell happened, and they said he was out of town, so then I asked if I could talk to his editor and they connected me to some... well, some person!" Sam wishes that he had a more unfriendly descriptor to use, but he's honestly hesitant even about "person," since whoever he spoke to had been so flat and nondescript as to be essentially a robot. "They said, 'On what grounds would you like the review retracted, Mr. Silverman?' and I said, 'It's Adelson, actually, and on the grounds that it ripped us a new one over a series of things that I know aren't true, and also, I'm pretty sure Norman Endicott's never even been here! There was no fact-checking, and nothing about the seventy-five-year history of the place or the dying deli culture in Cleveland or any research or anything. I don't think it's fair to call us "an overrated, outdated stain on the otherwise delightful West Ninth Street," especially in a column that usually focuses on places that charge hundreds of dollars per plate. Places with Michelin stars!' And they said, 'Well, it's an opinion piece, Mr. Silverman, anyone can have an opinion,' and I said, 'Again, my name is Sam Adelson,' and they said, 'Oh, so sorry, I must have picked up the wrong extension then,' and hung up!"

Sam is breathing hard by the end of this little speech. Alphonse is looking at him like maybe he thinks that *Sam* spends too much time at work, which, in all fairness, would not be wrong. This is one of the dangers of having your apartment directly above your place of business, especially when that apartment technically still belongs to your aunt, and you feel guilty about changing anything around from the way she's always kept it.

Not wanting to share this with Alphonse, and hoping, at last, to set aside the topic of the Kiss of Death review, Sam sticks his head back into the building and yells, "Anyone need anything? Any new customers?"

"Doornail," Joey—the deli's current primary counter minder, cashier, and customer wrangler—calls from the front.

Sam knows all too well, especially after this last month, that by "doornail," Joey means it's as dead as one in there. He sighs hard, collapsing back a little against the brickwork. It's noon on a Friday. This should be prime time, lunch rush. Alphonse should be sweating and swearing and begging Eileen to jump in and assist whoever was supposed to be slicing the meat; Joey should be howling for help as they're mobbed by a horde of irascible zombies who can only be sated by corned beef. Sam himself should, right now, be experiencing the strangely blissful stress of being pulled in a dozen directions at once, with no time or energy to even consider his own problems.

Instead, in direct violation of his own intention from only moments ago, he mutters, "That stupid review, I swear to God. Did you know this could happen? That some jackass critic could just write up a hit piece based on basically nothing and kill your traffic like this?"

Alphonse winces. "I mean... yeah, man. I've never seen anything go quite as, uh, wide as this has, but crappy Yelp reviews killed the last two places I worked at."

Sam freezes, briefly stunned into loaded, unpleasant silence. Silverman's can't *die*. Individual Silvermans, of course, could die, and did all the time. The deli's history is pockmarked with loss, like any place that's handed down through a family. But Silverman's, the location, the *institution*, has loomed so large across Sam's life as to become something unkillable, beyond such petty concerns as mortality. It's like suggesting a mountain could die, or a continent.

The very idea rocks Sam's internal landscape to a degree he's a little embarrassed by.

"Let's try not to get ahead of ourselves," he says instead. "Maybe it's just an... unrelated slump. It wasn't this bad last month after the review came out, right?"

Alphonse winces; Sam knows why. While it's true that traffic had taken a few weeks to start dropping, it's hard to agree with the idea that last month wasn't bad. It was differently bad, that was all. So many regulars coming in to say they were sorry to hear the deli was closing, and then looking at Sam with pity when he insisted it was not, would be hard for anyone to describe as "good."

With forced brightness, Sam says, "Okay, last month sucked, too, but it's just a couple of quiet weeks, and it's probably the weather anyway. People are easily convinced to stay inside by this point in the winter, you know that. But it'll turn around, you'll see! It might not be from the review at all, and even if it is, just because the stupid column is called Kiss of Death doesn't mean it actually *is* one."

"Yeah," Alphonse says doubtfully, "maybe not," but Sam can tell his heart isn't in it.

Sam goes inside, because it's high time he walked away from this conversation, and cloisters himself in his office. Well, it's not really his office, not technically. Like the deli, like the apartment above it, this is really Deb's office. They're her books on the shelves, and her files in the cabinet, and her framed photo of Talya, her wife, on the desk. It's her name on the door, even, although about six months ago Alphonse did stick up a Post-it below that reads, + *Sam Adelson!*

Every time Sam looks at it, it embarrassingly makes him feel a little burst of... well, of something, anyway. Not entirely pride, certainly, since it's a Post-it note, but *something*.

But if he wants more than the Post-it—if he wants his name to really be on the glass windowpane of this office door—he's going to have to do more than sit here and woolgather. That's the deal he made with his aunt, who, understandably, had some hesitations about handing over the reins of the family establishment to her then freshly twenty-nine-year-old nephew, the one she originally took in as a troubled teen. This whole last year has been an audition of sorts, and while it's just Sam's luck that something would go haywire in the last few months before she's due back to town, he can't let it all slip away from him now. He wakes up his computer—Deb's computer—abruptly flush with noble intentions of getting a jump on next week's payroll documentation.

He finds himself, instead, pulling up the stupid horrible life-ruining Kiss of Death review, a moth to a raging inferno. He's read it so many times, first in shock and then in horror and then in rage, that he more or less knows it by heart. Still, he skims over it now, his eyes lingering briefly on choice phrases as he scrolls. "Like eating a mouthful of fishy cement" whizzes past, followed shortly by "Couldn't have been more poorly seasoned if they were trying" and "If this place ever had the juice in the first place, you can rest assured it is long, long gone."

He stops scrolling when he gets to the bottom, his gaze settling, as it always does, on the little italicized paragraph after the article's close. It sits next to a thumbnailed headshot of a round-faced white man in his mid-fifties—a larger copy of which is currently pinned to the dartboard in the break room—and reads, "Norman Endicott is a restaurant critic and reviewer based on the West Coast. To protect his safety, his inbox, and the integrity of the review process, we do not share his contact information publicly. Please direct any questions, concerns, complaints, or tips to help@hearth.com, subject line 'Kiss of Death.'" This, above all else, irks Sam. The integrity of the review process, fine, whatever. But Endicott's safety and privacy? Sam wants to talk, that's all. Just talk. Nice, normal talking, at a reasonable volume, with absolutely no throwing of pickled herring, or hosing him down with a squirt gun loaded with expired clam juice.

God, maybe the *Hearth* policy has a point.

Sobered by this thought, Sam decides it's best to step away from the computer, and technology at large. What the situation calls for is Sam being visible, and friendly, and waving to passing customers who might be on the fence about stopping in. There's a large photo of his grandparents right across from the door: his grandmother, who started the place, is sitting on his grandfather's lap just in front of the register, obviously laughing. Sam inherited her sharp cheekbones and aquiline nose, not to mention his grandfather's athletic build and dark, unruly hair; any time he stands in front of the photo, someone passing comments on the resemblance.

So that's Sam's best move right now: being present. Generally reminding everyone that this is a family place, one that has been here for generations, and they don't need to take their advice from some snotty douchebag on the internet who's proven he can't be trusted.

As if to punctuate this thought, the bell on the front door goes off. From the direction of the walk-in, he hears Joey yell, "Can someone grab that? I'm halfway through refilling the mac salad," and Sam jumps up, energized.

"I got it," he calls back, already hurrying towards the front. He's glancing around as he walks towards the counter, mostly trying to make sure he doesn't bump into anyone who might also have answered Joey's summons, so he only takes in the vague shape of someone standing in front of the register. He starts talking as he approaches, the patter so familiar as to be second nature: "Hi there, welcome to Silverman's! What can I get for—"

"Jesus Christ." The voice is shocked and so obviously strained that it pulls Sam's focus back to center at once. His gaze wrenches forward to the waiting customer and...

... freezes, just like the rest of him, as he realizes exactly who he's looking at.

Jake Thompson, of all people, is staring back at him from the other side of the counter.

TWO

THEN: SEPTEMBER, FOURTEEN YEARS AGO

The tech booth in the Horseshoe Heights High School auditorium was small, cramped, and poorly lit. It was about the only part of the building that was. Since starting classes there a month before, Sam had discovered that nearly everything about his new school looked like it had been ordered out of a catalog called "Fancy Furnishings for Rich Educators." The classrooms, the teachers, and the students themselves all seemed to gleam as though polished to a high shine.

Even the manual for the light board, when Sam finally found it in the back of a filing cabinet, looked as though it had been well-maintained. Some previous member of the student stage crew had taken the time to tab the relevant pages, and Sam, flipping through them, was impressed and amazed to realize that not a single tab had a rude drawing on it. Not one.

All of this was atypical of Sam's experience of schools, which was both vast and unfortunate. By age sixteen, Sam had been enrolled as a student in six different area districts, moved around as his parents' medical careers dictated. The moves had slowed down somewhat after David and Mara both finished their residencies and had the triplets, but HHHS was still Sam's second high school.

His first one, not to mention both middle and all three elementary schools, had taught him a lot.

Most of what they'd taught him was that he was a weirdo and a loser who was never going to fit in anywhere. At sixteen, it felt like hard truth.

So when his parents had cracked a bottle of champagne and told him that they were moving to glitzy, expensive Horseshoe Heights, Sam had come up with a plan. He hadn't managed to make friends in far less hoity-toity school districts than this one, so he obviously couldn't rely on the strength of his personality alone. He'd just... try to be a little cooler, that was all. A little more dangerous, enough to balance out the ways people seemed to find him boring. It wouldn't be lying, exactly. It was more of a Fake-It-'Til-You-Make-It situation, at least in concept.

In practice, however, it *was* lying. This was because full-on, flat-out lying turned out to be the only way *to* make himself look cool. Without the lies he was still the same old Sam who spent most of his spare time reading or making up imagination games to play with his little sisters. The same old Sam who could manage a conversation with any adult, but never seemed able to pick up the rhythm with people his own age.

New Sam could pick up that rhythm. New Sam knew how to do all kinds of things, and within a month, any student at HHHS would have been able to tell you so. New Sam could ride a motor-cycle, and hotwire a car, and get in touch with at least four different high-profile musical artists. He'd been to seven countries and two jails, and could tell you how to navigate through each. He had never yet encountered a test he couldn't cheat on.

It was a shame, really, that all his claimed knowledge wasn't possessed by Actual Sam, sitting within and watching himself tell whopper after whopper to his new classmates. He was the one who had to suffer the consequences of, for example, the series of lies that led him to the tech booth on that particular afternoon.

First he'd lied to his parents. He'd told them he'd try out for the school musical to get them to stop insisting he sign up for an extracurricular. Then his father had offered to drop him off at the Saturday morning audition call on the way to his squash game. Sam had no choice but to go into the building and try to find something less embarrassing to do than mangling an innocent song in front of his classmates.

He'd been happy to encounter the HHHS Stage Crew, who dressed all in black as Sam already did, and ideally never sang at all. They asked him if he'd ever done stage crew before, and he lied; they asked him if he'd ever used a light board before, and he lied; they asked where he'd used light boards in the past and a story poured out of him about a series of raves he'd helped run. He had, in fact, never attended a rave—he'd pulled the entire tale from an episode of a terrible television show—but this seemed to convince them.

It would not occur to Sam until well into adulthood to wonder if they'd found this convincing because they, too, had never been to any raves. If he had, he might have found exactly the acceptance he was seeking in that collection of bright, offbeat teenagers.

Instead, he'd broken into the tech booth after school in hopes of teaching himself to use the damn light board before anyone worked out he was a liar. Now he flicked through the manual desperately and, praying that there weren't any adults in this part of the building, followed the instructions to turn up the main stage lights.

As if on cue, he heard the backstage door slam open. Sam froze with his hand still over the board, sure it was a teacher and deciding on some deep internal level that trouble followed the same rules as the T. rex in *Jurassic Park*: If he didn't move, it couldn't find him.

But, to his surprise, a boy stepped out onto the stage. His narrow face was loosely familiar to Sam. They didn't have any classes together, but Sam was pretty sure the guy was in his grade, and that his name was Jake. Sam had seen him hanging around amongst the upper echelons of the Popular Kids. Jake—assuming that really was his name—didn't have to beg for scraps of attention through unearned notoriety the way Sam did. Everything about him seemed to suggest he'd belong anywhere he was, without even needing to try.

Jake didn't seem to notice that the stage lights were on and shouldn't have been. Or, at least, the lighting didn't stop him from taking his shoes off and stepping out of his sweatpants to reveal a pair of skintight leggings worn beneath them. Without putting his shoes back on, he did a series of lithe, graceful stretches, pulling his long limbs into a variety of shapes, his thigh and calf muscles clearly visible under the clinging Lycra. Sam found this... upsettingly hard to look away from. It went on for nearly fifteen minutes before Jake straightened up, cracked his back, pulled a pair of battered-looking slippers from his bag, and slid them onto his feet.

Then Jake began to dance, and Sam forgot to worry about looking away, or learning how to use the light board, or anything else. He just leaned forward on his elbows and watched.

Sam didn't know enough about dance to have a real sense of what he was looking at. All he could tell was that it was ballet, and that Jake was *incredibly* good at it. This last point would be obvious even to a toddler. Or a dog. Or an alien who'd never heard of dancing before. Jake moved across the stage so fluidly that he seemed almost to be a marionette, spun around and lifted high into the air as if on invisible strings. And if there *was* some hidden puppeteer moving Jake around, then they had a generous grip on the capabilities of the human body. It almost looked, in certain moments, as though Jake was flying.

There wasn't any music, at least not any that Sam could hear. Jake was wearing headphones, an iPod shuffle clipped onto the band of his leggings, so whatever was playing was audible only to him. It didn't matter. As Jake leaped and whirled, carving sweeping arcs into the air and then pinioning himself down into intricate steps on the tips of his toes, a story seemed to move with him. It was almost as though he was two people instead of one, the emotion radiating out not only from his face but, in a way Sam couldn't begin to understand, his movements.

Sam realized somewhere around the two-minute mark that it was the most beautiful thing he had ever seen. Not just the dancing, but Jake himself: his long-limbed grace and the joy that radiated from him, enveloping Sam from across the auditorium. He moved as though the laws of physics were only guidelines, with which he could disagree at will.

After a few more minutes, Jake lifted his arms in a long, smooth motion as he leaped and his shirt lifted, too, exposing a glimpse of bare skin, toned abdominal muscles. Sam found his mouth suddenly bone-dry. His palms were sweating.

He was surprised to find himself standing up, moving towards the door in the side of the tech booth. As if pulled by one of the invisible strings that he'd imagined carrying Jake through the air, Sam hurried down the stairs into the auditorium on light feet. He sucked in a breath when he stepped out among the empty seats, and then immediately became transfixed again by the performance in front of him. His feet moved of their own accord, taking one step after another, until he was close enough to the stage to see that Jake's eyes were closed.

Sam doesn't know how long he stood there, lost in watching Jake. But he knows that when Jake stopped dancing and opened his eyes to find Sam standing in front of him, he didn't do any of the things Sam would have done in his shoes. Sam would have jumped, or screamed, or yelped, "Jesus Christ! How long have you been here?"

Jake only widened his eyes very slightly. He looked Sam over, assessing. Then he smiled, pulling his headphones down to hang around his neck.

"Well, hello," Jake said. His voice was light, amused. There was sweat patching his shirt in a few places—why, exactly, did Sam find that so attractive? "I'm pretty sure you weren't in here when I started."

"Um," Sam said, blinking up at him in amazement, looking for the words. "That was... You were... I mean, it was *incredible*. Holy shit. Wow." Then, his brain catching up to what Jake had actually said, he quickly added, "And no, you're right, I wasn't. Or, I mean, I was, but I was, uh." He gestured up at the tech booth, feeling himself flush as he finished, "Probably would have been less creepy if I'd just stayed up there, right?"

"Oh, no, absolutely not." Jake folded gracefully down to sit on the edge of the stage, his legs dangling into the orchestra pit. "Just staying up there would have been *way* creepier. Much better to announce yourself."

"In that case," Sam said, with a sheepish little shrug. "Hi, and sorry to crash your breaking and entering with... well, with my breaking and entering. And, uh. I'm Sam?"

Jake laughed, shaking his head. "Jake. No worries on the B&E —we're in a mutually assured destruction situation now, right? And I already know who you are. I'm, like, almost one hundred percent sure you're my back-door neighbor. You're on Park Lane, yes? Your family moved in this summer? The house with the big red roof?"

Sam stared at him, stunned. The idea that someone like Jake had the faintest idea that Sam existed, let alone where he *lived*, was so novel that it took him a beat too long to say, "Yeah... yes. My parents call it the Red Roof Inn, actually."

He regretted saying this immediately—there was nothing cool about quoting your parents' jokes—but Jake laughed again. Then, his tone going low and amused, he said, "I thought so, but don't worry. When I heard someone say the other day that you lived inside a secret speakeasy underneath the pizzeria, I didn't breathe a word of the truth."

Sam winced, putting a hand to the back of his neck. In only a month it had become second nature to lean into the rumors, to double down on any pushback he got with an even more outlandish fib. But from that very first conversation, part of Sam thrashed and kicked at the idea of lying to Jake.

Also, though Sam wouldn't understand this until he was much older, it was kind of a relief the way Jake seemed to know from minute one that it was all so much bluster and nonsense. A squirming, uncomfortable sort of relief, maybe, but a relief all the same.

"Yeah, I feel kinda bad about that one," he admitted. "For one thing, I'm sure people are making it weird for the staff at that pizza place. Do you know I've never even been there? We've only lived here a few months, and my parents *really* don't like takeout."

This time when Jake laughed, it was more a snort of amused disbelief than anything. He hopped easily off the stage as he said, "Wow, man, our parents are *not* the same. But it's fully insane that you haven't been to Perry's. A slice of their pepperoni with a root beer float is one of life's greatest pleasures." Glancing up at the tech booth, he added, "What were you doing up there, anyway?"

Sam made a face. "I have to learn how to use the light board before dress rehearsals start, because I told everyone on stage crew that I learned how to use one running a bunch of raves with a guy named Carl T. Danger—"

Jake wrinkled his nose. "God, really? Like in that episode of *Teen Terrors*? And they believed that?"

"A little too well," Sam said, with a guilty glance up at the booth. "I'm kind of afraid I'm going to end up ruining the fall musical."

"That," Jake said, grinning, "would honestly be very funny. If nothing else, we'd all get to watch Mr. Thornapple's head pop off." Mr. Thornapple was the high school's drama teacher, and tales of his temper were so legendary that even Sam had heard a few of them. "Don't worry, they haven't even cast the thing yet, and once they do that there'll be at least three weeks of fighting about the sets and the costumes and the blocking and the props. Also, if you stay here much longer, the night janitors' shift will start, and they'll catch you for sure. Come get a slice at Perry's with me instead."

"Oh," Sam said, blinking. He hadn't expected this, and wasn't prepared. When he said, "Are you sure?" his voice was high and reedy, and he immediately wanted to sink down into the floor.

But instead of tightening into mockery, Jake's expression warmed and softened. He closed the space between them to slap a hand on Sam's back and started pushing him towards the door. "Dude, yes. Of course I'm sure. It's *wrong* that you've been living here for months without eating at Perry's—in fact, it's illegal. Refuse my offer at your own risk, but don't come crying to me when the cops pull you out of class and force-feed you mozzarella sticks in front of a jury of your peers."

"Oh, okay, I get it now," Sam said, as Jake led him out into the sunshine. "It *looks* all shiny and expensive, but this is actually the school from *Matilda*."

Jake burst out laughing, and then started talking about how the students in the film should have staged a revolt roughly forty minutes earlier than they did. "I mean, you have a moral obligation, don't you think? To do something when your principal is holding assemblies to torture your classmates? And why don't any of the parents care about their precious children being shoved into the tetanus closet? Seriously, somebody should have sued."

They talked the whole walk to Jake's little green Volkswagen, and then the whole drive to Perry's Pizzeria, which was less a restaurant and more a quaint, plexiglass-windowed roadside shack. Jake pointed out a small sign on the back wall, which looked like it had been hand-painted by someone's grandmother and did indeed read, PERRY'S PIZZERIA: A SLICE OF OUR PEPPERONI WITH A ROOT BEER FLOAT IS ONE OF LIFE'S GREATEST PLEASURES.

The pizza *was* amazing, piping hot and oozing cheese over a paper-thin crust, the pepperoni perfectly spicy. It slowed the conversation for the handful of minutes it took them to demolish a whole pie between them, but Jake picked up the last dropped thread the minute he finished eating and they were off again, chatting back and forth the whole way home.

Sam wondered once or twice if it was a date, but he didn't dare to ask. It couldn't be one. Jake didn't try to kiss him, or say anything suggestive at all. He didn't even take Sam home; he instead drove them back to his own house, and showed Sam a spot behind the hedge at the back of the yard. To Sam's amazement, there was a little retaining wall back there made of stacked cinder blocks, which could serve as either a step up or a makeshift seat. When

Sam climbed over the fence, he found a similar setup behind the hedge on his side.

"No choice but to be friends, then, is there?" Jake said. "It'd be such a waste, otherwise. See you around, Sam." Then he waved and walked back to his house, and Sam whistled to himself as he returned to his own, turning the word "friend" over and over in his mind.

THREE

NOW: MARCH

"Jake!" The word bursts out of Sam's mouth, startled and pitched a few octaves higher than his normal speaking voice, in the same moment that Jake whispers, "*Sam?*"

They stare at each other, and, on top of everything, Sam suffers a moment of horrible gratitude for whoever wrote the stupid Kiss of Death review; he's glad the deli is empty right now. He's not sure what he'd do if he had to manage this with a fifteen-person line, hunched old Mr. Schecter somewhere at the back hollering that they better still have whitefish salad left when it's his turn, even though they've never once not had a serving of whitefish set aside for him in thirty years. Pulling it had been the very first thing Deb had tasked him with when Sam started working here in his late teens, and after meeting the man only once, he'd understood why she'd described it as "critically important for my sanity and yours."

Hell, Sam can't be thinking about old Mr. Schecter right now; he needs to *focus*. His mind is always doing this to him in the least convenient moments. He swallows, and squares his shoulders, reaches within the suddenly churning, writhing core of himself and grasps desperately for something to say.

Tragically, all he finds is a deeply ingrained, hard-earned sense of the rules of Midwestern politeness. This is why what comes out of his mouth is a jovial, if still slightly too loud, "Long time, man! How've you been?"

It's a stupid, useless question. It's been more than a decade since he's laid eyes on this man. They'd both been *boys*: on the cusp of adulthood but still grasping for it, their fingers not quite catching the edge.

But it's still the only thing he can think of to say. He can't very well go with, "You seem extremely not dead! I, for one, think that's neat," or, "I want you to know I haven't stalked you on social media at all, which I think shows a lot of restraint, unless you acknowledge the reality that I *would* have stalked you if your accounts were not private, which they are. Can you tell me what you've been up to and whether or not it aligns with what I've imagined, when I've allowed myself to imagine what your life might be like now?" It would be weird, for one thing, and for another Sam doesn't *do* stuff like that. It's the better part of dignity not to, and, honestly, only one person in his whole life has ever left him twitterpated enough to ramble on like that, like an overwhelmed teenager with a crush.

That person clears his throat, and shrugs, and drops his gaze down to the counter. "Oh, I've been, uh..." Jake laughs, lightly and humorlessly, and, without looking up, says, "You ever see that meme? How does it go—something like, 'You know a Midwesterner is having the worst day of their life when you ask them how it's going and they say, 'It's going?'"

"Ah," Sam says, sympathy creeping over him in spite of himself. "I gather it's going, then?"

"Gone, actually," Jake mutters, and then looks up, and offers Sam what looks like a fairly forced smile. "Sorry, that's nothing. Just, ah, weird to see you. Good? Weird. Hi."

"Hi," Sam says slowly, wishing suddenly but profoundly that he could go stick his head into the sink full of clean water in the dish pit. "Good and weird to... see you, too."

"Right," Jake says faintly. "Right."

Again, Sam finds they are staring at each other. This time he's able to absorb some details; when they did this a few minutes ago, the only thing Sam retained was, *OH MY GOD YES THAT REALLY HONESTLY IS JAKE ACTUAL THOMPSON,* the truth of it blaring loud in his mind like an alarm.

Now, with marginally more of a grip, he's able to take in things he missed the first time. Jake is—older, obviously, of course he is, they both are. So his structures and angles have changed a little, rounded cheeks hollowing down into a slightly narrower face than Sam remembers. His chestnut brown hair is cut shorter, and has a looser, more matte, less gelled finish now than it did when he was in high school. He wears round-rimmed glasses these days, which is a surprise, and carries a cane, which isn't. It would have been more surprising if he *wasn't* carrying a cane, and the one he's got makes the ghost of a smile tug briefly at the corners of Sam's mouth; it's covered in stickers, the way his water bottles and devices and the bumper of his crappy teen jalopy always used to be.

But there's something... different about Jake. Or maybe it's more accurate to say that a lot is different about him, but they're all expected things, normal things, except for one. It's in his eyes, Sam realizes, and the set of his shoulders, the twist of his mouth—something that had shimmered once is now barely glimmering, a hint of shine in the darkness.

Sam cannot, obviously, say this. "What happened to your effervescent sparkle, my guy? You misplace your joie de vivre somewhere?" would be unhelpful.

Jake clears his throat, looks away again, and says, "So, uh. You work here, I'm guessing? Unless I'm, like, interrupting you in the middle of some kind of bizarre, complicated con job—" He chokes himself off, eyes bugging behind his glasses, and then hastily corrects, "Not that I'm suggesting that you would be doing something like that! I wasn't—"

"Chill, man, it's all good," Sam says, lifting a hand, amused in spite of himself. This, at least, is familiar. Jake was often one little inconvenience or badly landed joke away from tilting into a frenetic verbal tap dance, as though throwing enough new syllables at a problem would make it go away. "And yeah, I work here. I run it, actually, although it's kinda a trial period situation, for now. It's my family's place."

For some reason, this makes Jake look at him as though Sam's not only grown a second head, but one from an entirely nonhuman species. Housefly, maybe, or anaconda. After a long second, blinking hard on it, Jake says, "No it's not."

This, admittedly, throws Sam for a proverbial loop. "Yes it... is," he says, his brow furrowing as he watches Jake's face crease into a mulish expression identical to the one he sometimes wore as a teen.

"*No*," Jake says sharply, the old light seeming to flare in his eyes if only in annoyance, "I know for a *fact* that David and Mara didn't quit the medical profession to start a *deli*, they're the scariest doctors I've ever met, it makes no sense! And—" He looks wildly around him, mutters something under his breath that sounds like, "God help me, there's not even any *branding* in here," and then his gaze seems to land.

Jake stalks over to the wall of photos that's practically required at an old-school deli like this and points, with the flair of the high school drama student, at one in the center. Sam squints at it; it's from the early seventies, when the sign had last been updated. With his finger hovering over the sign, Jake intones, "Silverman," and then, turning to point at Sam, "Adelson! So! Check and mate, I think you'll have to agree!"

Sam is torn. On the one hand, this is... odd, even for Jake, who always was a little odd, in a fun, distracting sort of way. What does he care who owns this deli? On the other hand, Sam's more than a little touched that Jake's remembered his parents' names all these years. He's even a little pleased Jake's remembered *his* last name, an upsetting realization he files away to review later, at a better time.

So he shrugs, and says, "It's, uh, my aunt's place? For now, anyway; hopefully, mine soon. She's Deb Silverman, and my mom was a Silverman, too, before she married my dad."

"So you're... here," Jake says, staring at him. "In this building.

Like. Every day? It's not just that you have, uh, specific shifts or whatever, you're *running* the place. I mean. You're probably a pretty regular visitor, right?"

"I live in the apartment upstairs," Sam says, cocking his head slightly in surprise at this reaction. "So less a visitor than a... resident? But, yeah, I'd say I'm here pretty regularly regardless."

This is neutral information, strictly the facts, but Jake cringes so drastically it changes his whole face. "Oh my God, I have to go," he says, and before Sam can even reply, he's turned on his heel and power-walked right out the front door.

Sam blinks, startled, after him. He's not sure what part of that conversation he should attempt to parse first; actually, he's not even sure he has the necessary mental equipment to parse it at all. When he'd been a teenager, being around Jake had often made him feel as though a giant was wandering across his mental landscape in steel-toed boots, gleefully kicking at particularly load-bearing areas and things he had, up until that point, been certain of. But, in retrospect, Sam had chalked that up to a side effect of *being a teenager*. Until now, it hadn't occurred to him that the problem would persist into adulthood, if only and specifically with this one man.

Of course, Sam hadn't imagined he'd ever get the opportunity to test it out. Until five minutes ago, Jake was as much a part of the past as VCRs and Sam's long-dead Digipet. Even in his wildest imaginings, the embarrassing, maudlin nights where he was maybe a little overserved at one of the West Sixth Street bars and let himself consider What Happened To Jake, Sam never imagined them meeting again. It had seemed so unlikely as to be unworthy of the effort; surely if Jake ever did see Sam out anywhere, he'd hurriedly turn the other way and pretend not to have seen him, or, if there was no escape, refuse to talk to him.

God, Jake *talked* to him. He talked to him like... well, not like he'd talked when they were teenagers, exactly, it was more stilted and panicky than that, but *still*. He talked! He didn't say, "Sam Adelson, I spit upon thee and upon this deli, and curse you for all your days." Admittedly, that was probably because he wasn't, say, a medieval witch, but it was a better conversation than Sam had ever dared to hope for.

"You... good?" Joey asks, sidling over in a way that they obviously mean to indicate they have only just returned, but in fact demonstrates that they stood and shamelessly watched the whole thing play out. Probably the whole staff did, carefully positioned in long-since-perfected spots in the kitchen that allow for overhearing without being seen. Testing this theory, Sam jerks his shoulder like he's planning to turn around, and sighs when he's rewarded with the scuttling sound of everyone scurrying back to their more usual spots.

Still. "Yeah," Sam says, and is surprised to find he means it for the first time all week when he adds: "I'm good."

And he is good. He spends the afternoon and early evening buoyed, a lightness in his step that's a little unfamiliar. Sure, it was a weird conversation. Sam can acknowledge that. But to have had any conversation at all, even an odd one, feels wonderfully like closure. Even if he never sees Jake again, which he has to imagine he won't, something sits easier in him to know their story now technically ends on a slightly different note.

Except that five hours later, as they're preparing to close, Sam is wrapping up an unusually productive run of paperwork when he hears a bit of a commotion through his closed office door. Last he checked the deli was still stone-dead, so he sighs, expecting some belligerent, early-evening drunk who has stumbled in from the bar scene a block over.

Instead, he opens his office door in time to hear Joey holler, "SAM! That weird guy from earlier is back! He wants to talk to you! He seems weirder than before!"

Yeah, Sam, go ahead and hire the sweet, awkward college student who can't keep their foot out of their mouth for three seconds, Sam thinks sarcastically to himself as he hurries up to the front. *It's not like you know anyone you're worried about mortally offending. What could go wrong?*

He'd never say it out loud, of course; it wouldn't be kind, fair, or needful. Anyway, Joey's particular brand of unfiltered honesty is never malicious. Sometimes it's even helpful.

Today, though, he says, "Why don't you go ahead and take off for the night, Joey?" when he gets to the front. He's prepared to offer an explanation and to finish their closing tasks, but he doesn't have the chance; they're out the door in ten seconds flat, calling a thank-you over their shoulder, clearly afraid he'll change his mind given half the chance.

"Sorry," Sam says, with a slight wince, to Jake, who looks a bit wild around the eyes. "They can be a bit blunt. They didn't mean anything by it."

Jake blinks at him, clearly thrown, and then, realization dawning: "Oh, that? No, that's fine, that's whatever. I am weird. And weirder than before. Call 'em like they see 'em, who could fault them for that?" There is a brief pause, after which Jake adds, in a faint, despairing sort of voice, "And also hello."

"Hello," Sam says, trying to fight down the urge to smile.

"Right," Jake says, before Sam can add anything to that single word of greeting. "The thing is, I was going to be so normal about this, I psyched myself up all afternoon. 'Be normal, Jake, don't make it weird, it's going to be so much weirder if you're weird about it, these things happen, apparently, and it's not like it was on *purpose!*'" He takes a deep, shaky breath as Sam, slightly alarmed now, shifts his weight in impatience to know what's going on. "But then I walked in here and remembered, oh, right. I can't do it normally, because I can't do anything normally, because you have to be normal for that! So I have to just... tell you, right now, even if it's weird and bad, and let the chips fall where they may. It's my only move. Right?"

"Uh," Sam says, lost, "I'm... not sure, to be honest. You're acting like you sold my organs on the black market."

Jake snorts out an obviously unwilling laugh, then runs a hand over his face, then groans. Sounding mortified, he takes a huge breath and, too fast, says: "The thing is I just moved back to Cleveland, because of—reasons, it doesn't matter—but I've been in Los Angeles for ten years, okay? So you have to believe me when I say I didn't know, I didn't know you lived here, I would have found another place, another *neighborhood*, I swear!"

Sam feels his eyebrows climb. "What are you talking about?"

"Christ, Jake, *say* the *words*," Jake mutters, clearly to himself. Then, louder but like he wishes it wasn't actually audible, "I moved into the building *behind* this one, Sam. Like. The one directly behind it. Like we're—"

"Neighbors," Sam says, his eyes widening very slightly. "Again."

"I'm not a stalker!" Jake waves the hand that isn't on his cane frantically as he says this. "And this isn't some kind of weird—I don't know, Hitchcockian nightmare scenario! It was an accident! And I'll *move*, okay, it just might take me a second to scrape the money together and I *knew* we'd run into each other again before then and it would be more awkward if I *didn't* tell you—"

"Hey," Sam cuts him off, unable to entirely keep the laugh out of his voice. "Slow down; you don't have to move." He runs a hand briefly through his hair, noting regretfully that he's at least three weeks overdue for a haircut, and probably looks like the sort of guy who doesn't believe in deodorant or regular showers. "And I don't think you're planning to *Rear Window* me."

"*Rear Window*!" Jake slaps a hand to his forehead. "That's the one, I couldn't remember the title, all I could pull up was *The Birds* and I knew *that* wasn't it."

"Yeah, admittedly, if you have to Hitchcock me, don't do that one," Sam says, grinning. "If nothing else, the health code violations—"

"I'm not going to *Hitchcock* you," Jake starts in the same moment, and then, glancing up at Sam's face, pauses. "Wait. You're... joking, aren't you?"

Sam nods.

"Because... this isn't as big a deal to you as I thought it was going to be?"

Sam nods.

"And... it's not going to be weird?"

Sam shrugs, and then, when Jake raises incredulous eyebrows at this non-response, crosses his arms over his chest and admits, "I mean, I can't promise that. I don't think anyone who works here would describe me as normal—"

"We wouldn't!" someone calls from the back. "We're not liars!"

"Case in point," Sam says with a sigh. "So, you know... odd, but fine? Should be fine. Can't think of any reason it wouldn't be."

This seems to stun Jake into silence for a moment. Then, very quietly, he says, "Are you sure?"

Their entire history flashes before Sam's eyes in an instant, brilliant and wretched by turns. Every shining, perfect moment; every brutal, devastating choice; every action that felt so right at the time. Every consequence.

"I'm sure," he says, and smiles when Jake does before jerking a thumb at the menu. "You want anything? We're closing up, but I can throw something together for you out of the case."

"Oh no, that's... No," Jake says quickly. Sam notes with interest that he's already edging backwards towards the door, like a spooked horse. "Thank you, but I have dinner at home, and you're closing, and I said what I wanted to say. I should go." He pauses, and then slaps a hand against his forehead again as he adds, "Hell, wait. Hold on. I came in here originally to say that there's a big van that says 'Silverman's' in what's supposed to be my parking spot? And to be honest with you, given the givens here, that's whatever. I would have street parked for the next thousand years to avoid having this conversation. But if you don't move it before tomorrow morning, my landlord will definitely have it towed, and that doesn't seem—"

"Oh, for God's sake," Sam says, turning an incredulous eyebrow towards where Joey was standing a few minutes ago and then remembering he sent them home. Shaking his head, he turns back to Jake. "*Sorry.* Joey delivered an order to the Katzenberg shiva earlier, and they promised me they'd parked it in our spot when they got back. I should have checked, though, because they're painfully bad at remembering *which spot that is*. I'll talk to them, and obviously move it myself right now, and, seriously, sorry for the inconvenience."

Giving him a slightly queasy smile, Jake says, "I think maybe don't? Apologize to me? Since I'm the one who has... well. Moved into your backyard?"

"I mean, fair play to you; I basically moved into yours when we were younger," Sam says easily, with a little shrug. "Look: Welcome to the neighborhood, okay? And seriously, don't worry about it—I get that it was a coincidence. Things happen. It's fine."

Jake's face twists into a complicated expression for a second, but he sounds genuine enough, like he really means it, when he says, "Okay, um. Cool, then. Thank you."

"Sure," Sam says again, not even sure why this time, and Jake turns towards the door in earnest, and Sam expects that to be that.

But when Jake's halfway out of the restaurant, he pauses, shakes his head, and turns around in the doorframe. His tone and his expression both suggest that he can't quite help himself when he asks, "Would your biggest concern with me inflicting a real-life version of *The Birds* on you *really* be the health code violations?"

Sam grins, a little sheepish. "I mean, yeah, probably, honestly. Do you have any idea how hard it is to fully sanitize a place like this after something like that? It would be a nightmare."

"Christ," Jake says, shaking his head and looking oddly pleased, "you really did grow up, didn't you? Became a full-on adult? Incredible." Then his expression shifts to an amused one, and he laughs as he turns back around and finishes leaving, calling, "Those birds murder people, Sam! They murder people!" over his shoulder.

Sam watches him go, not sure exactly what he feels. Then, like he does every night, he closes the restaurant, picking up any tasks his employees have missed. He shuts off the lights and, in the dark, grabs some of whatever's about to go out in the deli case, which looks to be roast turkey and mac salad tonight. He goes upstairs, and sinks onto the couch, and eats while he watches... well, *usually* he eats while he watches something, anyway.

Tonight he stares out the window at the tiny brick apartment building behind his, wondering which unit is Jake's, and doesn't realize he's forgotten to turn on the television until long after his food is gone.

FOUR
NOW: MARCH

Sam sleeps fitfully that night, in and out of the past, his dreams merrily ripping things he buried years ago up out of his internal earth. He wakes for good after a merciless, brutal nightmare; it might be more accurate to call it a flashback, but whatever it was, it *sucked*, and it propels Sam up and out of bed immediately. Even being up for his day at—God help him and his entire staff—3:28 a.m. is better than an encore of that particular show. It might still be pitch-black outside, and the chilled March air might be slipping in through the building's old windows, but that's still an improvement over what was happening in his sleep.

He keeps early hours anyway. The deli opens at 8 a.m., and deliveries start coming in as early as 6:30 a.m., so it's only two hours or so before his alarm would have gone off. That should, in theory, be fine. Sam should be able to operate with perfect functionality on two fewer hours of sleep than usual, even if what sleep he did get was a little broken. He's not even thirty, for God's sake; a few years ago he was cheerfully pulling all-nighters! Granted, it was mostly to do things most people would not find very exciting, like keeping an eye on the smoker while it was full of briskets, or rendering down a freezer full of chicken fat scraps into proper schmaltz, but so what? Sam had still done them and, importantly, stayed up all night to do them, and he'd always been fine the next day. Perfectly fine.

It becomes apparent fairly quickly that today Sam is not going to be perfectly fine.

He trips walking down the hallway to the bathroom, first of all, over a rug that's always been there and that he habitually steps around to avoid going flying. He goes flying, landing with a winding "OOOF," on his stomach despite trying to catch himself on a nearby side table, and only notices when he gets up a few embarrassed moments later that he scraped his knuckles raw in the process. Annoyed, he wraps a paper towel around his hand to stall the bleeding and then tries to get on with his morning.

Sam makes toast, which he burns, and then, figuring he has the time to do better and he might as well use it, makes pancakes instead. He burns those, too, his attention so consistently drawn to staring out his window at Jake's building that he keeps missing his opportunity to flip them. In the end he eats the two that are least charred and, after a particularly unpleasant bite, attempts to wash it down with the power of coffee.

The coffee, too, is burnt. It's still only 4:37 a.m. Sam despairs briefly of being alive.

He decides, in the circumstances, that he has no choice but to go and get Pastrami.

Pastrami plays a variety of roles in Sam's life; it is, of course, a meat available for purchase at the deli, and one about which, if he happens not to have it in stock, a few specific people will get really annoying. But Pastrami is also the name of Sam's dog, chosen because, when she was a puppy, she'd looked as though she planned to grow into a small-to-medium-sized white dog, with a thick coating of black speckles. When Sam found her digging around in the trash behind the deli four years ago, she'd been skin and bones, barely a few months old, and the speckles had reminded him of the pepper on the outside of a piece of pastrami.

The name had stuck, even though Pastrami herself had seemingly decided that she was not interested in being a white dog with black speckles, or indeed in being either small- or medium-sized. She had, instead, grown up to be quite a surprisingly large black dog with white speckles, long, slightly floofy fur, and one ear that was constantly flopping over her eye while the other one stood ramrod straight. Her veterinarian, after some thoughtful consideration, had filled in the section of her file marked BREED with eight question marks.

Sam had not intended on getting a pet of any kind, let alone one so big that she took up half the couch he once promised Deb he'd never let her sit on, but... she was a good dog, that was all. And she'd needed his help.

She'd been the helpful one, in the end. Pastrami is good with people, laid-back and happy to entertain anyone, chill about nearly everything. After a while, Sam had started bringing her down to hang out in the deli during the day, and then, at the suggestion of one of his customers, had her certified as a therapy dog. Now, a couple of times a month, Sam takes Pastrami to entertain kids in the cancer ward, or hang out with people struggling with their mental health, or very gently rest her head on the laps of a variety of old folks. It's.... nice. Or, at least, Pastrami clearly enjoys it, and it allows Sam to feel obliquely as though he's making up for something.

Right now, Pastrami is at the triplets' apartment, because it's finals week, and Sam always lets his sisters borrow her for finals week. This, too, allows Sam the relieved sense of making up for something, although in their case it's probably moot, since he's pretty sure Luce, at least, would break in and kidnap Pastrami if she wasn't freely lent.

Sam paces around his apartment waiting for it to be a reasonable hour, and then goes downstairs, does a variety of opening tasks for the deli that aren't even his job, and starts pacing around again. Eventually, he finds himself prowling the front of the house, peering dramatically under tables as though that will tempt fate to put an interesting problem below one of them. Fate doesn't oblige. All that's underneath the tables is the perfectly clean floor, which

Sam mopped himself last night after sending Joey home in a fit of mortified desperation.

But when Sam turns around at the sound of the back door creaking as today's openers arrive, Jake is walking past the deli's large front window, a backpack over his shoulders. He's moving quickly, his cane looking more like an extension of himself than an assistive device for a second; he's clearly so used to using it that he's moved past perfecting the art and into not thinking about it at all, the way you don't have to think about using your hands.

And the way he moves... *That same old dancer's grace*, Sam thinks, a little shocked to remember it, and thus to realize he'd somehow forgotten. Jake had been like that even as a sixteen-year-old. Not always, but in certain unpredictable moments, his movements would take on this hideously distracting elegance, a control and grace that Sam could only dream of. It's not like he was out doing pirouettes on the lawn or anything—it was in little things, mostly, but there whenever you looked for it. The way his hand moved when he picked up a glass; the way he'd leap over an obstacle in his path and then wince, automatically, like he knew he wasn't supposed to; and the way he walked, something so inimitable about it that nothing has reminded Sam of it in twelve years.

It's not that it's such a distinctive walk, even. It's just that it communicates so clearly Jake's utter, pinpoint awareness of his exact position in space that it has always made Sam's mouth go a little dry.

Jake turns, now, as Sam stares at him. He almost flickers, for a second, in Sam's vision—younger, as he was, and then back to normal again. He waves.

Sam waves back, then turns on his heel, and goes to get the van.

The triplets live in University Circle, on the other side of downtown; they also aren't generally at home to visitors before roughly eleven in the morning. Since it's still not even nine, Sam drives the deli's delivery van a few minutes in the wrong direction, crossing over the Cuyahoga River as he makes his way to the West Side Market. The whole place was a train station once, all elegant, intricate brickwork and high ceilings, but it's been a public market for more than a hundred years, and it's one of his favorite places in the city. He takes his time wandering the narrow, packed aisles between stands, visiting the butchers and bakers and spice merchants and fishmongers and other vendors fairly aimlessly. Without thinking about it, he picks up coffee for his sisters—iced vanilla lattes for Iris and Daisy, cold brew and a splash of cream for Luce, stealing the Sharpie from behind the counter to correct it when the barista writes *Lucy* on the cup. Technically that is her name, but she started asking to go by Luce when she was about thirteen, and Sam takes seriously being the only member of their immediate family who has bothered to consistently do so. He also picks up a red eye for himself, not that he imagines it will help.

Then he buys the triplets some groceries, too, because he feels guilty about taking the dog back. Then, as an apology for arriving so early, he buys them all empanadas to have for breakfast.

Admittedly, most of the reason he decides on empanadas is that Dani, his best friend from ages nine to fourteen, usually works the early shift at the counter that sells them. Though they grew apart over the years, dropping from "best friends" to just "friends" in a way that felt both natural and almost inevitable as Sam bounced from school district to school district, they never entirely lost touch. It's always nice to come and see her here, like it's nice when she stops by the deli for lunch, which she does every once in a while. It's even nice, in a horrible way, that when Sam orders more empanadas than he usually would, she raises her eyebrows and waggles them suggestively. "What's this, Sammy? Entertaining an extra guest? Have you taken a lover at last?"

Sam makes a face at her. "Don't use that word," he commands, hopelessly, "especially not in this case, since they're for—"

"Oh, don't tell me," Dani interrupts in long-suffering tones. "They're for the triplets. And so is the coffee, *and* the groceries. Aren't they?"

Sam nods. When Dani sighs dramatically, looking put out, he laughs. "Honestly, D, you should give up on me. My one true love is the deli; cut me open and you'll find the Silverman's logo stamped on my heart."

"Now, see," Dani complains, passing over his order with a shake of her head and clearly despairing of him, "that isn't *funny*, Sam. Just because you say it like a joke doesn't make it funny! You're a perfectly nice-looking guy, solid job, a good head on your shoulders. There's a lot of men in this town who could do worse, that's all I'm saying."

"Well, I'll let you know if I meet any of them," Sam says, with a slightly forced joviality, and starts backing up before...

"I could always set you up with one!" Dani says, raising her voice as Sam gets farther away. "You know, like I've been asking to, for years—"

"Bye, Dani!" Sam yells, and retreats, for the second time this morning, to the safety of his van. When he gets there, to his extreme displeasure, he discovers that it is only 9:45 a.m.

He makes the rest of the journey to the triplets' apartment anyway, trying to put Dani and her stupid crusade out of his mind. She's always trying to set him up with some guy or another, and it's never a good fit, never worth the agita of bothering. He thinks that maybe they're wired differently. Dani is a serial monogamist, someone who finds it deeply uncomfortable to be unattached, and so she must find Sam's long-term refusal to settle down an agony.

Sam himself isn't that bothered by it. It's not that he doesn't get lonely, but. Well. He's never been the kind of person who could get out of bed for anything less than the real thing; for anyone who doesn't make him feel, in whatever way, like all his nerve endings are on fire. He's never seen the point. So while he's been on an enormous number of dates—most of them set up for him by Deb, Talya, or Deb's best friend, Joanie—and even turned a few of those dates into relationships, he's never been with anyone longer than about six months. It always fizzles out, and a year or two ago, Sam decided to do his best to stop expecting anything else. The last thing he needs right now is to add Dani to the list of people who have permission to call him up and instruct him to meet a potential match somewhere.

Forcibly, he turns his mind to other subjects.

As they usually do on the way to the triplets', Sam's thoughts turn to Luce. He worries about her. The situation is an unusual one. Daisy and Iris are identical, like carbon copies of one another, but Luce isn't, for all they were born at the same time. It's a strange, rare thing for that to happen, and David and Mara had been thrilled by it, wanted to talk about it long after the pregnancy was done. Sam thinks it wasn't so bad for Luce when they were all small children; she looked enough like Iris and Daisy then that people assumed all three of them were identical, and didn't single her out.

But early in their teen years, Luce's looks diverged from Daisy and Iris's, making the distinction clearer. Daisy and Iris both have their mother's heart-shaped face, while Luce has their father's more squared one; Daisy and Iris both have glossy, smooth, medium-brown hair, while Luce's, like Sam's, is both darker and less tamable; Daisy and Iris are both tall and willowy, while Luce is shorter and stockier. Ever since the differences between them became obvious—and probably, if Sam's honest, since before then —the dynamic between the three sisters is one that Sam can't help but think Luce doesn't enjoy.

Even the apartment itself reflects the way things work between the triplets. It's a nice enough place, the second floor of a well-maintained duplex on a little street called Delaware Drive, at the top of Cedar Hill. That means that for Iris and Daisy, it's only a few minutes' walk to Case Western Reserve, where they're both seniors; they're even able to catch a university-funded shuttle to and fro most of the time. But Luce, studying at the Cleveland Institute of Art, has a half-hour walk each way to get to her classes, with no way home that doesn't involve ascending a punishing slope.

Sam sighs as he pulls the van up in front of the curb. This is in part out of sympathy for his sister, but, admittedly, it's partially because through his open window, he hears a voice that sounds like Daisy's call, in a slightly singsong tone, "It's Saaaaaam. Lucy, do you want to maybe hide your bong?"

I'm not your dad, Sam thinks, not for the first time; not that he's ever been able to bring himself to say it out loud. *I'm only eight years older than you. How far into adulthood do we all have to get before you stop looking at me as an authority figure I never even asked to be? I was a kid, too, you know. Just because I was older than you doesn't mean I knew what I was doing, and that's still true, right now.*

On the other hand, Sam notes wryly, he *is* walking up the stairs to their apartment unannounced, laden with bags of treats for them, and offended that they don't want him to see their bong, so. Maybe he has a lot of nerve being annoyed that they see him as a father figure.

Regardless, when he knocks it's Iris who answers. She's irritated to see him so early until he offers her the coffee, which seems to placate her somewhat. Never particularly food-motivated, she's indifferent to the groceries, but Daisy's excited by the various snack options, and Luce—the only one of the three who'd ever bothered to pay attention when Sam attempted to teach them to cook—is clearly pleased by the ingredients he's chosen. Sam's glad; some of them are expensive pantry items, things like tahini and cashews and good chocolate, and he's relieved that someone appreciates them. She kisses him on the cheek when she takes her coffee, and Daisy gives him a bubbly one-armed hug. Iris raises an eyebrow at him over the rim of her cup, but that, for Iris, is fairly demonstrative, and he smiles back.

At this point Pastrami, who was until now, presumably, sprawled unconscious on Luce's bed and sleeping the deep, luxurious sleep of a dog who has been given both a glut of attention and too many liver treats, bursts from the bedroom. She barrels towards Sam at a dead run, leaps into his arms, licks every inch of his face with a frankly unsettling efficiency, and then leaps back to the ground again. She circles him three times before she settles on the floor at his feet, panting happily.

Sam would have had to train that jumping out of her if she did it with anyone else, but only he has ever had this particular reaction from her. He'd be lying if he said he wasn't proud of that.

"She needs out," he says, instead of this. "Do you want me to—"

"I've got it," Luce says, standing and stretching, coffee still in hand, without spilling a drop. Then she smiles slightly at Sam and adds, "But you can come with, if you want."

Sam nods and waits patiently while she clips Pastrami into her leash and puts her shoes on. Then they descend the stairs together, Daisy crying, "Bye! Have a blast! Love you!" as Iris gives them both a curt, brief wave. They've always been like that, the two of them, as though the personality traits that were meant to be split evenly between them simply went one way or the other instead.

Luce is more like Sam: somewhere in between two extremes, warily trying to bridge the gap. She listens more than she talks, like he tries to, and does her best to be helpful, like him. He wonders, sometimes, if she's like him in less visible ways, too; if deep down inside she's often more upset, or angry, or hurt than she lets on.

He hopes not. It's a complicated hand to be dealt.

Regardless, they're enough alike that they walk in comfortable silence for nearly ten minutes. The sky is gray and vaguely threatening, but Sam's pretty sure it's bluffing, and it's just starting to feel pleasant to be outside again after a winter of cursing the weather. Pastrami has the time to use the facilities and move on to smelling absolutely every object they pass, in search of, Sam assumes, news of the canine world; Sam gets the chance to notice that Luce has dyed a small section of her hair neon yellow, and another bit lime green. It's not finals week for her so much as it's been finals *year* since last August—it turns out that art school is more about long-term capstone projects than exams, at least in Luce's program—and he wonders if she's managing the strain all right, without knowing how to ask her at all.

Finally, he clears his throat, steeling himself. It's ridiculous, he knows, to feel afraid; she's his *little sister*, for God's sake, and Pastrami is *his* dog, and, anyway, of the triplets, Luce's the kind one. "Listen, I'm sorry to do this, but I need to take Pastrami back early."

"Oh," Luce says, blinking at him in surprise. He notices her pull the leash towards herself a little, though he doubts it was on purpose. "Um, okay. How early?"

Sam winces. "I was thinking like. After this walk?"

Luce might be the Kind Triplet, but she's still his little sister, and thus subject to the laws of little sisters everywhere. She groans, a slightly whining element thrown into it, and briefly sounds like the seven-year-old she once was as she snaps, "But *Sam*, come *on*, it's *my* turn with Pastrami!"

"And yet, is it ever your turn with Pastrami when she's eaten half a pound of cocoa powder and needs her stomach pumped, I wonder?" Sam muses aloud, reflexively defending his territory the way he can't quite help with his sisters sometimes, even Luce; even now. "I mean, if we're moving to a taking turns model here, that implies shared ownership, right? So, let's see, this month your half of pet insurance would be—"

"Ugh, Sam, God. Fine," Luce snaps, rolling her eyes at him. "I know she's your dog, it's just... during their finals week Daisy and Iris get a little—oh, whatever. It doesn't matter." She sighs, and as a stab of guilt sinks deep into Sam's abdomen asks, a little plaintively, "What do you need her for so urgently anyway?"

Glancing briefly up at the sky for strength, Sam says, "I have a new neighbor. In the building behind the deli."

Luce stares at him. "So?"

"So," Sam says, and winces in spite of his best efforts not to, "it's... Jake Thompson."

Luce stares for another second. Then she whistles, shaking her head, says, "Dude," and passes him the leash without any further argument.

. . .

Another long stretch of silence, one that lasts for nearly half of the next block, and includes a cross-street where they could turn back towards the apartment. Wordlessly, without looking at each other, they don't, opting instead to take the longer route, to Pastrami's obvious and ecstatic delight.

After a while, her voice thick with sympathetic horror, Luce says, "And you're... sure it's him? It's not... I don't know, like a thing where you got wrongly delivered mail that said that name, and so you're *assuming* it's him, but it could be some other Jake Thompson? He could be a fifty-five-year-old car salesman from Poughkeepsie—"

"Oddly specific," Sam points out, a question for all it isn't one.

"Yeah, so, there's a girl in one of my sculpture classes who should wear a T-shirt that says, 'Ask Me About Catfish Hunting,'" Luce says, shaking her head and grinning. This results in a brief conversational detour, in which Luce explains the recent digital misfortunes that had befallen, indeed, a fifty-five-year-old car salesman from Poughkeepsie. Sam doesn't feel bad about laughing at his misery. The guy was pretending to be a twenty-six-year-old actress online in order to con people, so Sam thinks he got what was coming to him.

Sam also thinks Luce might have a serious crush on this so-called catfish hunter, but he doesn't mention it. That's not the way the two of them talk about things. Born loners in a family full of people with little to no sense of what boundaries are supposed to look like, the two of them have always given each other the grace to bring things up when they're ready to discuss them.

Usually, anyway, because as they round the next corner and her story draws to a close, Luce says, brightly, "Anyway, about Jake —if, that is, it's even him—"

Sam groans a little on the words, "Yes, Luce, it's him. It's him! He came into the deli; I talked to him."

At this, Luce comes to a dead stop. Sam, surprised, nearly tangles himself in Pastrami's leash in turning around to stop, too, and raises his eyebrows at her. He tries to keep his expression cool, calm. He tries to look like someone whose stupid heart has never even thought about pounding like a runaway jackhammer.

"You talked to him?" Luce's eyes are wide; Sam nods. "And was it, like. Okay?"

Sam shrugs. "Yeah, sure."

She stares at him.

"I mean it wasn't... not okay," Sam says, putting a hand to the back of his neck.

She stares at him some more.

"Okay, fine, I don't have any idea how it went," Sam snaps, and starts walking again, leaving her to keep up. She does. "I don't know how a person is supposed to tell? In these circumstances." He thinks of the shadows in Jake's eyes, the way he'd run off and then come back half-crazed with the awkwardness of the whole situation, and still been so... so...

"He was... Jake," Sam says, helplessly, with a broad shrug. "You remember Jake, right? I mean, it's okay if not; you *were* basically an infant."

Laughing, but also lightly shoving him, she says, "Dude, I was like eight when you started bringing him around; you're not *that* much older than us." Then, more soberly, she adds, "And I was ten —we were ten—when it all, uh. Went down? So... plenty old enough to form memories, I think."

Sometimes, in moments like these, Sam considers the merits of assigning randomized names to traumatic events, the way they do with hurricanes. It would be so much easier to talk about the whole thing if Sam could say, "Hey, you don't have to dance around The Hasselhoff Event, we all know what happened and we can all agree it was terrible. I don't need you to baby me."

But Sam can't say that. He *does* need her to baby him—his baby sister, indignity of indignities—because there is no fake name with which to sum up what happened. There is no shorthand, no way around it: Talking about it would mean talking about it, and Sam hasn't, not in over a decade. Not with anyone.

FIVE

NOW: MARCH

Sam makes it another three days without looking Jake up on the internet.

In total, he has more or less resisted the impulse for over ten years, which Sam feels is a lot more impressive. He *has*, a few times, looked Jake up on various social media platforms, found his accounts to be private, and then sat and stared in agonized indecision at the "Request to Follow" button for longer than he cares to admit. But that only happens in particularly grim moments, and it's been ages since the last time. Months, if not years.

He never did hit the follow button, on the theory that it wouldn't be sporting. Sam's theory was always that he, himself, wasn't difficult to find, and if Jake had never found him, it was because he didn't want to.

But he'd never gone so far as to type Jake's full name into an actual search engine and click enter. *Type* it, sure, dozens of times; stare at the letters and feel as though they were accusing him of a crime, absolutely; close the tab feeling deeply ashamed of himself, of course. That was as far as Sam had ever let it go, because it had been made clear, when it all fell apart, that Jake wanted to be left alone. Sam could do that much for him, at least.

However, Sam cannot help but feel, now, that Jake has

changed the terms somewhat. He came into the deli, and then *back* into the deli, and also is living basically a few yards away, closer than he was even in high school. Maybe he's trying to rationalize his own curiosity, but Sam keeps butting up against the argument that it wouldn't be so awful to see what's out there and publicly accessible. Things simply are not as they were even a few days ago.

Still, when he finally cracks it's by accident, his subconscious playing a nasty trick on him. He's at Harmonious Realms, the odd little shop next door to the deli. Joanie, the owner, has been there since the late nineties selling, as far as Sam can tell, whatever she feels like. About half the store is crystals and bundled dried herbs and tarot cards, books with titles like *Witchcraft and You* or *Could You Be Psychic?* The other half is densely packed with a rotating assortment of fascinating items she finds at thrift shops and estate sales.

The store is never particularly crowded, and Sam thinks she'd probably have been driven out of the neighborhood decades ago if she was subject to the same dramatic rental hikes the rest of the street faced, over the years. But Joanie's shop is technically part of the building housing Silverman's, which Sam's grandmother had purchased outright after years of scrimping and saving—mostly, according to family lore, to get one over on the previous landlord, whom she despised. And Deb and Joanie have been best friends since basically the day Harmonious Realms opened its doors, so as long as Silverman's survives, Joanie's does, too.

Of course, that means the reverse is true, too, a fact that's been sitting like so much lead in Sam's gut since the Kiss of Death review. Joanie's more or less family, and he loves her in spite of her erraticism and sincere belief in an assortment of ideas he himself would never entertain. He doesn't want to ruin what she's built any more than he wants to ruin Silverman's, and he knows her foot traffic is down, too, with fewer customers stopping by after lunch at the deli. The guilt is eating at him, even if she does wave him off any time he tries to apologize.

Regardless, he's dropped off a turkey sandwich for her, and he's waiting while she "takes a quick second" to grab something from the back she wants to show him. However, because he knows "Let me take a quick second to find something" is Joanie-speak for "I will be at least ten minutes, get comfortable," he pulls out his phone to get some work done. He's deep in a search spiral, pricing out a potential switch of the restaurant's launderers to save a little extra money, when Joanie calls, "Nearly found it! One more second! Don't go anywhere!"

Sam looks up, amused, fully aware that this means, "I have no damn idea where it's got to and I'll be ten minutes more." And it's at this moment that he catches sight of Jake across the street, chatting pleasantly with someone holding a clipboard. They must be collecting voter registrations or petition signatures or something, because after a second Jake takes the clipboard, scribbles on it, and hands it back. He says something that makes the other person laugh and then walks on, out of Sam's eyeline.

When Sam looks down, all traces of professional restaurant launderers have vanished from his phone. Instead, his treacherous thumbs have typed "Jake Thompson" and hit enter for him, without bothering to ask him if that's what he wanted.

It is what Sam wanted, though. He knows it the minute his eyes lock on the screen; a hunger for the information blooms wild and insatiable within him, only intensifying the longer he scrolls.

Searching Jake's name did not, as Sam had always rather expected it would, produce a string of random articles and corporate biographies about various wrong Jake Thompsons. Instead, he finds himself confronted with both a wide selection of photos of the correct Jake Thompson, and a series of links to celebrity gossip websites discussing him. In the photographs, Jake is always featured alongside a middle-aged man whose very appearance suggests sharp edges; in the articles, Jake's name is always accompanied by the name "Walter Gallagher." And in every place it appears, the name "Walter Gallagher" is always clickable.

Sam clicks. And then clicks again. And then clicks and clicks and clicks and clicks, so many times that he loses track of himself and where he's standing and what he's supposed to be doing until Joanie, returned now, very pointedly clears her throat.

"Oh!" Sam jumps, so badly startled that he accidentally tosses the whole phone in the air. It whips in a nerve-wracking arc through the shop, narrowly missing two large crystal displays and a delicate porcelain baby before landing, luckily, in a basket of crocheted bat plushies next to Joanie. Wincing at Joanie's raised eyebrows, he adds, belatedly, "Sorry."

"What for? Not like it broke anything." Joanie's small, pointed face is entertained under her curly blond-and-gray hair, which has been cut into a springy bob for as long as Sam's known her. She fishes the phone out of the basket and, glancing at the still-illuminated screen, laughs. "What, are you embarrassed to be caught reading TMZ, Sammy? I'm hardly going to judge you. Although, I will say, if Walt Gallagher is what does it for you, then we have very similar taste in men, and I'm sorry. That's a real tragedy for anyone."

"No, it's not that, it's..." Sam pauses, frustrated, trying to think of a way to explain this incredibly bizarre situation without having to get into any of it. He is, however, distracted almost immediately, because: "Wait. You know who Walt Gallagher is?"

Joanie rolls her eyes. "You think I'm that old? That I rode a dinosaur to school each morning? That I learned the alphabet from cave paintings on the wall and—"

"*I* didn't know who he was until just now," Sam interrupts, because if he lets her get going, it'll be five minutes of riffing. "I'm still not sure I do, except that it looks like he's, uh. Some kind of media mogul?" *It also looks like he's Jake's ex*, he adds, to himself. *Jake's rich, famous, handsome, professionally styled ex. Hell.*

"Did you seriously never watch *Fund or Fall*?" Joanie demands, crossing her arms over her chest as though the very thought of this offends her. "I thought everyone had seen that show. I thought they pumped it into every doctor's office waiting room in America."

Sam shrugs instead of saying, *I wouldn't know, Joanie; I'm the product of two doctors, and so I'll do almost anything to avoid going to see one.* "Don't know what to tell you. If I have seen it, it didn't leave a mark."

"*Well,*" Joanie says, in the gleeful-bordering-on-menacing tones of someone who is about to explain their favorite television show to you whether you like it or not. "Basically, it's sort of like *Shark Tank*, right? Except that the people who go on have to be so willing to stand behind their product that they agree to jump out of a *plane* if they don't get funded—"

"*What?*"

"With a parachute, with a parachute," Joanie says hastily. "It's a skydive, not... murder. Makes for good television, though, I tell you what."

Sam thinks it sounds like exploitative television but decides not to say so. He doesn't want to spoil her fun; he knows she's not naturally inclined towards it. Instead, he says, "And what, exactly, does this have to do with Walt Gallagher?"

"Oh, he's one of the judges!" Joanie's eyes have lit up with enthusiasm, and she sighs slightly wistfully as she says, "He's the *mean* one."

"Great," Sam says, trying not to sound as sarcastic as he feels. Both that statement and the way she said it bode fairly ill for Jake: Joanie really does have tragic taste in men.

The conversation moves on. It turns out Joanie wanted to show him a sad, desiccated pickle she found at the back of the shop fridge, and to ask his professional opinion on whether or not she should eat it. He tells her no, and gets her a fresh pickle from the deli, and then goes back to his day. He leaves the entire topic of Jake, and Walt Gallagher, and their very public, very long relationship aside. He *is* a professional, after all. These are his work hours. Sam's not about to let anything get in between him and his aunt's sign-off, a chance to run this place the way he wants to. Not even if that thing is Jake Goddamned Thompson.

That night, when he's alone in his apartment and Pastrami is flopped bonelessly across his lap like a weighted blanket, is another story. Sam is not usually one for reality television, although he does watch that show where Gordon Ramsay goes undercover in restaurant kitchens, mostly out of paranoia. Otherwise, he avoids it. It's not any sort of holier-than-thou affectation or anything—his brain wasn't built to follow unstructured narrative, and he's medium face-blind, and too many people talking at once on a screen makes all the audio impossible for him to parse.

So he's not expecting the glitzy, emotional-whiplash-inducing onslaught that is *Fund or Fall*. The show introduces you to hopeful small business owners, all with great ideas, and then brings them before the judges to desperately make their pitches. In spite of the editing and musical overlay, the nerves radiating off the contestants are nearly always palpable, and for good reason: The judges are allowed to interrupt them, interrogate them, demand demonstrations they didn't plan for, and, of course, force them to jump out of an airplane.

Also, when they're done presenting, Walter Gallagher tears every one of them—every one!—down to confetti-like shreds, leaving their hopes and dreams littered across the soundstage. Even the ones he *funds*, he finds a way to attack first, pecking and poking at them merrily, a curious robin tormenting an unfortunate worm.

Sam feels concern for Jake swell in his stomach like a balloon and tries, unsuccessfully, to pop it. Instead he reads several more articles in which Jake and Walt appear together. This stops when, after a few minutes of glaring at the inaccurate photo caption reading WALT GALLAGHER AND PARTNER JAKE THOMAS ATTEND MET GALA, Pastrami jumps up and smacks him in the face with her tail. Sam tells himself this is the act of a top-tier therapy animal completely attuned to his every need, even though he's pretty sure it's just time for her last walk of the day.

Of course, about ten minutes later he's doubting she was ever a top-tier therapy animal. This is because, despite normally being utterly relaxed on walks, she has broken the clasp on her collar in her urgency to barrel towards the person across the alleyway from them.

This person is Jake Thompson.

"Pastrami, NO," Sam cries, horror-stricken. Why now? Why today, of all days, and with *this man*, has Pastrami decided to lose track of her famous chill? He runs after her, hoping to restrain her before she can jump on Jake or knock him over or do whatever it is she suddenly and uncharacteristically—

Huh. Sam stops, confused, because Pastrami has also stopped, about six inches from Jake. She is snuffling with wriggling enthusiasm at the coat draped over his arm, not seeming at all interested in jumping or otherwise bothering him. Also, Jake is laughing, although there's a slightly helpless, rueful edge to both it and the expression on his face.

"Pastrami, for the love of God, sit," Sam says wearily. Pastrami does, somehow managing to look slightly prim about it, and then resumes sniffing the coat as Sam ties her broken leash around her collar. She is, Sam notices, drooling. "Jake, listen, I'm so sorry, I swear this isn't like her. I mean, she's a therapy dog, for God's sake! I don't know why—"

"No, no, stop," Jake says, half-chuckling, shaking his head. "It's not her fault; it's me. I... God." He looks briefly up at the sky, as if in search of something, and then, brightly, making eye contact with Sam, "Well! It seems I have no choice but to embarrass myself before you again, my apologies, not my first choice, either, etcetera, but. What can you do? The truth is, I was at my sister's engagement party, and they ordered a crazy amount of food, and money's kind of tight right now, so. Uh." Jake winces, and admits, "My... jacket pockets may or may not be... full of pierogies?"

Pastrami barks, as if in confirmation, and wags her tail.

"Ah," Sam says, trying not to laugh. "That would explain it, yeah. Pierogies are basically her favorite food."

"And yet," Jake says, smiling down at the dog, "you called her Pastrami, right? Not Pierogi?"

"She *looks* like a pastrami," Sam tries to explain, even though he knows there's no point. He's had this conversation a hundred times, and people always look at him as though he's lost his mind and tell him they don't see it.

Instead, Jake cocks his head, stares at her for a second, and then says, "Okay, I'll grant you—yes she does. But it's not like she *chose* what she looks like, whereas her love of pierogi is a matter of *preference.*"

"Are you seriously campaigning for me to rename my dog right now?" Sam's amused, not annoyed, but a little incredulous all the same. "On merit of... what, freedom of expression?"

"Look in her eyes, Sam," Jake says, a note of mock-pleading slipping into his voice. "She *wants* to be a Pierogi; can't you see that?"

"You're misreading the signals," Sam says dryly. "She wants *a* pierogi."

There's real pleading in Jake's voice this time, as he says, "Hey, can she have one? They're like—potato and cheese, I think, not, uh. Chocolate and grape and... I don't know, other things dogs can't have. Rat poison?"

"That'd be a weird pierogi," Sam agrees, not bothering to keep the note of laughter out of his voice this time, "but: sure. If you don't mind, that would make her night."

He watches in a mixture of sympathy and the well-concealed horror of a food service professional as Jake does, indeed, pull what appears to be a loose pierogi from a ziplock bag in his jacket pocket. Grinning, he tosses it to Pastrami, who snatches it gleefully out of the air and then, instead of scarfing it down in one bite the way most dogs would, carries it off a few feet, to the end of her leash's tether. She settles on the ground, places the pierogi carefully in front of her, and then eats it in tiny, careful bites, her tail wagging furiously.

"She just does that," Sam says, when he notices Jake staring at her the way people often do the first time they encounter this particular quirk. "At least with any food she finds particularly high-value. I think she's savoring it? Hard to ask her, though."

"A gourmand," Jake says, his voice far away. "Dog after my own heart." Then he seems to snap back to himself and adds, "I mean, guess that makes sense, doesn't it? If she was brought up in your deli and everything."

"Honestly, she's been given a lot more hot dogs than she probably should have," Sam admits, only half thinking about it. The other half of him is stuck on the idea of Jake stuffing his pockets with food at family events in order to eat. Surely his parents would help him, if he was really in trouble? Sam knows the Thompsons are loaded, and not the kind of loaded that might have semi-recently diminished to merely "comfortable." That was old, handed-down money, money stuffed away in so many different bonds and stocks and assets that you'd have to really, really try to ever come close to running out.

On the other hand... Well. Sam learned the hard way that what you might expect a parent to do for their child in a difficult situation and what they *actually* do can vary wildly. Maybe Jake's parents are out of the picture now, or uninterested in helping him; maybe Jake's been too proud to tell them anything's wrong. Maybe nothing *is* wrong, and it wouldn't be any of Sam's business if it was, and he should leave it alone.

Instead, he asks the normal, polite questions about Lila, Jake's sister, and her groom-to-be, who is apparently called Brian. While Jake sneaks Pastrami another pierogi and talks around what are obviously some doubts on the merits of Brian, who does indeed sound like a bit of a tool, Sam studies him, trying to decide what to do. He doesn't want to hurt Jake's pride, or God forbid insult him, but he can't quite bring himself to let it go, either. There's something nearly gaunt in the way Jake's skin is sitting across his chin and cheekbones; his clothes, which Sam can tell now that he's seen all those articles are fancy, high-end pieces, are loose on him in a way that Sam can't imagine was intentional.

If Sam were a completely honest person, the sort of person to let his authentic truth fly no matter how audacious or embarrassing, he would say, *Hey, Jake, looks like maybe you're experiencing the symptoms of malnutrition for reasons of your own, none of my business, would you think it was weird if I started cooking you several meals per day? Please say no.*

However, the very idea of doing this makes Sam want to explode into ten million pieces, so instead, as the conversation starts to dwindle down towards its natural end, he says, "Listen, uh. If you wanted to, come by tomorrow, around three? We close down for an hour and do family meal, to cover shift change and so the staff can eat. Food might be weird—it's my day, and it's my only real chance to get creative—but it'll be edible, at least."

"This is your fault," Jake says, with what Sam is pretty sure is joking severity, to Pastrami. She gazes up at him with guileless delight. "You made me look so pathetic that now Sam thinks I'm going to starve to death in my apartment, when the truth is that I suffer from an incurable pierogi addiction—"

"I don't think you look pathetic," Sam interrupts, unable to contain it a second longer. "And I don't really think you're a pierogi addict, either? Look, just... come, all right?" He rubs a hand against the back of his neck, uncomfortable. "Or don't, if you don't want to, but lots of other folks from the neighborhood pop in. It's a nice way to meet people. And we're always cooking up whatever needs using; it would just go to waste." Smiling as he watches Jake slip her a third pierogi, he adds, "And, anyway, I owe you for Pastrami's dinner now, so. You might as well."

"Hmm," Jake says, and then, "Yeah, all right, maybe. I'm not sure what tomorrow looks like for me but maybe. We'll see."

"Well," Sam says, with a shrug, "we do it every day at about three, so. Open invitation, if you want it."

Jake stares at him for a second as though unsure how to respond to this before finally, nodding slowly, he says, "I think that I do, thanks. Thank you. I have to... go now, but I'll see you, uh. One of these days, I guess." And then he smiles at Sam, this bright, brittle smile that somehow looks both happy and sad, the expression fleeting but haunting in its intensity. "Have a good night, Sam. Pastrami."

And he turns away, hurrying off towards his own building, only waving a hand over his shoulder as Sam calls a goodbye.

SIX

THEN: MAY, TWELVE YEARS AGO

Sam absolutely did not intend to throw a house party.

Well, no, that's not strictly true. It's teenage logic, calcified and fossilized in his brain all these years: He did intend to throw a party, and he did intend that party to take place at his house. He just hadn't intended it to be a *big* house party. Every previous time in his life he'd invited friends over without permission while his parents were out of town—and that, admittedly, had been a number of times—only the people he'd invited had showed up, and things never got particularly exciting. Usually they watched a movie or, if the night got wild, played a few rounds of Settlers of Catan.

At seventeen, Sam had not understood party mechanics. It was for adults and more popular teenagers to know that after a certain point, a party is more than just the sum of its guests. These days, he's aware that if you gather enough people together in the spirit of having a raucous, no-holds-barred good time, that gathering will take on a certain life of its own. You can't work in his industry and not know that. In the right conditions—even, remarkably, in an entirely sober crowd—people will do things they'd never consider in any other circumstance, driven by the spirit of the party.

But Sam hadn't known that then. What Sam had known was

that if he asked twelve people to come by on Saturday night and hang out, maybe six or seven of them would show up. Still, he dutifully made enough frozen pizza rolls for thirteen and then waited for the first person to arrive, nervous as always that no one would.

An hour later, that worry had transformed into a blissful daydream, one Sam tried to wrap around himself as he walked around his parents' home in horror. In another, better world, no one had shown up at all, and Sam had been a little sad, maybe, and then he'd read a book, and gone to bed.

In this world—one Sam was beginning to suspect was, in fact, hell—every student he'd ever passed in the halls of Horseshoe Heights High was crammed beneath the rafters of the so-called Red Roof Inn. They'd poured in through the front door like a swarm, one right after the other. They'd brought speakers, and plastic cups, and a variety of high-end liquors stolen from their parents' carts and cabinets. In retrospect these were the weird alcohols, least used and thus unlikely to be missed. At the time, Sam had assumed that among the most common drinks in the world was the combination that was on trend amongst his peers: peppermint schnapps and Sprite.

There were people in every room of the house. He'd walked into them all, perversely curious, needing to know how bad it was and then regretting finding out. Someone was smoking a joint on his parents' bed, and there was a sort of Olympics of Bed Jumping being held in the triplets' room. God, who even were all these people? He didn't recognize most of their faces. Should he call the police? But wouldn't *he* be the one to get in trouble, if he called the police? But they were destroying the house—oh, his parents were going to *kill* him.

But then someone came up and clapped Sam on the back. He was a football type, big, wearing a senior letterman jacket. Sam never actually learned his name, because they never interacted again. But he shone with the unquantifiable light of popularity visible only to teenagers, and he grinned at Sam, and said, "You're like the biggest badass in HHHS history, bro. I mean, these fools are wrecking this place and you're just vibing. Cool as a cucumber. Guess it's true what they say about you, huh? Anyway, congrats on a dope party."

He handed Sam a drink and ambled away, and Sam stared after him, thunderstruck. It shouldn't have mattered to him, but that approval, in that moment, had felt like the sun rising. Sam hadn't been cool as a cucumber: He'd been frozen, horrified, ripping himself into little stressed-out shreds. But to that tall, popular, linebacker-shaped senior, he'd come across as a chill and unfazed badass, calm and in control.

Sam had wanted to feel calm and in control for so long, by that point. He's not sure that, before that moment, he ever really had before.

He took a breath. He took another. *You're a badass,* he told himself, and tried to believe it. *You're a badass, and it's too late to do anything about it, so you might as well enjoy your stupid party. You are, after all, going to die for it.*

When he took a step down the stairs, someone caught his eye, and enthusiastically gave him a pair of cheerful finger guns. Someone else called, "Cool party, man!" A girl he'd been in math classes with for two years—a girl who had once, when Sam asked her if she'd dropped a pencil, stared at him for a full minute but refused to respond—waved coyly at him, and blew him a kiss.

Well, that was that. Sam could tell himself all day he was a badass, and he might even be able to believe it, but there was nothing he could tell himself that would make him want to kiss a girl. God knows he would have found it already, if such a thing did exist.

When he got down to the first floor, he realized someone had set up a keg in the foyer, using his great-grandmother's hand-embroidered footstool as a balancing device. One of the legs had broken off of it and was sitting forlornly to one side. It looked up at him accusingly, as if to say, "You've killed me, Sam! You and you alone!"

Sam decided to get some air.

He walked back down through the party, briefly and half-heartedly thrashing along with the group blasting music in the living room and spilling a bit of his untouched drink, then choosing to ignore two boys ripping the hose attachment out of the kitchen sink faucet. He gently pushed aside a couple making out aggressively against the back door, and then stepped outside, relieved to take a breath of air that didn't smell like sweat, beer, or pot smoke.

Then he looked out into the yard and was relieved all over again: There on the other side, leaning up against the fence next to their shared hedge, was Jake.

He met Sam's eyes, and smiled.

The walk across the yard that night is etched in Sam's memory like stained glass, leaded in place and catching the light even now. He's never been entirely sure why. Maybe it was that sense of blooming possibility, the still-solidifying idea that his life was his own, and he could do anything with it he wanted.

Maybe it was the way Jake was smiling at him, a small, private smile, one Sam would normally only get to see through the gaps in the fence.

"Hi." Sam was breathless by the time he reached Jake, for exactly no reason at all—it's not as though it was a taxing walk. "You came. I thought you had... You're not usually around on Friday nights."

Jake's smile shrank down, his lips pursing slightly as he glanced down at his nails. "You sound oddly glad I'm here," he remarked, "for someone who didn't actually invite me."

"I didn't actually invite anyone," Sam admitted, leaning up against the fence next to Jake. "Or, I mean, I invited a few people from my English class to come over and watch the movie version of *Rebecca* so we wouldn't have to actually read it—"

"What's so wrong with *Rebecca*?" Jake said, crossing his arms over his chest and sounding genuinely affronted. "Gothic mansions, undertones of lesbian obsession, hot murdery husbands —it's basically a perfect book!"

"You think Maxim in *Rebecca* is hot?" Sam asked, wrinkling his nose.

"Do you *not*?" Jake seemed astounded by this. Then, before Sam could answer, he added, "Hey! And you've *clearly* read it."

Sam shrugged and felt himself flush slightly, caught. "Ah. Yeah. A few times."

"So you invited your English class"—Jake looked doubtfully out over the yard and house, both packed with teenagers—"and maybe every English class there's ever been, over to watch a movie... to avoid reading a book... that you've already read several times?"

Wincing, Sam said, "Honestly? My parents are in Michigan with the triplets, taking them to tour sleepaway summer camps—"

"Ew," Jake commented.

"I know," Sam agreed, still bitter about it. *He'd* never gone to sleepaway camp. He'd never so much as gone to day camp, not even the free ones you could sign up for in most cities if you got on the list early enough. "But I just. I don't know. It felt too lame to do *nothing*, and you're usually..." Sam paused, and only didn't say, *Out with your actual friends*, by the skin of his teeth. "...busy, on the weekends, so. I figured I'd have a few people over. Only those people told people, and those people told people, and now... well." He gestured out at the yard, and sighed. "Here we are."

Meditatively, Jake said, "Your parents are going to kill you, you know."

Sam sighed again. "I know." He looked wistfully into the windows of the house; he'd never seen them like that before, every one alight, shadows alive and moving in every room, and he never would again. It was nice, in a strange, complicated way. Looking at it made him feel a bit sick and weirdly proud of himself at the same time. "But it really was an accident, and there's nothing I can do about it now."

"You could ask them to leave," Jake suggested.

Sam rolled his eyes. "Do you think they would?"

"No," Jake admitted, on a sigh. "They might have a few hours ago, or if they didn't all think you were some sort of semiprofessional daredevil, but as it is: no. Probably not."

"Right. So." Sam shrugged, and cast Jake a slightly hesitant sidelong grin. Lifting his drink, he said, "Might as well enjoy it? Since it's literally my funeral?"

Jake narrowed his eyes, but then he said, "Oh, give me that." He tasted it, made a face, and said, "Oh, God, it's the awful mint Sprite thing; what is *wrong* with everyone," and handed it back to Sam, who took one sip, gagged, and precipitously tipped it out into the hedge. They exchanged a look of utter exasperation with it all: the bad taste of their classmates, and the demands and restrictions of their parents, and the whole unsettling, exhausting experience of being teenagers.

But then Jake said, "Why can't you tell them the truth, Sam? I don't understand why you have to act like you're this other person. Like you've done these things you just... haven't. Wouldn't it be the same party either way?"

Later, Sam would come to realize that the answer to that question was no. It would have been a different party if he'd been presenting any different version of himself: the honest one, or a different set of lies, or any of the fairly normal spaces in between where most teenagers build some sort of construction or another. Part of what made that night what it was *was* Sam's out-of-control reputation, the sense people had that whatever they did, it couldn't possibly be any worse than what *he'd* do. The fact that he didn't end up doing much of anything didn't matter. It was potential that powered the rumor mill, rarely what actually happened.

But Sam hadn't known that then, so he'd given Jake the best answer he could, which was, "Look: I've gone to a lot of schools, okay? And sometimes it's gone well, and sometimes it's gone... less well." He swallowed and thought of elementary school in Euclid, where he made a bad first impression that kept getting worse, and was thus relentlessly bullied by his classmates until his parents, thankfully, moved. "The truth is I'd rather—ugh. I'm just... trying to get through high school. Aren't we all trying to get through high school?"

Jake's gaze had sharpened for a moment, then softened. "Yeah," he'd said. "I guess we are." He'd tapped his fingers against his thigh for a second and then added, "You know what? You're right. We should enjoy your funeral. Come on; let's get a drink."

Sam could have said, "I don't drink," or, more accurately, "I didn't drink until that sip of foul swill a few minutes ago, and if that's alcohol, I am all set for the rest of my life. Thank you so much and, very sincerely, yuck." But he didn't. He smiled, instead, achingly pleased to be asked, and followed Jake inside.

Inside was a carnival of fascinating horrors.

Jake made them both a drink. He told Sam it was a 7 and 7, although some years later Sam ordered one at an actual bar and was delivered such a different drink that he's sure, now, that it must have been something else. He wasn't watching while Jake put it together, too distracted by the wreck of the kitchen.

Sam had only been outside for ten minutes, and the kitchen had been fine when he left it, setting aside whatever tragedy had befallen the sink. But while he was away, conditions had deteriorated. It had at least emptied of people, but the window over the sink was broken, a still-lit joint next to its now-misaligned frame, smoking gently inside a ceramic flower Luce had made in art class. The freezer *wasn't* broken, at least as far as Sam could tell, but it might as well have been: the door was hanging wide open and it had been stripped entirely bare, nothing left within but shelves and a few popsicle stains.

This was a mystery: Where had it all gone? Surely they hadn't eaten it all—some of it was raw meat, for God's sake—but Sam didn't get a chance to investigate. He'd caught sight of the stove, on which a pot full of something that he suspected had once been ramen was beginning to smoke. He pulled it off the heat, then turned off the burner, then noticed that one of the cabinet doors was fully off one of its hinges and barely clinging to the other, as though having recently survived a bear attack.

"God, Aunt Deb is right: People are animals," Sam muttered under his breath. She'd been saying it for years, any time they were out to dinner, or at a store, and someone behaved badly; it always made his mother roll her eyes.

"These people, anyway," Jake said brightly, coming up next to Sam and pressing a glass into his hand. "You should take this; you're going to need it."

Then he dragged Sam into the dining room, where Sam immediately solved the mystery of what had happened to the contents of the freezer.

The dining table, which normally sat in the center of the room, had been pushed up against one wall. Ranged upon it was a collection of teenagers, some sitting, some sprawling, some standing. They were all yelling—cheering, really—for the group standing in front of the table. That merry band had a laundry basket filled with the contents of the freezer, and they appeared to be taking turns sliding them as hard as possible, one by one, across the hardwood floor. The goal, as far as Sam could tell, was to make the item explode impressively against the opposite wall. And it was, Sam had to give it to them, fairly impressive how much they'd changed its color in such a short amount of time.

On the other hand: "I can't believe both of my parents are going to prison for life," Sam said, mournfully and under his breath, to Jake. He took a long sip of his drink, which he didn't like, but it seemed like the thing to do. At least it wasn't the peppermint lime nightmare.

"Oh, I don't know," Jake said back, equally low. "There was a party like this at Jasper Collinwood's house last year, while his parents were in Barbados for a second honeymoon, and his mom is Judge Collinwood, so. They might just get a slap on the wrist for murdering you in cold blood."

"Comforting," Sam said, dry, and Jake grinned at him and shrugged.

"I live to please," he said, with a little bow, and then turned when someone called, "Jake! Bro! I thought that was you—come on! We're spinning out here, and you gotta defend your title!"

Sam, resigned, braced himself for It to happen. Jake was one person when it was just the two of them, hanging out behind the hedge or in one of their houses, or even during the occasional moment they caught together at school, when fate was kind or Sam was skipping class. But the minute one of his friends interrupted them, the minute he had to start putting on The Jake Thompson Show, he was as remote from Sam as someone who lived on another planet, instead of the house behind his own. Sam had become used to it. It didn't bother him very much, so long as he didn't think about it.

Except that night Jake had rolled his eyes, and groaned, and said, "God. Sam, have you ever done a wine spin?" Then he'd taken Sam by the wrist and dragged him outside. Sam had not ever done a wine spin, and looking back from the clearer vantage point of adulthood, he's pretty sure no one ever *should* do one. The wine spin is not, as a concept, a good idea.

But he still watched in horrified fascination as Jake sat down in an office chair—Sam's father's leather office chair, Sam realized with a distant but very real pang of terror—and someone held what appeared to be a plastic bag full of red liquid over his head. It was, Sam surmised from context clues after a moment, what came inside one of those huge, cheap boxes of wine. There was a spigot on the end, which Jake made a great show of wiping off with his sleeve and then placed in his mouth.

Someone flicked the spigot, and someone else started spinning the chair, and the person holding the bag ran to keep up as Jake chugged with the impressive but also frankly upsetting ease of someone who had done this before. The crowd began to chant, "Wine spins! Wine spins! Wine spins!"

Sam found himself wanting to chant, "Your liver! Your liver! Your liver!" He was aware that it was not at all in line with the reputation that led to this entire calamitous evening in the first place, so he kept it to himself.

It was around this point that a small mental package finally made its way to the central chamber of Sam's brain, appearing only after it had survived an arduous journey. It was a battered, beaten thing, torn and stained and marked with something that looked like a footprint, and stuck with notices that said things like, *Please! For the love of God! Someone get this up to the control room!* It contained a single piece of paper, which contained a single sentence, which read:

Perhaps, on reflection, there might be some unfortunate conse- quences to telling so many people so many lies.

The reality of the party—the enormity of the mistake—washed over him like a mudslide, sweeping him away in the debris that remained over the first floor of the house. What was he going to *do?* What was he going to *say?* His parents were getting back in two days; he couldn't possibly clean it all up in time. God, there had been an assembly at *school* about that party at Jasper Collinwood's house. Could he get a professional crew in, maybe, to clean it? But where would he get the money? Maybe Deb would help him? But ugh, no, she'd probably think it was *funny* that the house got wrecked, and anyway he hadn't seen her since that Yom Kippur his parents hosted last year, where she and Mara had that blowout fight.

Abruptly but profoundly, he started to feel like he was going to be sick, not sure if it was from nerves or the very drink he'd been sipping, and he stumbled away from the crowd and down the porch steps with Jake still spinning under the bagged wine. Under any other circumstance Sam would have stayed and kept an eye on him, but he couldn't bear it anymore, this swimming mass of almost-strangers who were looking at him but seeing someone else. What had felt good, early in the night, the nods and acknowledge- ment of his fellow classmates, abruptly felt twisted, horrible. Each one ratcheted up his sense of guilt another notch.

That wretched walk around to the side of the house seemed to take an age. He was so panicked, so upset, that he could hardly put one foot in front of the other. The whole night up until that point he'd been at a sort of automatic remove, not yet ready to face the reality before him. He'd run through every possible punishment he could think of: being grounded for a year; having his laptop run over by a semi-truck; being forced to babysit every day until the triplets turned eighteen; having his bedroom moved to the unfinished section of the basement; being left for the summer on top of a mountain with a tent and crate of protein bars to meditate upon his crimes. But it hadn't even occurred to him that that night—the damage, and the expense, and the fight Sam and his parents had about it, and the way they'd all been with one another, after— would be the penultimate stair on a flight he'd never noticing himself descending, one that led to him being told, in no uncertain terms, that he'd have to finish high school in someone else's house.

He'd been pretty freaked out all the same. He'd gone and sat on the dilapidated, half-rotted wooden bench on the left edge of the property line, which had been there when they moved in and which David and Mara had never quite managed to bother removing, and put his head between his knees, laced his fingers behind his neck. Firmly, and exclusively, and over and over again, he thought: *Don't vomit, Sam. Do. Not. Vomit.*

After an interminable age that was probably, in retrospect, about ten minutes, someone said, "Sam? You okay?"

Sam looked up and it was Jake, looking remarkably sober for having been Wine Spun, and holding a bottle of water. He passed it to Sam, who took it gratefully, taking a few desperate swigs as Jake folded neatly down next to him on the bench.

"Not really," Sam admitted, as he wiped his mouth and attempted to pass the bottle back. Jake refused it, indicating that Sam should keep it, and Sam tried to smile; based on Jake's returned expression, it didn't go very well. "It's kind of all... hitting me? How bad it is?"

"That makes sense," Jake said, sanguine. "It is, I'm sorry to say, *very* bad."

Sam laughed, not with much humor. "You don't want to maybe sugarcoat it for me a little bit?"

"I don't think you'll enjoy that," Jake said, "but sure, we can try it." He adopted an affected, old-Hollywood-ingenue sort of voice and said, "I know it seems grim now, Sammy, but I really *do* think your parents are going to love the new color of the dining room wall—"

"Oh my God, stop, stop," Sam said, laughing for real, even if it was half in horror. "God. You're right. That's worse."

"If I were you," Jake said, his voice abruptly serious, "I think I might be relieved. Not because David and Mara aren't going to kill you, they definitely are, but. I don't know." Sounding unsure, like he wasn't entirely certain it was the sort of thing they had permission to say to one another, he added, "I guess I just feel like... why would you do all of it, you know? Not this, I know this party was an accident and/or the horrible act of a vengeful God, but... the rumors, the vandalism. Why would you do that if you didn't want, on some level, to get caught?"

"Seriously?" Sam said, trying to laugh on it. "You think I *want* to get in trouble? That this is all, what, some sort of half-cocked scheme, and deep down I just want my parents to *care* enough about me to—" He stopped, cutting himself off, because he could hear the razor-edged truth in it even though he desperately didn't want to. It settled, heavy and unignorable, into Sam's bones like lead.

Jake shrugged, looking pained. "Isn't it?"

"Sometimes I wish your mom wasn't a therapist," Sam muttered, staring down at his hands, and was surprised when Jake laughed.

"Sam," he said, with real feeling, "sometimes we all wish that."

Sam still couldn't quite muster up a laugh, but he turned his head and smiled at Jake, amused and rueful at first. But Jake was staring back at him with an expression of such fierce concentration that Sam's smile slid into something smaller, more confused. He said, "Jake...?"

"Realistically," Jake said, his brow still creased in thought, "what's the shortest amount of time you expect your parents to ground you? Like when do you imagine there's a glimmer of a chance you'll see the daylight again?"

Sam sighed, grimacing. "Oh, I'd say seven? Eight, maybe? We're talking thousands of years, right?"

"Of course," Jake agreed. He still seemed to be somewhere else, his gaze fixed but nearly vacant. "That's about what I thought. It's just... I mean, the timing's really *bad*, obviously, but I guess it *is* my last chance to do it before... Hmm."

"Your last chance to do what?" Sam swallowed, wondering if he should be alarmed. If Jake had secret aspirations towards setting the hedges on fire, for example, it would be a terrible time to find out. That didn't really sound like Jake, but a few hours earlier Sam wouldn't have suspected his classmates of wanting to throw a frozen turkey across his living room like it was a bowling ball, so he wasn't looking to take anything for granted.

Then Jake said, "This," and grabbed him by the T-shirt, and kissed him.

It was a *bad* kiss, which shouldn't have been a surprise; it was, after all, Sam's first one. But Sam was so profoundly not expecting it, was so sure his feelings for Jake were one-sided, that Jake was so far out of his league that he couldn't possibly see Sam that way. He gasped in shock against Jake's mouth, which, combined with the driving force of Jake's enthusiasm, caused an unfortunate meeting of teeth. They both pulled back, Sam not sure if he wanted to wince at the awkwardness or grin for the next several eternities at the amazing, impossible news that Jake wanted to *kiss him*.

And then Jake smiled, and shook his head, and said, "Let's try that again, shall we? Once more, from the top."

Sam changed his mind. He didn't want to wince or grin; he wanted to do this, and nothing but this, forever. When he looked back on the moment later, he'd be appalled by his inexpert technique and fumbling hands, but at the time he'd felt as though he and Jake were *inventing* kissing there on the rotting old bench, the first two human beings in history to ever discover it.

Somewhere in the back of his mind, a siren began to caterwaul, as though alerting him to the opening of a secure door, one meant to protect something valuable. He ignored it at first, only managing to break away, breathing hard, when he realized the howling of sirens was not within, but without—approaching from a distance, but louder all the time. Resting his forehead against Jake's, he murmured, "Shit. Those are for me, aren't they?"

"Ohhhh yeah," Jake said, sounding apologetic about it. "No doubt about it. And, so you know, no offense or anything, but I *will* be jumping the fence before they get here. It's not you, it's just that I'm not interested in being arrested and then executed by my father, especially not so close to your own untimely death. You understand."

But he waited, without moving his head away, until they could see the flashing lights turn down the street, blue and red and blinding.

SEVEN

NOW: MARCH

Sam has no idea if he should expect Jake to take up the invitation to swing by for family meal. He knows there's every chance that Jake never will. It was probably weird and presumptuous of Sam to even offer, in retrospect. Jake's from a wealthy family, and was semi-recently in what certainly looked, in Sam's research, to be a long-term, monogamous relationship with an incredibly mean celebrity who got famous for being rich. He's probably fine, and doesn't need a random mid-afternoon meal at the deli, and might even have been slightly offended by Sam's offer.

That's what Sam tells himself when Jake doesn't turn up at the appointed time the afternoon following their conversation in the alleyway. That inviting him was stupid, a mistake, and Sam shouldn't get his hopes up for ever seeing him in the deli again at all.

So he probably looks a little too excited—excited enough that Alphonse raises his eyebrows and hides a smile behind the back of his hand—when he hears the front doorbell chime a few minutes after three, and a familiar voice call, "Sam? Are you here? I know you said I could come by, but the sign on the door says, 'Employees Only Until 4 p.m.,' so if you're, like, having a meeting or something... Oh. Uh. Hi."

This last, slightly surprised, is because Sam has come dashing out of the back to meet him, only his nonskid shoes saving him from careening into the counter and being thrown over it by his own momentum. Knowing it's entirely doomed but committed to his bit anyway, he tries to sound casual as he says, "Hi."

"It would seem you are indeed here, then," Jake says. A small smile bounces around his mouth for a moment, not seeming sure where it wants to land—it lifts first one corner, then the other, before dropping both into a slightly confused expression. "Is that... Um. Are you supposed to be... holding that?"

Sam stares at him, uncomprehending, for a long moment. Then he follows Jake's gaze down his own arm, where he realizes, to his surprise, that the raw chicken he was seasoning for tonight's special—Wednesdays are always the roast chicken dinner—is still in his gloved hand, dangling from its drumstick.

"No!" Sam says, with a somewhat forced joviality, and then, "You should come on back, and I should... uh, put this down. Follow me." He lifts the folding counter with his non-chickened hand to let Jake through, and then, stepping in front of him, adds, "Oh! But stay on the rubber mats, yeah? You don't have—"

"Nonslip shoes? I do, actually." When Sam turns to glance at him in surprise, Jake shrugs, putting a hand to the back of his neck. "I was a barista? When I first moved to LA? So I had to wear them then, and, uh." Wincing slightly, not quite meeting Sam's eyes, he shifts his weight, lifts his cane off the ground and wiggles it a little in the air. "Turns out they're not just helpful in a kitchen? You'd be amazed how much wet ground can mess up my day."

"That makes sense," Sam says, after the barest half second where he strangles back, *I am history's greatest imbecile, kindly have the mercy to kill me where I stand.* He proceeds far enough into the back to grab a bowl and slap the chicken into it; Alphonse passes and whisks it away in seconds, before Sam can even finish taking his gloves off, giving him a reproachful look. It's clear he'd also give Sam an earful if it weren't for Jake standing just behind him.

"Also," Jake says, "they're helpful at the dance studio up the street, where I work. Madame Louisa likes a very specific finish on her floors, which I appreciated a lot more when I was a student."

His chin tilts up defiantly as he says this, as though daring Sam to... what, exactly? Say something asinine and insensitive about Jake's disability? Disparage teaching as a profession? Delve into their shared unspoken past by pointing out that he remembers Madame Louisa's name, mostly because he'd spent a lot of time cursing it, since Jake regularly had to cut short stolen afternoon hookups to get to her studio? Surely he knows Sam well enough to know he'd never do any of those things... doesn't he?

Of course he doesn't, a little part of Sam points out, sounding a lot like Deb. *It's been more than ten years, and you were kids back then. He doesn't know what's going on in your head any more than you know what's going on in his. Do you want to be scared, or do you want to be curious?*

"I didn't know you were teaching dance," Sam says, tossing his dirty gloves in the trash. "Ballet, I'm assuming?" When Jake nods, most of the defiance drains from his expression, leaving something smaller, shyer. "God, that's cool. I bet you're a really great teacher. How long have you been doing that?" He gives Jake a tour of the back of house, gesturing at his/Deb's office, and towards the walk-in fridge and freezer, as Jake explains that it's his first teaching job. It's part-time, Madame Louisa taking a chance on him. Though Jake doesn't say the next bit out loud, it's pretty clear that she's doing this because he's had such a rough few years, and that he would rather do anything than detail those years to Sam right now. Sam doesn't make him. It's not any of his business, and anyway Jake's clearly skittish, nervously glancing around like he's expecting someone to tell him to get out at once. The last thing Sam wants to do is push him.

When they finish the tour in the main section of the kitchen, Sam looks around and realizes it was a lucky thing that Jake chose today to come by. Sam wasn't exactly *lying* when he said members of the community drop in—he does his best not to do that kind of thing anymore—but it might have been a bit of a stretch. It was a well-polished version of the truth, of which the unvarnished edition might sound something like, *Well, Joanie usually comes, because we cook ninety percent of the food she eats, and occasionally this weird guy Gerald who works at the fish place around the corner? A lot of other people around here have been invited, technically speaking, but if you want to talk technically, most of those people don't usually... show up. Usually, it's just me and the restaurant staff on shift that day, but that sounds a lot more awkward, doesn't it?*

Today, however, a few off-duty staff members have swung in for a bit, and a couple of the delivery guys from the sandwich joint up the block have also decided to drop by. Sam introduces Jake, slightly nervous about how he'll be received, which is stupid. It's not as though his staff is ever anything less than lovely, excepting Eileen, and Sam somehow can't imagine that Jake, in the last twelve years, has completely lost his almost preternatural gift for making friends.

Sure enough, Joey grins at him and says, "Oh, hey, it's you! Weird guy!" and pretty soon they're chatting it up like they've known one another for years. Sam leaves them to handle the rest of the introductions and turns back to the food. It's his turn to cook family meal in theory, although in practice he's sort of flipping back and forth between actually doing it and helping Alphonse prep the special.

He's making a bastardized, improvised version of kreplach, and he finds himself relaxing into it, the way he always does when he's doing this kind of cooking. Mostly what's made in the Silverman's back of house are the same classics they've been making for seventy-five years, tried and true favorites that have stood the test of time. These days Sam isn't doing much of the Silverman's cooking, only hopping in to cover when there's a call-off or a rush, but over the years he's probably made enough blintzes and open-faced brisket sandwiches to feed an army.

But at family meal, Sam gets to cook with what's around and, within those confines, make whatever the hell he wants. Today what he wanted to make was kreplach, only fried in a pan instead of boiled in soup, which he's realizing only now is probably because his conversation with Jake last night got him thinking about pierogies. A kreplach and a pierogi aren't so different, really. The doughs aren't quite the same, and, obviously, neither is the cooking method, but a dumpling is a dumpling, after all. When he'd noticed they had a bunch of them lying around, premade in the standard quantities for a pre-Kiss of Death review week, and they didn't have room for them all in the freezer, he'd immediately decided he was better off frying them in onions and butter for the staff than letting them go to waste. Slightly embarrassed, and hoping Jake won't pick up on the connection, he evacuates the latest batch out of the pan and into the waiting tray and replaces it with the next round. It smells good, at least, onion and garlic and mushroom and fresh thyme, the nutty undertones of the butter Sam browned, the rich note of schmaltz he added to the pan, even the scent almost coating the tongue. And the kreplach themselves have a deeply familiar aroma, since Sam has made the fillings hundreds of times over the years: Some are ground beef and onion, some chicken and mashed potato. All of them are seasoned with garlic and freshly cracked pepper and the dried shallot powder they make in-house, because it was Sam's great-grandmother's secret ingredient in about a third of her dishes, and neither Silvermans nor Adelsons excel in the art of changing or letting things go. That's why the menu has stayed basically the same for seventy-five years: the family tendency to stick with what works.

Sam's never quite been sure how he feels about that: if it's nice, a preservation of traditions that serve as guidepost for life, or stifling, a heavy stone from under which they're all forever struggling to crawl. Drawing in another breath of the complicated smell, familiar and new all at once but wholly delicious, he wonders if the answer is that it's both.

As if hearing this thought, Jake steps up next to him and says, "Jesus Christ, okay, you either need to cook that faster or make it smell worse. Criminal, that's what it is, to make me stand here and smell that without letting me try some—"

"Pastrami begs like this, you know," Sam informs him solemnly. She, curled up in her bed in Sam's office across the hall and watching the proceedings in lazy, unbothered entertainment, lifts her head at the sound of her name and gives Sam what he feels is an unimpressed look. It compels him to add, "She's more subtle about it, of course."

"Yes," Jake says thoughtfully, "that was my takeaway last night —that she's a very subtle creature when she's hungry. Discreet, some might say. *I* wouldn't say it, since she immediately and utterly blew up my spot with absolutely no remorse at all, but some might."

"In her defense, that was pierogies," Sam starts, and then, remembering he'd meant to *avoid* drawing any attention to the concept of pierogies, tries not to look at the pan as he tends to the kreplach. "Which are her favorite, so. It's hardly a fair sample."

Damn; Jake peers down into the pan himself, and then flicks a glance up at Sam, and then smiles, small and pleased and... something else, Sam thinks. Something that might be wishful thinking on his part. Something he would, in any other context, categorize as hunger, and not for kreplach. Not, in fact, for food of any kind.

But that can't be what it is. After everything that happened between them, Sam is lucky Jake's speaking to him at all.

Still, there's a new tone to Jake's voice, one Sam can't help but find thrilling. If he were any other person, Sam would call that tone *flirtatious*. "I mean, I'm not trying to be a dick here, but. Are these... *not* pierogies? Because, I'm just saying, they look a little bit like pierogies."

"No," Sam says, with as much dignity as he can muster. It's... not very much. "They're *kreplach*. Fried kreplach." Jake raises his eyebrows, and Sam groans and admits, "All right, all right, yeah, fine, it's basically the same. But these were going to go out anyway, and kreplach usually go in soup, you know."

"I know what a kreplach is, Sam," Jake says, sounding amused

sideshow act. Joey has their chin on their hands, and Alphonse is giving him a look that says, as plain as day, "You and I are going to be having a little talk later, and that little talk is going to be very, very funny for me, and excruciating for you."

"Oh," Sam says, glaring at all of them with absolutely no effect, and then turning back to the stove and Jake on the theory that it's too late to do anything about their audience. "You know, uh. Tradition, and all that. It's been the same menu the last seventy-five years, more or less. Part of the whole schtick, or at least that's what my aunt says. The place lives and dies on being a stitch in time."

"Hmm," Jake says. It's a sound of genuine curiosity, as opposed to one of doubt, and his face creases as though he's seriously considering the logic. Thoughtfully, he says, "There's definitely merit to that theory. The nostalgia angle plays, for sure. But at a certain point you have to strike a balance, don't you? If nothing *ever* changes, I think it's easy to slide from nostalgic into boring, and once the joy is gone, the product—" He cuts himself off, and Sam, glancing sideways, sees his eyes bug out a little in alarm. "Jesus Christ, not that I'm saying this place is boring, or that the food is! At all! I'm just, you know, talking like, generally, as a rule of thumb—"

"You're fine, dude, chill," Sam says, grinning at him, feeling abruptly and utterly sixteen. How many times had he said that to Jake, back in those early, easy days? How many times had he heard, 'rom his own side of the fence, Jake puffing himself up like an enor- ous, anxious balloon, and reached through the slats in the wood th a tiny verbal pin?

It's as satisfying now as it was then, to see Jake catch his breath, then Sam's eye, and smile back, and say, "Thanks." Horribly, it t be *more* satisfying. Back then, Sam hadn't known it would be ᾱ rare feeling. He hadn't known he'd spend twelve years 'ng for its like, for even a shadow of it, and never even brush of his fingers across anything that came close.

'oesn't get to say anything else, though. As he's opening his reply, Joanie bursts in through the employees-only back door Sam has begged her a thousand times not to use and bellows, "Samuel Deborah Silverman! How dare you make such a delicious smell infiltrate my sacred space! I insist you compensate me with lunch at once."

Sam, despite feeling himself flush, manages to sound calm and unbothered as he says, "Hello to you, too, Joanie. I think we can all agree that isn't my name, and that of course you can have as much lunch as you want, and that *you're not supposed to use that door*."

"A witch uses whatever door she likes," Joanie says haughtily, throwing her hand-dyed scarf over her shoulder, and then she glances at Jake. Sam sees her eyes widen very slightly, but he's pretty sure no one else does, and when her gaze slams over to meet his, he can almost see the cogs working in her brain, sorting out the particulars. He panics for a second, kicking himself for not thinking this through. She's a fan of Jake's ex, so she'll have seen Jake in photos and interviews with him, and have watched all the stuff Sam forced himself not to. She *knows* who Jake *is* and she'll *say* something and Jake will panic and bolt and *move* and probably *starve to death* and—

—and Joanie is smirking at him, and rolling her eyes, and Sam realizes in a wash of sheepish relief that he is underestimating her. Joanie's odd, and off-beat, and believes in a lot of things that Sam himself is far too young a man to categorize as "hokum" and does anyway. But she's shrewd, and smarter than she lets on by a wide margin, and more discreet than he tends to give her credit for. She enjoys gently embarrassing him—hence greeting him by shouting an inside joke that sources back to before Sam could legally drink— but she wouldn't call Jake out, make him uncomfortable, because she isn't like that. He's a stranger, and one she's bound to find interesting, so she'll approach him carefully and curiously, in the interest of drawing more information out.

Sam wonders, in a distant and somewhat fatalistic way, how bad it is that he's already feeling this protective of Jake. On a scale of one to ten, one being, "Perfectly healthy, fine and normal, well within the bounds of reasonable things to feel, not setting yourself up for heartbreak at all," and ten being, "As completely, disastrously bad as the filthy dreams I keep having where we break into Horseshoe Heights High and end up having sex in the locker room," Sam thinks it's about an eight.

Joanie just says, "Oh! A new face. Who's this, then?" She sounds for all the world as if she really doesn't know. Sam gives her a grateful look as he introduces her to Jake, and they start chatting, and then the food is cooked and Sam's serving it up and then they're all talking, exchanging stories, complimenting the kreplach, joking and laughing. Family meal isn't always like this. There have been a lot of days lately, in the wake of the Kiss of Death review, where they've all hunched over their plates in miserable silence, eating for sustenance instead of joy.

But Jake, just as he always did, has this *effect* on people. Sam thinks it's partially his willingness to throw himself on the sword of looking a bit foolish, and partially the sheer irrepressibility of his personality. It's hard not to like someone being so obviously dragged by the ankles behind his own peculiar nature.

The staff must agree, because Jake fits in well for the whole meal, and leaves having eaten two helpings and promising quite cheerfully to return. He fits in well again two days later, swinging by before his afternoon class of middle school dancers, and the day after that, dropping in exhausted after a morning spent teaching the under-six group, and then suddenly he has become such a regular part of family meal that Sam has a hard time imagining it without him. He starts to look forward to it, that hour where he's all but guaranteed a chance to bask in the warmth of Jake's presence, and then to rely upon it. Upsettingly quickly, it becomes the linchpin around which his whole day is constructed, the carrot he uses to lure himself through difficult moments.

Maybe that's why the next month evaporates like water on a hot griddle, a flash of billowing heat in the blink of an eye. Or maybe it's because, aside from the highlight of Jake, there are quite a lot of difficult moments.

For the first couple of months after the Kiss of Death review,

Sam tried to stay positive. He told himself it was the slow season anyway, that traffic was always lower in that weird, slushy period between winter and spring.

But in the weeks Sam spends getting used to seeing Jake every afternoon for family meal, he also has to get familiar with the quarterly earnings reports. They are... grim. Or, more accurately, they're perfectly flat and normal, in fact slightly higher than usual year-over-year, right up until the Kiss of Death review.

Then they start to tank. Hard. Scarily hard.

Many businesses, Sam knows, are designed to carry with them a certain amount of insulation against financial ruin, a layer of cushioning stuffed with money. But Silverman's isn't like that, because restaurants, by and large, aren't like that. There are too many moving parts. Traffic and demand are both highly variable; the product you produce is perishable, and so must be sold or lost in a tight window; ingredient costs fluctuate based on a market over which you have no control; the list goes on and on. It's an industry of slim margins, and part of being a good manager is learning how to weave through the gaps like an otter through an angry river, darting and diving and never losing track of the essentials. Sam likes it, usually, the thrill of knowing things could go snarled up and wrong if he let them, if he didn't have a firm grip on every interwoven strand of this place. It makes him feel necessary, fulfilled, in a way he's accepted but isn't entirely proud of.

But if Sam doesn't find a way to turn things around soon—like, in the next month or two—they're going to hit a point he's not sure they can come back from. As it is, he's already changed suppliers on more than half their ingredients, axed all their chocolate desserts (to Eileen's shrieking fury) because the price of cocoa was killing him, cut his own salary down as low as he can take it without running out of money for his and Pastrami's basic bills and upkeep, and cancelled a number of large, long-standing back-stocking orders. He's also convinced Casey, their apple guy, to let them float a few months on credit. Unfortunately, Sam's pretty sure the only reason he does this is because a few years ago, before

Casey met his now-husband, Deb set them up, and they went on one of the most awkward dates of Sam's life. There was so little chemistry between them that, halfway through the appetizer, three strangers slid into their booth, assuming they were the business associates they were meant to be meeting; to say things have been awkward ever since is an understatement. But, on the plus side: In times of trouble, Sam can always count on his apple delivery, even if he knows they'll all taste vaguely of pity.

It isn't enough. But all he can think of otherwise is raising prices—a terrible idea when they're trying to lure spooked customers back in—or firing someone, which is just. No. He can't do that. There has to be another way.

Technically, Sam knows there is one. He's painfully aware Deb's gotten offers to sell the building over the years, lucrative ones. The neighborhood has changed a lot since his grandparents invested their life savings here, and the building sits on what is, these days, fairly prime real estate. There's even a local restaurant group who has mocked up a concept for what they'd put in the space if Silverman's was gone, which Sam knows because they send over a copy every month, along with an offer to buy if they're ever interested in selling.

He and Deb had talked about it, just once, right before she left town. She'd offered to give him some of the profits if she sold; he refused. She pointed out that he could start his own place with the money, call it Adelson's, do everything the way he wanted to do it; he refused. He'd been a little afraid that she *wanted* to sell, was feeling him out in the interest of moving forward, but she'd grinned at him with tears in her eyes and hugged him, whispering, "I knew you were my favorite nephew for a reason." Sam, touched, had refrained from pointing out that he was her only nephew. It hadn't seemed like the right thing for the moment.

Sam has spent his life, with a few brief blips of teenage exception, trying to be a helpful person. It's at the very core of who he is, that burning drive to do *something* for *someone*, to feel useful and important. Overall, it's one of the things Sam likes best about himself, but, like everything, it has its drawbacks. *Being* helpful is a joy, something Sam wishes he could do every minute of the day, but asking for help? Sam would rather, in all honesty, tell Mr. Schecter they're out of whitefish.

It turns out that when push comes to shove, Sam would rather do something personally excruciating than destroy his family's legacy and lose his home and cost a bunch of people he loves their source of income, so. He decides, hating it, to put his damn hat in his hand and ask around.

EIGHT

THEN: NOVEMBER, TWELVE YEARS AGO

It was a long, terrible summer, the summer before senior year. Physically, mentally, and emotionally, Sam crawled into bed most nights at the very end of his rope, only hanging on by the barest grip.

His parents had been furious about the party and the wreck it left of the house, of course. Sam had expected them to be furious. Actually, Sam had expected them to be apoplectic, which they were, and he'd also expected them to punish him extensively, which they did.

But he hadn't expected their rage to be quite so... apocalyptic, and he *really* hadn't braced for the nuclear winter that settled over their relationship in the weeks and months that followed. Sam had thought, after a lifetime of making his own sack lunches and sometimes his mother's, father's, or sisters'—after being left more than once to wait anxiously because someone forgot to pick him up— that he understood how it felt for his parents not to bother with him. He thought he'd had that all packed away, nice and neat, in a box on a shelf where it couldn't upset him at all.

He'd been wrong, though. As each new bill came through for the repairs to the house—as David and Mara cancelled the triplets' summer camp plans because they had to redirect the funds into undoing the damage—his parents seemed to turn to glass, cold and empty and brittle. They didn't make eye contact; they barely looked at him at all. He tried, dozens of times, to explain: that it had all spiraled out of control, that he hadn't meant it to happen, that he'd been lost in trying to be someone else, that he was so sorry. That the very next Monday he'd gone to school and, when someone had asked him whether it was true that he threw parties like that every weekend, snarled, "I made it up! I made all of it up! I've never lived *anywhere* but the suburbs of Cleveland, I'm not wanted by the FBI, I've never been in the mafia! I don't throw parties like that every weekend; I read *books* and try to cook *soufflés* and look after my stupid *sisters*! I made it up!" That the other kids in the hallway had all stared at him, and then silently dispersed. That whispers had followed him through all his classes, circling like vultures but never approaching, still waiting for him to die. That his social standing had dropped like a stone all afternoon, and by the time the day's last bell rang, he was an even bigger loser than he was at any of his previous schools, epic party or no. That he didn't care, and it didn't matter, because all that mattered to him was how sorry he was, and how much he never wanted anything like this to happen again.

Nothing broke the glass. It all bounced off his parents with a high-pitched, slightly sickening peal, as if each strike brought them that much closer to shattering entirely.

So it was a hard, horrible summer. But there was, as there always seemed to be when Sam lived in that house, one bright spot, beaming up like the sun itself from behind the hedge in his backyard.

It wasn't like they meant to start hooking up or, God forbid, talked about what it meant. It was just that something had shifted, somehow, after that party. After that kiss. Suddenly, the adult world with its adult consequences seemed to be looming just above them, no longer a safe distance away. Jake was fixated on the idea of going to Juilliard to study ballet, and had been dreaming of it since he was practically a baby. There was no question, at least as far as Sam was concerned, of Jake's talent; he couldn't imagine a world in which Jake didn't get in. But Juilliard was all the way in New York, and while that was great for Jake, Sam knew to his bones that *he* wasn't going to end up in a big city like that, if he ended up at college at all.

A certain urgency began to enter their conversations, replacing the caution with which they'd both approached the heavier topics before. Questions started to become more loaded; areas which had once been safe to tread were suddenly seeded with land mines.

But hooking up? Hooking up was safe. Jake couldn't bring up the five hundred miles he was hoping to move away if Sam's tongue was in his mouth; Sam couldn't blurt out some stupid, embarrassing question about what exactly they were to one another if Jake was making him forget his own *name*. Neither one of them could accidentally take things too far if they were busy *taking things too far*. Or, as Sam remembers it, just far enough. He was reasonably certain they'd both been virgins when they'd kissed at the party, but was entirely sure neither one of them was by the time August rolled around.

So they didn't talk about it. They kept meeting up behind the hedge like they always had, talking like they always had, and, when they were sure no parents or siblings could possibly turn up and catch them at it, fooling around. It worked for them through the hot, sticky swelter of the summer and the fitful, mercurial rain showers of early fall.

It worked for them right up until the day of the accident.

It was November 21st; Sam likes to think he would have remembered it anyway, but that date was stamped across so many court documents that he couldn't forget if he wanted to. It was a Friday, gray and bitingly cold, papery dead leaves rustling off tree branches with every gust of wind, and it had begun as a good one. He and Jake had started the day with twenty stolen minutes behind the hedge, waking up unnaturally early for teenagers to achieve it. It was an experiment, largely to see if they could get away with fooling around before school, and if it was worth the punishing hour and unfortunate temperature. They could; it was. They prepared to part ways pleased with their efforts, pink-cheeked and grinning at each other, and then, sounding shy, Jake said, "Hey, uh. Anthony's having a thing at his place tonight that's definitely going to get out of hand."

"Poor bastard," Sam said, with feeling. "He should put a moat around the yard and fill it with alligators."

Jake laughed, but only briefly, and sounded forced-casual when he said, "Well, sure, but there probably isn't time. Anyway, I thought I'd see if you'd be interested in watching someone else experience The Horrors. No worries if you're still perma-grounded, or just, uh, don't want to or whatever, but." He shrugged, the movement uncharacteristically stiff. "Just a thought."

"I *am* still perma-grounded," Sam admitted, "that's the thing about the 'permanent' part, but they can't keep me as their prisoner forever. Let me put out some feelers, see if I can slip away for a few hours? I'll let you know."

"Great!" Jake said, too loud, and then wincing dramatically: "Okay thanks bye!" He vanished into his own yard before Sam could say anything else.

Sam, at that age, had been many things, but he had been far from fluent in the language of romance. So it had taken most of the day, as he recalls, for it to occur to him to wonder if Jake had, in fact, asked him out. On a date.

Once this *had* occurred to him, it was all he could think about. He thought about it through his afternoon classes, and on the bus ride home, and as he remembered to his surprise and pleasure that his house was going to be empty for the evening. His parents were heading to the Horseshoe Heights High Fall Fundraiser, along with every other parent in town, and they were dropping the triplets off at a slumber party on the way.

It was the first time Sam had been trusted alone in the house for more than an hour since the party. This was the first stroke of bad luck in what must have been the unluckiest day of Sam's life: It might all have gone differently if everything hadn't felt so weighted, so important. If Sam hadn't been so nervous about making another mistake, or less fixated on doing what seemed like the right thing; if his parents had been slightly more paranoid, and one of them had stayed home that night to guard the house against teenaged hordes; hell, even if the *triplets* had been home, and thus Sam's responsibility, it all would have played out a different way.

Shame it doesn't work like that. Shame that whatever happens stays happened, even if you spend over a decade thinking through all the ways it might not have.

What did happen was that David and Mara left with the triplets around six. Sam didn't even wait until they were out of the driveway to dash back towards the hedge, but Jake wasn't waiting for him. His used Volkswagen was still in the drive, as were his mother's Range Rover and the black Mercedes sedan his father generally drove. This was odd: Sam knew that Mrs. Thompson was chairing the HHHS Fundraising Committee, and that she'd have murdered Mr. Thompson for skipping that night's event. They should have left an hour ago, at least.

As if in response to this thought, Sam heard the back door slam, and the sound of footsteps, voices he recognized as belonging to Jake's parents:

"Patrick, *please*. If you would calm down, we could talk about this."

"What is there to talk about? *Apparently*, the situation is what it is! Apparently, *everyone* knew but me—"

"We all thought you *did* know—"

"Oh, well, what a *comfort*." A brief, bitter chuckle; then a sigh. "Just get in the car, Lauren, all right? I can't do this right now, not if I have to go to this damn rubber-chicken dinner and make small talk with the likes of Barry Wheeler."

"I worked on this for a year; we are *going*! And you *like* Barry," was the last thing Sam heard Mrs. Thompson say. Then the voices were replaced with the sound of car doors opening and closing, and the thrum of the Mercedes's engine pulling them down the drive. He didn't think anything of it—the Thompsons argued all the time, about nearly everything—but he did wait for Jake for an increasingly embarrassing twenty minutes before resignedly going back into his own house.

He started making himself dinner, checking his phone for messages at shorter and shorter intervals while trying to tell himself it was fine. Of course it was fine. High school parties started late, that's all it was. The gnawing sense of dread in his stomach was from the Hot Pockets he ate when he got home, probably. Nothing to worry about.

It was about an hour later that Jake pulled into the driveway, honking the horn to announce his arrival and immediately giving Sam quite a lot to worry about.

The car he was driving was the first problem. It was not the little green car Jake usually tooled around in, which had been two of his siblings' before it was his, and their grandmother's before that. Nor was it his mother's frankly enormous car, which Jake was very occasionally given leave to drive if, for example, he needed to transport a huge number of PTA file boxes to the front office on Lauren's behalf.

No, that night Jake was behind the wheel of his father's maroon 1966 Jaguar E-Type convertible. Sam knew it was a 1966 Jaguar E-Type convertible because he had never heard Jake's father talk about it *without* rattling off its full name, and Jake's father talked about that car a *lot*. Once, when Patrick had happened past the house on a walk while Sam and his family were out front doing yard work, they'd all stood and chatted for a few minutes. After he'd walked away, David had muttered, "Good Lord. You'd think that car was his mistress, the way he talks about it," and Mara had let out a shout of laughter before slapping him on the arm and telling him to watch what he said in front of his daughters.

Jake should not have been driving the Jaguar. Jake should not, based on his father's general vibe and energy and also explicitly stated rules, even have been looking at the Jaguar. The car had its own special bay in the garage, its own dedicated rags and shammies, its own set of tools and polishes and oils no one else was allowed to touch. Patrick had joked more than once—enough times Sam himself had heard him say it—that he loved it more than any of his family members.

So it was worrying, to say the least, to see Jake sitting behind its wheel in Sam's driveway. But not as worrying as—after bursting out of the house and running over to the driver's side window to demand, "Okay, *how* are you driving the Jag?"—catching the smell on Jake's breath. Sam knew he was drunk from the first whiff, even before he started talking.

"Oh, I took it," Jake said, glassy and blank. "Juuuuust took it. Why shouldn't I take it! He's never going to like me anyway." His gaze focused on Sam and sharpened as he beeped the horn, suddenly grinning. "Anyway, come on, get in! We've got a party to get to."

"Jake," Sam said carefully. "I think maybe you should get out? So we can talk about, um. Whatever's... going on... first? It seems like maybe you've been drinking, and—"

"Oh my God, are you really going to do that?" Jake complained, pulling a face. "Be Mr. Responsible? Right now? You don't have to *babysit* me, Sam, you know."

Sam had felt, even then, that this was below the belt. It was especially rough coming from Jake, who knew that Sam resented how much time he spent left in charge of his sisters, and who was not typically prone to saying anything harsher than, "I'm so sorry to tell you this, I really am, but you are, in point of fact, off-key."

Jake must have been surprised by it, too, because he blanched, and his face fell, and he sounded genuinely remorseful—agonized, even—when he said, "Sam... sorry. I'm sorry. I'll get out."

True to his word, he turned off the car and got out, and Sam made his first mistake of the night: He did not immediately snatch the keys out of Jake's hands. It didn't occur to him that it was an option to do so, although it would later, and he'd spend a long time

kicking himself for not having done it. This was, at least, a productive mistake: More than once in the years since, Sam *has* taken the
opportunity to remove car keys from the hands of someone overserved, and he's fairly certain he's saved a few lives that way.

But that night Sam was too young to understand the mercurial
nature of the drunk, the way rationality comes and goes across their
internal landscapes like so much wind. So he didn't take the keys,
or insist that Jake come inside, or leave the Jaguar safely in the
driveway, or call his parents, or Jake's parents, or anyone. Instead
he peered down into Jake's eyes and said, "What *happened?*"

"What happened," Jake repeated, vacant, leaning back against
the car and tapping his fingertips against his thigh. "What.... happened." A pause, and then, in an oddly bitter tone for something
Sam would have thought would be good news: "Well, I got into
Juilliard, first of all. That happened. Early decision. Got the letter
today." His lip curled up into a slight sneer as he added, "Hooray
for me."

"Jake, that's great?" Sam wasn't able to keep the confusion out
of his voice. "I mean, isn't it? It's what you wanted, right?"

"It is what I wanted." Jake's voice was hollow; wobbly. "What I
want. It is."

Sam waited for more. When nothing came, he asked, tenta-
tively, "So... what's the problem, then? Do your parents not want
you to go or something?"

"Oh, no, they're thrilled," Jake said, and then his face twisted
and he added, "*Were* thrilled, anyway. It's so *prestigious*, you know.
Great bragging rights with the artsier circles they move in, and
they've already had one kid go through one of Ivies, so, you know,
it's all gravy, right?!" There was an edge of hysteria entering his
tone that didn't match the words, but Sam still wasn't ready for the
abrupt non sequitur: "Listen, I seem gay to you, right?"

In spite of the circumstances, Sam—who had still, after all,
been a teenage boy—smirked. "Well, yeah. I'd guess you seem
gayer to me than you do to most people, even."

Jake would have laughed at that, usually; he didn't. Instead, he pressed: "Sure, sure, but I mean. My vibe. My affect. It's not, like, particularly heterosexual, right?"

"Ah," Sam said, half-afraid it was a trap, but, "No, I wouldn't describe you like that, personally."

"Right!" Jake threw his hands in the air. "Nobody would! Because I'm not! And I thought it was, you know, one of those things we don't talk about in my family, because it's inconvenient, or uncomfortable, or whatever. Like Uncle George's pills, or Mom's 'tennis instructor,' or that whole weird thing with Aunt Elizabeth's job!" He scrubbed one hand over his face, laughing wearily. "Turns out my dad just... didn't know. No idea. Had never picked up on it once."

"Oh, God." Already knowing it must not have been good based on... well, everything, Sam asked again: "What happened?"

"Oh, you know," Jake said, in a fake-cheerful tone so played up it bordered on singsong. "First he made a comment about how I'd have to be careful at a school like Juilliard, and how we'd have to have a talk about the realities of the world, because I might attract the attention of a certain kind of man and not know what to do. And then my brother said, 'I think Jake knows exactly what to do with the attention of that sort of man,' and everyone laughed, except my dad, who said, 'What?' and I said, 'What?' and he said, 'What did he mean?' and then my sister said, 'Jesus Christ, Dad, do you *not* know Jake's gay?'" Jake sighed, heavy and hard. "And then, uh. It all got a little... shouty."

Sam winced. The Thompsons, he knew, could really shout; more than once he'd heard them from his own backyard. He'd often wondered if that wasn't what had driven Jake to find the hidden spot behind the hedge in the first place: hunger for somewhere that no one was yelling.

Sam's own parents had been very low-key when he came out to them. To his deep and secret shame, Sam felt they'd been a little *too* low-key. It's not like he'd wanted a blow-up fight, but "Okay, kiddo, pass the bread" had been a bit of a let-down. His father had said it in the same tone he would have used if Sam told him he was thinking about getting a burrito for lunch.

He did not, obviously, say any of this to Jake. He also did not say what he should have said to Jake: "Oh no, that's terrible, I'm so sorry! Why don't you come inside and tell me all about it." If he had just said that, they could have gone into the house, and Sam could have swiped the keys when Jake dropped them on the counter, and they could have waited until their various parents got home to deal with the Jaguar, which would have remained safely parked. Mr. Thompson would have been angry, probably, but Mr. Thompson was nearly always angry. It wouldn't have, say, altered the course of both of their lives.

But instead, because he was a teenager, and an idiot, and panicking, what he did say was, "Shit. Well. I mean. At least now it's all out in the open?"

Even years later, Sam doubts he'll ever forget the way Jake turned to look at him, the long, still moment they spent staring at one another. Jake looked empty, blank, and then briefly his eyes closed and his face creased in devastation, making Sam wonder if he was replaying the whole incident in his mind.

When he opened his eyes again, there was a gleam in them Sam didn't like at all.

"Out in the open!" Jake said, with a false, brittle brightness. "That's right! Always better that way, isn't it? To get things out in the open? That's what this whole day was *supposed* to be about!" His tone cracked into a snarl on the last sentence, and before Sam could stop him, he turned and wrenched the car door back open, throwing himself inside. "Come on, then, get in. We have a party to go to."

"Jake, please," Sam said, desperate, "please wait. I really don't think you should be driving, let along driving that—"

"Sam," Jake said, stonily calm, as he turned the key in the ignition, "I am taking this car, and I am going to this party, and there is nothing—do you hear me?—*nothing* you can do to stop me. If you don't want to go, fine. If you don't want to be seen with me, fine! Stay here, if that's how you feel. But I. Am. Going."

Over the years Sam has relived this night many times and many ways, spun out all the things he might have changed to make it go differently. But the next decision he made, he has never bothered rethinking. Sam, then or now, could not have let Jake drive the Jaguar away in that condition by himself. He couldn't have climbed into the passenger seat or thrown himself in front of the car, either. He'd heard too much from his parents about impulsivity and drunk drivers, and knew that doing either of those things was likely to end in injury or death for them both. So, although at any point before that moment he could have sent things careening down a different track, it was already too late when Sam said:

"God, fine, scoot over, then. If we're doing this, I'm driving."

Jake scooted down accommodatingly enough, clambering with drunken grace over the gearshift, but he smirked when Sam climbed in and slammed the door. "Do you even have your license?"

"Yes," said Sam, who didn't. What he had was a learner's permit and parents who, between them, had not been able to bring themselves to give him more than three cumulative hours of lessons.

But those lessons were certainly enough to know how to return a car to a home which sat directly behind his own. And that was, in all honesty, the only thing Sam ever intended to do. His plan was simple and direct: drive the car back to Jake's house, refuse to give him the keys, wait until he calmed down, and then invite him over to eat freezer-burned ice cream and watch terrible made-for-TV movies. It was well thought out, that plan. It should have worked.

They were halfway to Jake's when disaster struck.

NINE

NOW: MAY

Sam tries Joanie first, on the theory that she will probably have the most to say but also be the least helpful, so getting her out of the way is efficient. The ensuing conversation takes about four hours, with breaks in between for them to tend to their respective businesses. It ranges over a variety of topics, including "What happens to my rent prices if Silverman's goes under?" and "I mean it, Sam, what happens?" When Sam tells her, begrudgingly, that if it came down to it, Deb could always sell the building, the conversation turns into a discussion of Joanie's hatred of corporate overreach in neighborhood development, which is a topic she has a tendency to really settle into. It's ages before Sam finally manages to get her to circle back to her advice on what to do regarding Kiss of Death recovery.

This advice is primarily the suggestion that Sam seek revenge against the bastard who reviewed him. When Sam explains, not for the first time, that Norman Endicott has made himself more or less unreachable, probably because people might have ideas like that, Joanie shrugs and suggests he ask the Dark Web for help. At this point things veer into a discussion of what, exactly, Joanie thinks the Dark Web is, and the discovery that it is wildly incorrect, and after that Sam decides to wash his hands of the conversation and try someone else.

He tries a lot of other people, prioritizing seeking a solution over socializing, sleeping, and even celebrating his thirtieth birthday, which he shuffles past without looking directly at in mid-April. (Jake sends him a text with a balloon emoji and asks him when they're having cake, but Sam manages to distract him with a video of a squirrel completing an obstacle course.) He runs the options over and over again with Alphonse and Eileen, goes to bother Dani at the West Side Market, and asks his barber, the restaurant's new meat vendor, the restaurant's *old* meat vendor, a very unhelpful internet forum, and—to his great shame—all three of his sisters for their thoughts. Nobody has anything helpful to say beyond, "I'm sure it'll turn around, man!" or "I'll try to spread the word that people should come by!" Iris and Daisy don't offer him even that; Iris shrugs, bored, and Daisy winces, uncomfortable, and they leave together for some exercise class that Sam can't quite understand the name of.

But Luce says, "Let me think about that, okay?" and then turns up at the deli the next day with a huge canvas, her supply bag, and a collapsible easel. When Sam raises his eyebrows, she shrugs and says, "Listen, I have to turn in three paintings before June 1st or I don't graduate, and I figure having an artist in the window might draw people in, so. Thought if you're cool with it, I'd do them here, of the deli? Past/present/future sort of deal? What do you think?" She looks up at him with big eyes, and adds, in a slightly sheepish tone, "Not that you should let this sway you or anything but. I'd also, um. Love to spend a little less time at the old... apartment."

"I think it's a great idea," Sam says, smiling at her, even if deep down he doubts the power of art to move the financial needle. "You go ahead and get set up, okay? Let me know if there's anything you need."

Luce nods at him, grinning, and then strides right out the door. He watches her stand out there for a minute: framing the building with her hands, taking a few photos with her camera, reviewing them, repeating the process. Finally, she stares up at the building with one hand on her hip, the other shading her eyes, unwittingly imitating a photo of their grandmother that hangs across from Sam on the wall.

Sam takes a breath, turns around, and almost trips on Pastrami, who has curled up around his feet while he stood staring and fallen asleep. Stepping over her carefully, he goes into his office and calls Deb. His pride means a lot to him but isn't worth the deli.

She's warm from the moment she picks up. Of course she's warm. She's always warm, and Sam always forgets until he's talking to her that his internal version of her is a lot harder on him than she's ever been herself. Sam thinks probably it's all those years with his mother, preparing himself for coldness or indifference so it wouldn't hurt so much when it arrived.

It's a comfort, if a chilly one, that Sam knows he's not the only one who experienced his mother as something of an icebox; it was a joke, back when the sisters still spoke, that Deb and Mara were like fire and ice. Certainly, that had spilled over into the fight that ended their relationship for good, the one his father, afterwards, would sometimes refer to as the Great Yom Kippur Schism, although only when Mara was out of earshot. The two of them had battled out every grievance over the table: their childhood frustrations with one another; Deb's sense of betrayal over Mara's abandonment of the deli; Mara's rage at what she perceived as Deb's judgement of her parenting and life choices; the ways each felt the other had failed them while their parents were dying. Everyone else had quietly eaten their bagels and kept their eyes on their plates, and what Sam remembers more than anything either of them said was the way they were a study in opposites. As Deb pleaded and shouted and gripped the table so hard Sam thought she would break it, Mara grew colder and more clipped, until she seemed to radiate a cloud of frost like dry ice.

Maybe that's what it comes down to, then: Deb burns where Mara freezes, and so is warm more than she's not. Whatever the reason, her softer, easier energy is still a bit shocking to him even now, a delightful surprise every time.

It's obvious from "Hello" that she knows why he's calling, but she does him the courtesy of letting him work up to it. When he asks about how things are going on the dig, she answers at length, telling him about Talya's latest discovery and their funding struggles and the new graduate student on site who has, according to Deb, an "Indiana Jones complex."

After that conversational topic is exhausted, and after she's pointedly reiterated the birthday wishes Sam had demurred away from on the actual day, she does ask about the deli, but not in the way she *could* ask. She could say, "So, how are... things going... at work," with the loaded, heavy pauses of someone who knows the answer and doesn't like it. Sam knows she gets the same quarterly budget reports he does, and that she reads the daily roundup emails he sends her, and that she saw the Kiss of Death review. It would be easy to come at him from a tense, combative place.

But instead, breezily, she says, "How's work, then?"

Sam swallows, knowing he'll never get a better opening than this, and bites the bullet: "It's *terrible*, Deb. It's so terrible, oh my God, it's never been this terrible, I didn't know! That one review! Could just send everything off the *rails* like this!" He takes a deep breath, reining it in, aware that this is not the way to present himself as someone worth trusting with his family's seventy-five-year-old business. "I'm sorry, I really am, but I need. Some help? If you have any thoughts or ideas or anything, I can't—I can't figure it out on my own." He hangs his head, ashamed of himself but knowing it's the truth, and his only move. He *does* need help, and she's the most qualified person he knows, at least when it comes to keeping the doors open at Silverman's.

There is a long pause at the other end of the line. Then, thoughtfully, Deb says, "Do you know what, kid? I gotta jump off right now, but I'm really glad you asked me that. Not that I have an answer for you, except to tell you that this is an insane situation and you're doing all the right things, the things I would do, but still.

Real glad you asked. I'll see you soon, Sammy, okay? Keep your head up; haven't I told you what Gram always said?"

Sam sighs, smiling a little in spite of himself, and recites: "'Even the best restaurants are at least thirty percent luck'?"

"That's the one," Deb says, with a little chuckle. "So sometimes, it's about having faith that yours will turn around."

This is a lovely sentiment. A sweet one. It does not, however, change the facts, and Sam finds that there is only so much faith he can muster in the face of numbers so low.

In the end, having exhausted all his other options, he asks Jake for advice.

In spite of having tried all the alternatives, Sam still doesn't entirely mean to ask for Jake's help. It feels wrong, like Sam doesn't have the right—like Sam is, in more ways than one, paying back old debts, and couldn't possibly ask for more credit.

But Jake's set up with his laptop in the deli one Thursday afternoon after family meal, the May sunshine bright across his face, tapping away at some freelance task, as has become his habit in the last few weeks. Sam's sense of what freelance tasks they are is vague, mostly because it's become clear Jake's taking whatever he can get to supplement his income at the dance studio. One day he's complaining about the quality of the audio on files he's supposed to be transcribing, and the next muttering that he hadn't expected such painful boredom in finding and removing dead links from old articles. Sam doesn't comment; Jake is prickly about anything adjacent to money, work, or his life in LA, which Sam thinks makes sense. It's obvious that there's a wound there, and one that's still bleeding underneath the thick layer of dressing Jake keeps firmly wrapped around it.

That particular Thursday, Sam finds himself in a bit of a daze after getting off a call with the deli's accountant. Geraldine was kind, cool, and matter-of-fact in executing what had felt like a conversational axe murder: Sam was correct that they wouldn't make it to next quarter if he didn't turn things around, and that there wasn't any wiggle room to free up additional funds, and also, just as an FYI, property taxes were going up, so his monthly numbers were even shorter than he thought.

After hanging up, Sam sits and stares at the office wall for a while, and then stands up and begins prowling around the deli in something closer to a sleepwalk than anything else. All the staff take one look at his expression and edge away from him, finding some task or another to busy themselves with, which Sam thinks, distantly, is fair enough. They've all seemed a little cautious around him since the day last month when Alphonse had cheerfully asked what they were going to do for his thirtieth. Sam had stared at him with blank, uncomprehending horror for a long minute before, bleakly, saying, "Oh, enjoy my last birthday in the deli, I guess," and wandering off. It wasn't exactly Sam's personal best, leadership-wise, but he didn't realize it would spook them so much, and he wishes he could take it back.

Jake glances at him, does a double take, and then immediately uses his cane to push out the chair across from him as he says, "Jesus, who died? Sit down; you look awful."

Sam sits down. He puts his head in his hands. He stares down at the woodgrain of the table, familiar from hundreds of childhood brunches and thousands of after-close wipe-downs. Pastrami, who has been following him around with obvious concern, settles down next to him, sticks her head into his lap, and gives him a mournful look.

"Okay, listen," Jake says, urgent now, "if someone *did* die, then I'm very sorry I said that. I never learn! Every single time this happens I'm like, 'Jake, you idiot, stop asking people who died because sometimes someone *really has died* and then you look like—'"

"Nobody's died," Sam says, in a tone of voice that sounds very much as though someone has. He clears his throat, and more audibly but no happier, adds, "I'm just going to lose the deli, that's all. Just my family's deli that I've built my whole life around, that my aunt trusted me with, after all this *work*, over one *stupid* review!" He takes a deep breath, trying to think steady, calming thoughts. "But things happen, right? No big deal."

There is a long, slightly awkward pause. Then Jake closes his laptop and, very quietly, says, "It sounds like a pretty big deal to me, Sam."

And Sam, to his own surprise and mild shame, tells Jake everything. With everyone else he spoke to—save Deb, who had already seen the numbers—he'd been conservative with how much he shared, not wanting to reveal the full extent of either his stress level or just how bad it is. He tried not to mention just how insanely viral the review had gone, or exactly how much that virality has affected things. If nothing else, it was easier to keep himself steady without talking about *Hearth*'s gigantic online reach, or the fact that it's read all across the country and even beyond, or the way Sam had gotten sympathy calls from friends in New England and Nevada. But with Jake it all comes pouring out of him: the nose-dive in traffic and profits, the changed suppliers, the horrible fights he had to have with vendors whose contracts he was cancelling after thirty years. The cuts to his own salary, and to their inventory and backstock, and the fact that it isn't enough.

Jake, unusually for him, doesn't talk much. He just listens, nodding and shaking his head and occasionally muttering, "Christ, Sam, I'm so sorry." Sam wonders when he learned that, how to contain his energy until the appropriate moment, the way he couldn't as a teenager. It's nice.

But something shifts when, at the end, Sam screws up his courage and says, "Anyway, I know it's a long shot, but I'm just wondering if you have any, um... ideas? About how to, maybe, I don't know... market this place? That first day you came in here you said something about branding—"

"Oh my God," Jake says, his hand flying to his mouth. He stares at Sam, his gaze going from shocked to accusing. "You *know*, don't you? You've known this whole time!"

Sam's brow furrows. "Know... what?"

"About *Walt*," Jake moans, running a hand over his face. "And LA and the whole hideous breakup and *all* of it. It was stupid of me to convince myself you *didn't* know, honestly, but hell, I'm going to miss believing it. That's why you're asking me, right? Because you know I used to be, like, fame-adjacent, and naturally everyone who is must know all about how to digitally promote things and make them go viral."

"Uh," Sam says, blinking at him. "No? Or, I mean, okay, I did look you up a little when you got back to town, and so I do, sort of, know about Walt. But not a lot!" he adds, holding up his hands when Jake groans. "I didn't read any of the weird personal-life articles—that felt like crossing a line; I just read a little bit about his professional background and watched a few episodes of that show, but then it started to make me feel, uh. Dead inside?"

"Yeah," Jake says, an odd expression on his face. "It'll do that."

"Anyway," Sam says, eager to press ahead, "it felt creepy to look any further, and I don't have any preconceived notions about your digital promotion skills? I've just asked, genuinely, everyone I know, and *no one* has been helpful. My hairdresser wanted to know if I'd ever considered selling some of my less-vital organs. Apparently, she has a guy for that."

Jake grimaces. "Should... she have a guy for that?"

"Probably not," Sam admits, "but I think it'll be fine, so long as we don't introduce him to Joanie."

Jake laughs—he's gleaned enough of a sense of Joanie by now to understand why that introduction would be dangerous—but then he narrows his eyes and peers at Sam suspiciously. "So you're really... just asking? This isn't a play for information?"

"I mean," Sam hedges, "it *is* a play for information, technically. But just like, marketing information? Nothing personal. And besides, it sounds like you don't know much about that anyway, so we can just forget I ever—"

"Oh, no, I can definitely help you with the marketing," Jake says, waving a hand. "That's easy. I was just being obnoxious before. You *do* learn a lot of that stuff being adjacent to fame. At least, you do if you're paying attention." He drums his fingers against the tabletop for a moment, his gaze far away, and then snaps back to attention. "Yeah, I think I should be able to have a proposal ready for you by... Does this time tomorrow sound okay?"

"*Tomorrow?*" Sam can feel his own eyes bugging out. "But I mean—thank you, obviously, but you don't have to do it by tomorrow!"

Jake shrugs, a pained expression briefly crossing his face before he shutters it off again. "It all sounds... pretty urgent, Sam." Quietly, like he doesn't quite want to know the answer, he says, "This is why you were weird about your birthday, isn't it? Why you changed the subject whenever it came up?" Sam's uncomfortable expression seems to answer the question for him, and Jake returns it before nodding sharply. "Right. So. Sooner seems better, yes?"

Sam opens his mouth to argue, grimaces, shuts it, and nods. He contents himself instead with, "Thanks."

"Don't mention it," Jake says, and then, confusingly, adds, "It's the least I can do." Sam's expression must give away his bewilderment, because Jake rolls his eyes and clarifies, "You feed me? Every day? Because your dog shamed me for my pilfered pocket pierogies?"

"I think you just wanted an excuse to say 'pilfered pocket pierogies,'" Sam says, forcing himself to stand up. It seems more dignified than going into a long diatribe about how he could feed Jake every day for the rest of his life and they *still* wouldn't be even, not for the way Sam's mistakes affected him. "I should get back to work. Thank you, for... for your help."

Jake rolls his eyes again, clearly unwilling to accept the thanks, and opens his laptop back up. But as Sam's walking away, Jake adds, "So you're *really* not going to ask about, like. The thing at the Met Gala, or the stories about the skydiving planes from the show, or... any of it?"

Sam pauses mid-step, turns around. On the one hand, he now does, just based on that question, have about seventeen things he'd like to ask Jake about. On the other hand: "It's not that I *don't* want to know what happened in LA, Jake. But I'm not looking to find out from the internet, or force you to tell me if you don't want to."

"Oh," Jake says; for some reason, he flushes slightly. "That's nice, actually. Thanks."

"Sure," Sam says, not feeling it merits thanks, with an awkward little shrug. Then he reconsiders the phrasing of Jake's original query, one practically begging for follow-up questions, and adds, "Of course, if you'd *like* to tell me what happened—"

"Now, who said that?" Jake's face is a picture of amused calm, but Sam notices that one of his hands is shaking slightly. Jake must notice it, too, because he whisks it under the table as he says, "Anyway, don't let me keep you. Haven't you heard? I have important marketing work to do."

Sam chuckles and decides to let the topic of Walt lie, and does, indeed, go back to work. The rest of the day is good, easy, nothing bothering Sam except a tiny thread of discomfort running through the back of his mind. He hardly notices it until he's alone, and when he finally does, he's surprised to find himself thinking again of Jake's casual, offhand, "It's the least I could do." As though Sam wouldn't owe him forever. As though Sam hadn't altered the course of his life.

That night, for the first time in years, he dreams of the accident. He can't say he's surprised.

TEN

THEN: NOVEMBER, TWELVE YEARS AGO

"You know," Jake said conversationally, as they turned off Sam's street, "if you're going to go this slowly the whole way to Anthony's, getting there is going to take ten thousand years."

That night the whole world seemed to be conspiring against Sam, a perfect symphony of disaster conducted by someone who hated him. Instead of saying this, or pointing out that he had no intention of driving this car anywhere but back to its appointed spot in Jake's garage, he muttered, "Duly noted."

Even the roads weren't working with him on his mission of questionable mercy. If Jake had just lived on a normal street, the drive from Sam's house to his would have taken, at most, two and a half minutes. But because he didn't, Sam had to drive a whole five minutes, and directly past the high school where his parents and Jake's were spending the evening.

Or he would have. They didn't actually make it that far.

Everything that rallied against Sam that night would irritate him for years to come, but surely, of them all, the most annoying blame to have to lay was at the feet of city planning. Scoone Avenue, Jake's street, had a cul-de-sac at one end, and was cut off by the lower portion of Scenic Lake at the other. There was only one way to get in or out, which was to go over the small iron bridge to the road that ringed the lake, Scenic Drive. It *was* a scenic drive, one with lovely views of the water and its surrounding woods and wetlands; there had been some legal fight in the sixties to turn the area into a nature preserve, and in the end it had been agreed that nothing new could be built on the land. Which is why there was nothing on Scenic Drive except for Horseshoe Heights High School.

They were arguing, Sam remembers that. He'd cursed the city planning then, too, if only inside his own head, because the way things were laid out meant Jake cottoned on to what Sam was doing almost immediately. He'd snapped, "Hey, this isn't the way to—oh my God, you liar! You lied to me! You *said* you were taking me to the party!"

"We can go to the party," Sam said, trying not to sound desperate. He drummed his fingers against the steering wheel as Jake made an assortment of outraged noises. There simply was no good way to say to Jake just now that a very loud, frightened part of him kept screaming things like, *This is a very expensive car*, and, *This is a very expensive car that belongs to the scariest man I know*, and, *This is a very expensive car that belongs to the scariest man I know and he knows where I live and I don't even have a driver's license, Jake, oh my God!* This was, in a word, unhelpful, especially since it kept drowning out different and more rational parts of him, which were saying things more along the lines of, *Remember, the brake's the LEFT pedal and the gas is the RIGHT*, and, *Just a note, Sam: You're supposed to know where the turn signals are and how to turn them on* before *you start driving.*

"Not from here we can't!" Jake snapped, gesturing around them as Sam eased them, at roughly seventeen miles per hour, up the road. "Not unless you turn off at Oakwood, but that'll take you all the way up the hill, and Anthony's is completely the other way! And otherwise this only takes us back to my house or to—oh my God, Sam, you're going to drive us past the high school. You can't do that! My dad is in there! Turn around! Abort mission!"

"You drove by it to get to my house," Sam pointed out, instead of saying, *Yes, Jake, I'm more than half hoping we get spotted and stopped. I think we might need an adult.* As he did, he had a glimmer of a thought older than his years: Perhaps Jake, too, had wanted to get caught, the way Sam had always sort of wanted to get caught every time he told a lie. It had been horrible, what happened with his parents and the house party—it had been awful living with their disappointment and rage—but it had been a relief, too, in a weird way. That he'd finally gotten their attention, maybe, or maybe just that they cared enough to be angry with him.

Sam glanced over at Jake as they were passing the intersection at Oakwood Road, feeling suddenly soft towards him. It would take him about five years of therapy, in the end, to forgive himself for that glance—to accept that there was no scenario where, as an unlicensed teenage driver, he would have known in advance about the dangers of the Oakwood Road intersection, and thus been paying more attention. To accept that even if he had been paying more attention, it wouldn't have mattered, because of those very dangers he would not in any scenario have known about.

Still: He glanced at Jake, and away from the road. So he wasn't looking, noticed only the abrupt change in lighting, when the car hit them.

The Oakwood Road intersection was dangerous for five reasons, all of which had been enumerated in a variety of city council meetings that Sam, as a seventeen-year-old, had neither attended nor heard about. The first reason was that Oakwood Road twined down the long, steep slope of Oakwood Hill; the second was that it met Scenic Drive just off a sharp curve, and thus was essentially a blind turn for both directions of traffic. The third reason was that only Oakwood Road had a stop sign, and the fourth was that said stop sign was mostly obscured by both the curve in the road and an unfortunately low-growing beech bough.

However, the fifth reason that the Oakwood Road intersection was dangerous was the most important one, and that was *where* it was in relation to the world around it. Most of Scenic Drive was surrounded by sparse, relatively young forest, but where it met Oakwood Road happened to be the only point along its run where it skated close to the lake it was named for. So close that between the road and the water, there was only a badly battered guardrail, barely standing, and a roughly ten-foot drop.

Sam doesn't remember screaming. He must have screamed—Jake must have screamed—when the other car hit them, but he doesn't remember that. He remembers that it was from behind them, and hard, like it had been flying down the hill and turned right into them without slowing down at all. He remembers his mind going perfectly blank, forgetting how to brake or steer even as part of him knew it was all happening too quickly for either to do any good. He remembers there was a tearing, crumpling noise as they went through the guardrail, and he remembers—God, like it was yesterday, he remembers—the sick, strange serenity of the approaching lake through the windshield, and making brief eye contact with a very surprised duck.

Then they hit the water, and the world went black.

Sam blinked his eyes open into a brief, muddy moment of confusion. He was wet; he was cold; he could hear strange, metallic creaking noises, distant birdsong, and the rush of water. Slowly, as if being filtered through mud, the realization that he'd been unconscious drifting towards him, though not for how long.

Why he'd been unconscious, on the other hand, was pretty clear. His head ached where it must have slammed against the steering wheel on impact, and he dizzily remembered Mr. Thompson saying something about this car being older than airbags—

—wait, why was he in—

—oh, *God*, he crashed the car into the—

"JAKE!" Sam yelled this, frantic, as he whipped his head around to look for him, and then cut himself off abruptly for two reasons. The first was that turning his head so quickly was decidedly unpleasant, and probably, in the circumstances, foolish; the second was that Jake was right next to him, still in the passenger seat where Sam saw him last.

Of course, that passenger seat was half-submerged in lake water, and Jake, bleeding sluggishly from a head wound, was fully unconscious, so Sam wasn't exactly counting it as a win. The water was a concern. Sam hadn't quite noticed it up until that point, but it was up to his own waist as well. For a second he was gripped with panic, sure both that they were sinking and that Jake was dead, before he realized the water level wasn't rising. Glancing over the edge of his door, he realized they seemed to be stuck somehow, the surface of the lake a mere inch from the top of the open cab, but the car not descending any further than it already had. This made no sense at all, but Sam decided to worry about it later.

In the interest of giving himself *less* to worry about later, Sam held a hand in front of Jake's mouth briefly and, when he felt Jake's breath brush against his palm, heaved out a sigh of relief so intense he nearly choked on it. At least Jake was alive; at least they were both alive. Sam was fairly certain, as he wincingly took stock of the wreckage around him, that it might easily have worked out otherwise.

Telling himself to approach the situation with a triage mindset and tackle the most urgent problem first, Sam found himself stuck almost immediately on determining what his most urgent problem was. The car was in the lake; it was late November, so the lake was just this side of freezing; the human body could only be in cold water for so long without developing hypothermia; these all seemed like fairly critical issues. But then, so did Jake's lack of consciousness, not to mention his head wound, not to mention Sam's head wound, not to mention—

—God, even in remembering it Sam struggles to make himself look down, which is stupid. It's not as though there was anything particularly gory to see, since by the time Sam did make himself look, both of Jake's legs were submerged under the inky black surface of the lake. But even without being able to peer under the surface, Sam knew something was badly wrong. He didn't know yet entirely what had happened, and wouldn't until he could see the wreck from the outside, but he could tell that Jake's side of the car had been damaged somehow, was bent into an unnatural shape that must have, within it, at least some part of Jake bent unnaturally, too.

Sam concluded, a little breathlessly, that he had too many problems to solve, but that luckily they all pointed towards the same next step: getting himself and Jake the hell out of this car. Half-assessing and half to reassure himself, he put two fingers against the pulse point in Jake's neck, absurdly grateful for every beat, as he gripped Jake's other shoulder and squeezed as much as he dared. He didn't want to shake Jake, or drag him through the water, if he had some sort of spinal injury, but it was equally critical that he talk to Jake to work that out, so. He said—maybe, if he's honest, he screamed—"Jake? Jake! *Jake*, wake up! Come on!"

"Y'don't have to yell," Jake muttered, irritable, blinking his eyes open. "M'head hurts—m'leg hurts... Oh, *shit*." This last he breathed out in a sort of long exhale of horror, although Sam wasn't sure if was at realizing their circumstances, which would have been entirely justified, or a result of the pain he was in kicking up a gear. Certainly he made a keening sound in his next breath and gasped, "Okay, wow. Okay! Leg really hurts, Sam. Really hurts, really fucking hurts, shit, *shit*—"

"Stay calm," Sam said. It was an absurd thing to say; how could anyone stay calm in a situation like that? He, himself, didn't feel calm at all, but the words sounded like he did, firm and convincing for all the command they issued was useless. "Do you feel like your spine is broken?"

Jake turned his head and made a face at Sam, somewhere between frantic, agonized, and annoyed. "How would I know? What does having your spine broken feel like?"

Sam was already unbuckling his seatbelt. "Well, yours probably isn't, because you just turned your head, so. Still—can you feel your arms and legs? Move them?"

"Feel them, yes. Too much. Move them..." Jake sucked in a deep breath, his face going very pale. "Mostly... yes. Left leg feels..." There was a pained pause, in which Jake took a couple of shallow, half-sobbed breaths, before he managed, "Stuck."

"Jesus. Okay. Got it," Sam said. "Just hold on, I'm coming around." He jumped over the edge of the door and into the water only an inch or so below him.

He'd worked out already that, strangely, the car didn't seem to be interested in sinking any further into the lake than it had while Sam was unconscious, and had filed this away as odd, but non-urgent. As he swam around to Jake's side of the car, the solution to this little mystery was made horribly clear to him, although he rather wished, then and now, that it hadn't been.

The Jaguar had landed in the lake, right enough. It was a long car, with the engine and front end taking up easily two thirds of its total body; the cab and the trunk were crammed into the back third of the machine, as though it had been an inconvenience to the designers to have to include them at all. This final third of the car had, at least partially, escaped submersion into the murky depths below, but as Sam paddled around to the passenger side, his whole body aching with the cold of the water, he realized why with a sinking heart.

Ringing Scenic Lake, spaced about fifteen feet apart, were low, round cement pylons, each one roughly the size of a log, sticking up about three feet above the waterline. These were affixed with a series of large sturdy metal hooks and were used as tie-offs for the boaters, mostly in kayaks or canoes, who enjoyed taking the occasional dip in the lake. And, in descending from the road above, the Jaguar had managed to land bang on top of one of them. Neither object had managed to quite destroy the other, but Jake's side of the car was crumpled slightly inward from its encounter with the useless guardrail, and, more significantly, upward by the pylon below. It was remarkable, at least from where

Sam was looking at it, that he only felt like one of his legs was trapped; it could easily, maybe even more easily, have been both of them.

"Shit," Sam said, horrified, treading water next to him. He was beginning to feel shaky somewhere deep in the marrow of himself, the numbing cold of the lake seeping past unpleasant and into alarming. He wanted to wait for the paramedics—what did he know about dealing with something like this—but he had a distant, nervous clock in the back of his mind, one that was counting down to one or both of them freezing to death. It happened, he knew, faster than people thought it in these kinds of temperatures, especially dealing with shock or adrenaline.

"Can you *do something*, please," Jake ground out, clearly strangling back a scream of pain, "your lips are turning blue and it also *hurts*, Sam, okay, in case you were wondering, it fucking hurts a *lot*—"

"Yeah," Sam said, his mind racing, "Yeah, I'll do something."

And the truth is, to this day, he doesn't quite know how he got Jake out of that car. Maybe it was an adrenaline rush, like those stories about mothers lifting their cars to rescue their trapped children; maybe it was luck, that night's single stroke of it. All he's completely sure of is that he'd swum around, and braced his feet against the submerged hood of the car, and sliced up his arms reaching through the shattered windshield to grip at a hunk of misshaped plastic and metal and heave upward, and he only remembers about his arms because of the scars.

It took a number of tries, he knows that. He knows he was sobbing and screaming, and that Jake was sobbing and screaming by the time Sam heaved so hard he was sure it would kill him, and Jake yelled, "Yes! Yes! I'm out, holy shit, Sam, I—oh, fuck," and visibly nearly passed out, going so pale he looked, frankly, dead. Sam has always assumed that it was trying to move his now-freed leg that had done that, but he'd never gotten the chance to ask Jake; the Freezing to Death clock in his mind had started to tick quite urgently, by that point.

He swam to shore on reserves he hadn't known he possessed, dragging Jake, half-conscious, behind him.

"Sorry," Sam whispered as he pulled Jake up on to the nearest bank, and Jake made a noise like a dying animal. "Sorry, sorry, I'm so sorry." He collapsed for a few seconds in the reedy mud, gasping for air, every part of him aching; then he stripped off his sodden sweatshirt and rose painstakingly to his knees, tied it in a makeshift tourniquet around Jake's injured leg. He wasn't at all sure it was the right thing to do—he wasn't, after all, a doctor—but certainly Jake was bleeding heavily, and Sam had been a practice dummy for his parents and their friends enough times to understand the basics of how it was done. When he'd managed that, he looked around, deciding quickly there was no way he'd be able to get the both of them up the slope to the road. On the theory that he might as well, he dragged himself around to sit at the crown of Jake's skull, crossed his own legs, and very carefully lifted Jake's head up until it was resting in Sam's lap.

Sirens began to wail in the distance, which was good; Sam's phone, which he'd forgotten even possessing, had surely drowned already. The other driver must have called 911. Sam had also forgotten that there was another driver, or, indeed, another car. His world had narrowed to a single point, no bigger than the space it took to contain himself, Jake, and the sick, abrupt horror of what had happened. It was jarring to suddenly remember there was anything beyond that, or ever had been. It couldn't have been more than twenty minutes ago, but Sam felt separated from the person he was when he got into the car by a gulf of years.

"Oh, God," Jake said. It was so thick with pain as to be nearly unintelligible. Sam was expecting what he said next to be, *My leg* or *Seriously, my leg*, or maybe just a long *Arrrgh* sort of sound. So it took him a second to process what he was hearing, and then another to get over the surprise, when Jake moaned, "The *car*."

"The *what*? Jake, it's just a car," Sam said, as gently as possible. "Your leg—no, don't! Don't look at it, keep looking at me, that's good—but it's, uh. I wouldn't worry about the car, right now."

"But it's *my dad's Jaguar*," Jake said, and moaned again. "It's in the *lake*. You don't *understand*, Sam; he loves that thing more than any of us! I didn't want to *murder* it, I don't have a *death* wish, I only wanted—oh my *God*, he's going to kill me. He's going to *kill* me, oh my God, oh my God—"

"Jake, c'mon, stop," Sam said softly, keeping his voice calm, soothing, through sheer force of will. It was too surreal, having this conversation while they were both sprawled out on the reedy edge of the lake, soaked and covered in mud and blood, Jake's leg mangled and hard to look directly at. He ran a hand through Jake's hair and, casting around for anything to calm him down, added, "Look, just focus on staying conscious, okay? I was the one driving anyway, so I'll just say it was my idea, how about that? When the police get here? He's not my dad; there's only so much he can do to me, right? Okay? Jake?"

However, in spite of Sam's request, Jake had lost his grip on consciousness, sprawled limp across the mud, his head in Sam's lap. There was no way to know if he'd even heard Sam's offer, let alone what he would have replied.

But Sam did it anyway, although it wasn't the police who arrived next. It was his own parents, who, as it turned out, had run down from the high school when the driver who hit them burst into the benefit yelling about an accident. The man was apparently a parent himself, speeding because he'd been running late to the event, and David and Mara—along with the handful of other doctors in the room—had immediately grabbed what supplies they could find and headed to the scene.

Sam doesn't think he'll ever forget his parents' faces, the way their expressions had gone from concern to shock to sheer terror between blinks as they realized it was him in the accident. His mother had let out a single, choked-off sound, more gasp than sob; his father's eyes had widened in brief, watering horror.

Then they were doctors again, the same doctors they'd been all Sam's life. They smoothed out into the versions of themselves he'd known best when he was small and regularly keeping himself a secret during their patient exams on days they couldn't find child-care. They asked questions and gave instructions and barked orders at the other people who had come down from the school with them. They told Sam it was all going to be fine, that he should try not to panic, that he'd done the right thing by tying the tourniquet. They made someone get Sam a blanket while they did what they could to get Jake ready for transport to the hospital.

They didn't ask who had been driving, whose car it was, whose idea it had been to take it. Sam allowed himself to believe that this meant that it wouldn't matter to them; the truth was, it just wasn't important in the moment.

And they heard him, anyway, when the police turned up a few moments later, an ambulance hot on their heels. They heard him talking to the cop; they heard him when he said it was all his plan, taking Mr. Thompson's car. That he'd pushed Jake into it; that Jake had only come along to keep an eye on the Jaguar.

The cop he talked to while Jake was loaded onto a stretcher by a team of paramedics was an older man with a face like a worn-in boot. It was obvious that he didn't believe Sam, even though David and Mara, stony-faced behind him, clearly believed him a little too much. The officer tapped his pencil against his notebook when he finished taking Sam's statement, frowning down at his own notes, and then looked up a point beyond Sam and whistled.

Sam turned to take a look for himself and grimaced. What had to be the bulk of the guestlist for the Horseshoe Heights High benefit had apparently decided to follow David and Mara, if at a slower pace. Fancily dressed rubberneckers who had escaped the event were now peering curiously down at them, muttering amongst themselves.

At the front of the crowd was Patrick Thompson, who, as Sam stared at him, got close enough to take in the full scene before him and then shrieked, "My CAR!"

Terrified of making eye contact with the man, who was rapidly turning purple, Sam twisted back around to face the cop.

Raising his eyebrows, the cop glanced at his notebook again

and said, "Right, so, just to confirm—you're sure this is your official statement? Your full account of what happened here tonight? Nothing you might have left out, or changed around?"

For a second, Sam considered telling him the truth. It was only a second; in the next one he caught a glimpse of Jake's ashen, unconscious face as he was loaded into the ambulance. A face that, if Sam had only been more careful, might be smiling and laughing at a party with him right now.

"I'm sure," Sam said, resolute. "It was all me." The cop sighed and shook his head, but didn't argue.

ELEVEN

THEN: NOVEMBER, TWELVE YEARS AGO

Unsurprisingly, the rest of the night went poorly.

When the ambulance left, his parents crossed over to him, tight-lipped, their movements stiff. "Come on," David said, hauled him into standing, "Let's go home."

Surely, he and Mara had driven to the event—Sam knew they had, having seen them leave in the car what felt like an eon before —but all three of them walked home. At the time Sam had thought it was a punishment, that he hadn't deserved a ride after what he'd done. Looking back now, he wonders if it wasn't just the thick cloud of shared shock.

Whatever it was, they walked in painful, loaded silence, and when they did get into the house, all Mara said was, "We've checked you and you're not hypothermic or concussed; that's good. Still, you should get some rest. Clean yourself up and go to your room, Sam."

"I should explain," Sam said. His tongue, he remembers, felt strange in his mouth, too heavy and ill-fitting, as though it had been swapped out for someone else's. "It wasn't... I wasn't really—"

"I said," Mara ground out, "clean yourself up, and go to your room."

So Sam cleaned himself up and went to his room. He got in

bed. He didn't sleep. For a while, he listened to the muted sounds of his parents arguing, the words inaudible, but the rising and falling tones suggesting raw unhappiness. Then the noise stopped and was replaced by the soft song of the night: crickets playing their low violins, frogs croaking in the nearby pond. Sam listened to that, too. He tried, as hard as he could, not to think about anything at all.

Around four in the morning, he got out of bed, walked silently down the hall to the bathroom, and threw up neatly and without fuss. If he cried, he didn't notice. Not because he didn't want to cry, not because he wasn't ripped apart with remorse and regret, but because what had happened was still too incomprehensible for tears. A real part of him was convinced that if he could just fall asleep, he'd wake up to the blissful realization that it had all been a horrible dream.

But it hadn't all been a horrible dream. Personhood is an exercise of chance and probability, every life a single marble sent rolling down a hill, and any little bump or twig might be the one that sends it careening down a totally different path. It was a hard truth to learn so entirely at seventeen. Even now, looking back, Sam doesn't quite feel old enough to know it.

Certainly, it kept him up that night, and because he didn't sleep, he didn't get the chance to awaken, relieved, in his familiar, undamaged world. Instead he walked downstairs the next morning hollowed out, trapped in the hideous new one.

David and Mara were at the breakfast table, stone-cold and silent. Neither one of them would meet Sam's eye. He tried, with increasing desperation, to tell them the real story. It was clear that with every word he said, they believed him less. Numbly, he realized that this, too, was a cost of having spun a web of intricate lies; the damn things had a half-life, still breaking down months after he'd abandoned the practice entirely. But the trust that had eroded away, bit by bit without Sam's even noticing, was gone now, lost seemingly beyond rescue or repair. The knowledge came upon him wholly, a perfect, unbroken understanding that had arrived far too late.

Sam doesn't remember now what else they talked about at that breakfast, if they talked about anything. All he remembers is thinking that he didn't care what they did to him, that nothing could be worse than what had already happened, and then how much he'd regretted, later, ever having had that stupid thought.

And he remembers that they were interrupted before he could clear up by the sound of tires squealing, a car door slamming, and someone bellowing in what sounded like rage from the front yard.

"Oh, God," Mara said, her already pinched expression tightening even further, as David sighed and got up to answer the door. She glared at Sam as she rubbed at a temple and snapped, "Do you see? Do you see the impact your behavior has on this family? I doubt whoever is out there on the lawn is screaming about me! Or your father! Or your sisters!"

"I know," Sam said, his head hanging, shame burning within him like a trash fire: all noxious gases and greasy, lingering fumes. "I know, I know, I'm sorry. I was trying to do the right thing—"

"By stealing a car, Sam? Exactly how much of a moron do you think I—"

But she stopped, because David had opened the front door, and the screaming outside had become both louder and more intelligible.

"You get him out here right now!" This voice was clearly Mr. Thompson, and Sam was surprised by how terrifying he found it. Usually, observing as an outsider, he thought the man's tantrums were a little pathetic, and sometimes wondered why Jake seemed so cowed by them. But being the target of his ire, knowing all that raw, uncontrolled rage was being directed at him, made Sam freeze in his seat as though glued to the cushioning.

Mrs. Thompson's voice filtered back into the dining room, trailing his thinly, like a wisp of smoke. "Patrick, honey, please, let's just calm down and talk about this. The neighbors are coming out now; they're all going to see—"

"I don't give a good goddamn about the neighbors!" Patrick was roaring now, so loud that Mara winced, and then glanced at Sam, and then sighed and pushed back her chair, stood up. "Let them all see! Let them all stand here and watch as I give that little pissant what's coming to him—"

"Whoa now." That was David, the calm, even voice Sam had heard him use dozens of times on unruly patients while Sam was, secretly and very much without official permission, hanging around the ER during his shifts. "I understand we're all upset here, but let's not escalate to threats."

"Oh, he doesn't want me to escalate," Patrick snarled. "Do you hear that, Laur? He doesn't want me to escalate!"

"I think the whole neighborhood's heard now, Pat," Lauren said. There was an edge of despair in her voice that rendered it almost unfamiliar, even though Sam must have heard her speak a hundred times before. "Let's just go home, or back to the hospital. This isn't going to fix anything."

"Who's trying to fix anything?" Patrick's voice grew, somehow, even louder: "I know you're in there, Sam! If you're old enough to steal from me, then you're old enough to face me like a man!"

"He's seventeen." That was Mara, clipped and cold. "And he took your stupid, ugly car for a joyride around the lake, not to a chop shop—"

"Stupid?!" Patrick's incredulous rage cracked through the word, splintering it. "Ugly?!"

"—and the important thing," Mara continued, as if he hadn't spoken, "is what happened to your *son*, which I'm sure we can all agree we feel sick about. But it was an accident—"

"Oh, a likely story—"

"And I know Sam's very sorry—"

"But not sorry enough to face the consequences, eh?"

"Sorrier, actually," said Sam quietly, stepping past his parents to stand before the mottled, furious Patrick Thompson. "Sorrier than I've ever been about anything in my life."

Far from looking mollified, the apology seemed to further

enrage Patrick. Then again, maybe it was just the sight of Sam that fanned the flame of his anger; Sam certainly wouldn't have blamed him. Or... looking back as an adult, Sam can't ignore the uncomfortable possibility that perhaps the man was just very upset, reeling after a series of blows that might have thrown off anyone's equilibrium, and had seized with relief the nearest available lightning rod.

Whatever the reason, Patrick snarled, "You should be sorry," as he stepped forward, jabbing a finger hard into Sam's chest and then repeating the gesture occasionally for emphasis. "You stole my car. You drove it into the *lake*! You *ruined* my son's life!"

"Patrick!" It was the angriest Sam had ever heard Jake's mother; she sounded near tears. "Don't—how could you say—Jake's life isn't *ruined*."

"Oh, no, of course not." Patrick's voice was sharp and bitter. "He's going to go off to study ballet at Juilliard next fall, just like he wanted! A completely pulverized ankle won't impact that at all! Those severed ligaments and crushed bones? No big deal! The surgeries and physical therapy and years of rehab he has coming to him definitely won't be an issue. Shouldn't be *any* kind of problem that his doctors don't know if he'll ever be able to walk on it again!"

At this point, Sam began to feel as though he might throw up in sheer horror for the second time in less than twelve hours. Not thinking about it, his body making the call for him, he crouched down and put his head between his knees.

This was a mistake. A moment later Sam was being grabbed by the collar of his T-shirt and hauled upright, held an inch from Patrick's now-purpled face. Everyone was screaming—Patrick demanding to know what right Sam had to collapse when this was his fault, Lauren begging Patrick to let Sam go, David threatening to call the police, Mara shrilly insisting Sam was only a child.

And Sam could have shouted, too. He could have told Patrick that Jake had stolen the car, that Jake had been drunk, that both of those things had happened as a direct result of Patrick's own actions. He could have explained that he'd only taken the driver's seat so Jake wouldn't crash it himself; he could have pointed out that the other driver was at fault, and that he couldn't have prevented it no matter how desperately he'd wanted to.

But he hadn't. He'd watched, instead, as Patrick pulled back his fist, and then he'd turned his head, waiting for the blow. He knew to his bones he deserved it; he wanted Patrick to hit him. Anything to make his outside match what churned within. Anything to feel like he was receiving some sort of just punishment for his unthinkable crime.

Patrick didn't hit him, though. In the end, after a hanging second, he muttered, "Saints above, what am I doing?" and let Sam go. And then... Sam had never seen anything quite like it, the way all the fight seemed to drain away from him, leaving something behind smaller and less certain than the Mr. Thompson who'd stormed out of the house the evening before. Some of the man's commanding presence was whittled away there before Sam's eyes on the doorstep, leaving him looking old. Sallow. Lost.

"You'll hear from our lawyers," he said, but it didn't sound like a threat so much as a weary promise. "Let's go, Lauren. Let's go."

Sam and his parents stood there together and watched them walk down the drive, climb back into Patrick's Mercedes, peel away. Normally, David would have made a crack about the wasted opportunity to simply walk around the block; he didn't. None of them said anything at all until:

"Sam, I would like you to go upstairs, and pack an overnight bag, and get in the car." Mara's voice was calm and dead and empty, a forest after a fire. "Right now, please."

Sam blinked at her, surprised. "Where—?"

"I said," Mara said, in that same blank voice, "right now, please."

It was a tone he'd never heard her use before, and it scared him; he didn't argue. He went upstairs and packed a bag, and then, at her instruction, he got in the car. His father, as they passed, said, "Mara, where are you—" and then, silenced by a sharp look, stayed in the kitchen, looking sorrowfully after them.

The drive was silent, too, not even music. Sam tried to break it a few times, but every time he did his mother's knuckles grew a little whiter on the steering wheel, so he stopped. The previous day's gray weather had given way to a sharp, sparkling snow, the kind that felt like knives in the wind and glittered like sequins as it fell. Each flake looked as brittle as Sam felt, as Mara seemed, as the energy between them had palpably become.

He was pleased, horribly, when they pulled up to Silverman's. He always had been, all his life. And he was pleased, as his mother dragged him inside by the sleeve, to see Deb behind the counter. That, too, had been true all his life.

But his pleasure had evaporated when Mara snarled, "Well! You know what, Deb? You were right! I was an unfit parent for him, just like you said, and I ruined him, just like you said, and it nearly got him killed, just like you said! And, as a bonus, he's become a monster, just like you might as well have said, so you know what! Fine! My bad! *You* do it. *You* get him through high school, if you think you know so much better than I do! I give up!"

"Mara," Deb said, wide-eyed, glancing between the two of them. "For God's sake, what are you even saying? Let's just talk for a second. What the hell happened?"

"Ask him," Mara said, her voice tight in a way it would take Sam years to realize meant she was holding back tears. "Ask *him*; I can't—" and then she was gone, turning on her heel and storming out of the deli without even saying goodbye.

Deb hadn't asked him, though. She'd taken one look at his face, pulled his bag from his hands, dropped it on the counter, and given him a hug. It was then—and only then—that Sam cried.

TWELVE

NOW: JUNE

Over the next few weeks, Sam does what he always has when life asks him to face the realities of the accident: He puts his head down and tries his best to get on with things.

The first time, when he was a teenager, he'd poured himself into work as a distraction, determined to learn and live by the laws of his new home too thoroughly to ever risk being thrown out. It's easy enough, now, to do that again. Or it would be, if Jake hadn't abruptly become such a central figure in Sam's professional life.

The marketing plan Jake presented the day after their conversation had been thorough. Surprisingly thorough. There were charts and graphs and sample posts and a suggested timeline, complete with a fully fleshed-out posting schedule. Jake had even made graphics, and mocked up merchandise, and a whole list of ideas for deals or promotions to run across their socials. Many of these had little notes with questions attached for Sam about feasibility on various points.

It had seemed an almost impossible amount of work for one person to have done in a single day, but when Sam said as much, Jake laughed and told him it was nothing. So Sam had smiled, and thanked him, and given him the okay to get started. If he found it amusing, not to mention a little odd, that Jake seemed to have aged into a sense of modesty, he kept it to himself.

In the weeks since, as summer has started to creep in around spring's fading edges, Jake's proved he had no need to be modest. Most mornings before the dance studio opens, and on the afternoons when he doesn't have classes, he spends a couple of hours in the deli working, filming people or typing furiously on his laptop. Social media posts for the deli go up even when Jake's not there, advertising specific dishes, specials, highlighting the staff. It's all stylized cohesively, the food somehow looking more appealing through the lens of Jake's phone camera than it ever did through Sam's. Every post feels polished and intentional, but still a little fun.

He makes Sam sit down for filming on one of his very first days at it, and says, "Forget the camera is here; talk about what this deli means to you. Tell me about what the last few months have been like." And then somehow he cuts the tangled mess of an answer that follows, one no one would call compelling or professional, into short videos where Sam comes off as both. He talks about his grandmother, about learning to make gefilte fish from her in the Silverman's kitchen, the way he still measures them out with her cherished wooden spoon. He talks about the loss of traffic recently, how desperately he doesn't want to see the place go under, all that history lost in the blink of an eye. He talks about finding Pastrami, who comes over at the sound of her name and does a series of tricks for the camera. He talks about his food-safety practices, and how seriously he takes them. He talks about how much it sucked to have been a fan of Norman Endicott, only to be squarely in striking range the one time he decided to punch down, not to mention lie.

The videos circulate well locally, or at least seem to. Certainly, Sam receives a number of messages from various people he's known over the course of his life saying they saw him, and he looked great, and they'll stop by the deli one of these days.

And something about that video must move something in Jake,

too, because in the weeks that follow, in bits and pieces, he tells Sam about his life in Los Angeles. He had, apparently, gone out there originally to see some specialist for his ankle, less than a year after the accident. He stayed with his brother, a UCLA student, because the treatment took a few months; in the end, he'd liked it enough to apply. He got in, did well for a year, and then met Walt; the man gave a guest lecture to one of Jake's classes about the business side of Hollywood, and, apparently, found it an appropriate place to look for dates. Sam has to read between the lines on some of the rest, because Jake gets embarrassed and strange whenever the topic comes up, but it sounds to him like Walt was controlling, intense, and did what he could to cut Jake off from both his family and any real source of his own income.

Sam tries, a few times, to tell Jake he's sorry about what it sounds like was a brutal time of his life, but Jake always brushes him off, rolls his eyes, and tells some story about celebrity, wealth, or excess he witnessed on Walt's arm. It's distracting, certainly, but it always makes Sam wonder if Jake is doing it on purpose: justifying what he went through on the grounds that it was worth it for the rarity of the experience.

Still, in spite of the chill that tends to fall over the conversation when Los Angeles comes up, the days get longer and warmer as June settles in, each one feeling more hopeful than the last. And as each one stretches towards the next, traffic gets a little bit better, diners trickling back in one by one.

It's interesting to see who returns, and in what way. There are people he expects to see, and doesn't; he's sad and a little surprised not to see Marty, the landlord of the building behind them, show his face. He'd been a near-daily visitor before it all went down, and had, in the initial aftermath of the review, promised not to abandon them before abruptly going radio silent. Embarrassing though it is, it kind of hurts that even now he doesn't trust them enough to return.

On the other hand, some of the once-and-future regulars

saunter back in as though there hadn't been any sort of intentional gap in their patronage at all, only the slightly forced edge to their performance giving them away.

Others are more honest. Amber Baumbach, who has for years insisted that her children are allergic to the coating on the outside of the pastrami, but not to the pastrami itself, nor to the layer of the same coating which makes its way into the center of the meat, comes in nearly weeping with remorse. None of the other delis in town, she explains, will cut the outside off the pastrami for her! They all called her crazy! She tells Sam she cancelled her subscription to that awful magazine and then, in the same breath, orders four pounds of mangled pastrami, which Sam dutifully cuts up for her, less annoyed by it than he ever has been before.

And a lot of people, their voices often lowered as though Norman Endicott might be lurking around nearby, have something disparaging to say about Kiss of Death. This is less gratifying than Sam would have expected, if he'd been expecting it. It's not that it isn't nice to hear them echo his own feelings about Endicott's trustworthiness and ethical failings, but... Well. Sam can't help but wonder now if they're all talking out of the sides of their mouths—if a few weeks ago, to other people, they were insisting that they, too, had seen rats at Silverman's, simply because that was the way the wind was blowing.

Still, slightly complicated though it is, it's nice to have his customers back. As traffic picks up, spirits within the deli seem to as well. In fact, there seems to be a certain air of things blossoming about the place, as though the restaurant's turnaround has triggered a willingness in everyone to trust that things will work out. Eileen, aggressively single since 1987, goes on three dates with the same person and isn't consumed with hatred by the fourth; Alphonse and his partner adopt the most adorable kitten Sam's ever laid eyes on; Lyle, one of the dishwashers, comes in for his scheduled shift one morning grinning ear to ear and says he just got married, up the street, at the courthouse, about fifteen minutes ago, and would Sam mind if he called off for his honeymoon? Sam lets him go, although not before Jake pops out from around a corner and demands that they replay this interaction word for word, so he can take a quick video.

There's also... whatever is going on with Joey and Luce. Sam doesn't like to involve himself in his sisters' romantic affairs for many reasons, the most pressing of which is the sheer awkwardness of the thing, but it's all so obvious that it's impossible for him to ignore. Luce has done six paintings of Silverman's, first of all, when she was only meant to do three; possibly that's because she's had to do *something* to fill the time she's spending at the deli, which is the vast majority of most days. Or, at least, she has to find something to do to fill the time other than standing and talking to Joey, or helping Joey restock soda, or following Joey to the back for their smoke break, or staring moonily at Joey from across the diner. Joey, for their part, is no better. Sam's had easily a dozen conversations with them that have started, "Luce said," or, "Has Luce ever told you," or, "Did you know that Luce...?"

It's cute, kind of. Or rather, it would *be* cute if it was anyone but his little sister, who in Sam's eyes is still the eight-year-old who made him sit and watch while she performed vital surgery on a Pop Tart. It's jarring to see her close in on what she wants in such an unmissable way; to realize she's just as much an adult as he is, if a less experienced one.

On the other hand, maybe Sam shouldn't judge. It's not as though Luce isn't being forced to watch what's going on with him and Jake, which is arguably just as obvious as what she's been up to with Joey. In fact, on the whole, Sam thinks it might be worse. At least Luce and Joey, having never met before encountering one another at Silverman's, are free to move forward at whatever strange, slightly awkward pace suits them. Sam and Jake are almost dancing now, whirling around and around the conversation neither one of them wants to have. But without having that conversation—without acknowledging the accident, and everything that happened after—neither one of them can make a move towards the other.

So instead they circle closer and closer to the thing without ever touching it, the way two opposing magnets can be made to spin around their own resistance to making contact.

Jake won't accept payment for his social media work; that's part of the problem. It's not right, letting him do all that for nothing, but he stands firm and won't be moved, so Sam has to find other methods of compensation. This, for Sam, means feeding him.

It would be less embarrassing, probably, if Sam hadn't already done this with Jake when they were teenagers—or, indeed, if demonstrating his value by method of producing a meal wasn't already basically his go-to move. If you gathered his handful of exes together and asked them to compare notes, they'd all agree that Sam's love language was cooking, and also that maybe, at least in this aspect of himself, he talked a bit too much.

But Jake seems to enjoy Sam's tendency to drop a plate in front of him, or bring him a fresh piece of rugelach snatched directly off a hot sheet tray while Eileen's back is turned. It might simply be a function of the fact that Jake's living, as best Sam can tell, as close to the bone as possible, but he doesn't really think so. Jake had been like this when they were younger, too: exclaiming appreciatively over every dish, eating heartily, asking for seconds. He seems to genuinely enjoy not just food, but *Sam's* food, and has an unerring tendency to notice and praise the ways Sam's making a recipe his own. If he's honest, that was part of what had driven Sam to improve his cooking skills in the first place: the thought of how impressed and enthusiastic Jake would be about homemade pizza or scratch brownies.

Only... the thing is, Jake never asks for food, so Sam tends to throw together meals or snacks for him when he's doing it for himself. And then Jake will notice that Sam has two plates, and invite him to sit down, join him. And *then*, without his meaning them to, whole hours will pass as they lose themselves in the simple pleasure of conversation—laughing about strange customers and the unlikely adult lives of the people they went to high school with, or sharing interesting tidbits of knowledge they've scraped up off the floor of some life experience or another.

They don't talk about: their families, the accident, the aftermath, Jake's messy relationship with Walt, Sam's messy relationship with himself, how increasingly obvious it is that they're every bit as desperately attracted to one another as they were twelve years ago. It's all too loaded, a whole chain of land mines just waiting to go off, and both of them are a little too aware of it for comfort, always tensed for the explosion.

But that doesn't stop the other variety of tension they're feeling for one another from... manifesting. Aggressively. *Embarrassingly*, some might say, especially since it's happening all over the deli.

It's all really stupid stuff, too; that's the worst part. Sam wouldn't mind it so much if he and Jake were debonairly swooning around like actors in a period piece, delivering devastatingly sharp one-liners and double entendres before raising speaking eyebrows. That would be... okay, not exactly *fine*, it would still be mortifying, but it would be better than what *is* happening.

That's because what's happening is that Sam, at the ripe old age of thirty, has forgotten how to behave like a human being. Jake does something particularly funny or kind or hot, and all the desperate confused longing Sam's been tamping down since high school seems to shove his higher thinking skills away and take the wheel.

Worse, the same thing seems to be happening to Jake, meaning that between the two of them they possess not even one person's worth of normal behavior. This dire circumstance keeps resulting in situations like the one just the other day, where Jake was behind the counter filming, Sam needed to put a stick of cheese away in the cooler behind him, and as he leaned the perfectly reasonable amount that was required into Jake's personal space, meant to say, *Don't mind me, just putting the cheese away.*

But instead he'd experienced an internal electrical fire the second he got within a few inches of Jake, abruptly unable to think about anything beyond how much closer he'd like to get. So what he actually *said*, staring down at Jake's mouth, was, "Don't, uh. Cheese."

And Jake, staring back up at him with wide, unblinking eyes, replied, "Oh. It—won't," as though either statement made any sense at all. There was a charged moment, one where Sam seriously considered demanding everyone get out of the deli so he and Jake could defile some tables, leaving undiscussed past traumas and the associated horrors to be solved for another day.

Of course, then Joey said, "Question: Is there like a joke here I'm not getting, or do you both need to go to the hospital? Those weren't, like. Sentences?"

Sam, grimacing, had to suffer the indignity of rescue by little sister, as Luce took their arm, laughing, and said, "It's your break now, right? Come out back with me and I'll explain it to you." They'd left, and he and Jake had exchanged a horrified look, which became a lingering, speculative look before, when they noticed this, becoming horrified again. Even Pastrami had seemed a bit embarrassed for them at that point, slinking away from them to hide underneath one of the prep tables with a whine.

It's all starting to feel a bit... unsustainable, Sam thinks, is the word for it. He's dreaming about the man most nights now, these sweat-soaked, sheet-twisting fantasies of Jake showing up in his bedroom half-dressed and wearing less by the minute, smirking at Sam's surprise, climbing into bed to straddle him. The details vary delightfully from there, but it always ends with Sam pinning Jake to the mattress, which he knows because more than once he's woken up to find himself grinding against his own. He's not sure how long a person can sustain this kind of desire before something breaks dramatically, and they end up entwined, naked and touching frantically, in the middle of a public sidewalk.

On the other hand, to snap himself out of it, all Sam has to do is try, for the thousandth time, to figure out how to clear the dreaded conversational hurdles that stand between him and satisfaction. Even the thought of the accident is like taking a series of punishingly cold showers, and the idea of *talking* about it is genuinely chilling, no matter what approach Sam considers.

So they carry on in limbo, leaning towards each other and away again, inching closer and closer to the critical moment of no return—

—until it arrives, with little warning and even less fanfare, the night of Joey's twenty-first birthday party.

THIRTEEN
NOW: JUNE

The night of the party, as a birthday gift to Joey, Sam lets the whole staff go early and promises to handle close himself. They're all going out to dinner before meeting up at a popular West Sixth Street bar, and Sam had tried his best to beg off from the whole evening, but no one he talked to had been willing to listen. They all insisted that Sam hadn't done anything for his thirtieth birthday, which was true, and that he owed it to himself to come out with them and make up for it, which was not. Sam felt that what he owed himself was a nice quiet night where nothing much happened and he was able to get really excellent sleep, but when he said as much to Eileen, she just slapped him on the back and said, "Jesus, you sound older than I do." This, in particular, shamed him, and he had no choice but to agree to come out.

But while Sam was invited to both halves of the night, he knows he's only really wanted at the second. It would have been different a few years ago, when Sam was just another employee; the footing would have been more equal, and the conversation, as a result, less awkward. But ever since Deb left him in charge, Sam's The Boss, and it changes the dynamic. She'd warned him that it would, not that her warning made it any less jarring when it actually happened.

Sam's used to it now, though. He waves them off, knowing as they shuffle out that the best thing he can do for Joey tonight is handle the closing tasks, have dinner by himself, and then drop in to the party for an appropriate, but relatively brief, amount of time. That's the professional way to approach this, even if it does put Sam in a slightly lonely position.

Or it would normally put Sam in a slightly lonely position. Instead, to his surprise and pleasure, he finds that after the staff have gone Jake is still lingering in the doorway, scuffing a shoe slightly awkwardly.

Sam raises a questioning eyebrow.

Jake grimaces. "Look, okay, it's not that they're not all lovely, right, it was so nice of Joey to invite me, I'm happy enough to stop in at the bar, but there's only so much twenty-first birthday energy I can take? It makes me feel old, first of all, but secondly, my own twenty-first was such a mess I feel like maybe I shouldn't get too close to theirs in case I jinx it." He gives Sam a slightly pleading look. "Can I help you close up?"

"Sure," Sam says, grinning at him, "if you tell me what happened when you turned twenty-one," and Jake groans and pantomimes being shot by an arrow and dying an ignominious death, but then grins back.

Really, Sam is the one who should be offering thanks. Jake seems to gravitate naturally towards the tasks Sam most loathes doing, like wiping down counters, wrapping the meats, and tallying inventory. This leaves Sam to tackle the stuff he enjoys more, like dealing with the floors and ovens, and the things he *can't* hand off, like entering the day's take into their tracking software.

As it turns out it's pretty wonderful to take what Sam thinks of as the Solo Close of Kindness—something he's done many times over the years—and make it a Dual Close of Camaraderie. He doesn't have to hover around and make sure Jake knows what he's doing in an unfamiliar area, because Jake has been documenting everyone's daily deli tasks for weeks. He doesn't have to worry that he's asking too much, being a pushy or overbearing boss, because he's *not* Jake's boss, and also, he's not asking. Jake just cheerfully turns to the next thing that needs doing every time he finishes something up. He even runs Pastrami out when she starts scratching at the back door while Sam's in the middle of drain duty.

And they talk the whole time they're working, shouting to each other to keep the conversation going while they're in separate areas. They revisit the shared memory of Sam's seventeenth birthday, which involved them both being thrown out of a double feature at a movie theatre after Sam had laughed so hard at Jake's increasingly hysterically whispered defense of the film's supposed villain that he'd spilled an entire large fountain drink over not only the two of them, but also the irate couple in front. This part of the discussion, at least according to Jake, is meant to act as a grounding counterbalance to the story of about his own twenty-first birthday: an evening that he apparently spent at an incredibly high-end party that had nothing to do with him, drinking more Lemon Drops than one person should ever consume, and eventually collapsing into a bush in front of a wildly famous celebrity. Jake won't tell Sam who said celebrity was, so this diverges into a sort of guessing game, with Sam yelling things like, "Russell Crowe!" and "Meryl Streep!" across the restaurant, and Jake calling back, "Nope!" or, "Hah, I wish, it would have been worth the embarrassment to meet her."

And then, suddenly, they're laughing together in the kitchen, and everything is done except the stove, which Sam left for last because—

"Oh, right," he says, suddenly sheepish, putting a hand to the back of his neck. "I was going to, uh. Make dinner? If you want some?"

"Oooh, sure. If you don't mind, that sounds great." Jake doesn't seem at all perturbed by the offer. After all, why would he be? Sam has been feeding him for weeks now.

But, as he gathers ingredients from the fridge and freezer, Sam is intimately aware that this is not like all the other meals he has prepared for Jake. And that's because every other time, they haven't been meals he prepared *just* for Jake. It was always family meal, or something off the line, or the occasional thrown-together sandwich, but that didn't count. Anyone could slap corned beef on bread and spoon a mound of potato salad next to it on a plate—that wasn't the same as *cooking* a whole *meal* specifically for *one person*, let alone sharing that meal with them.

Sam is... nervous, he realizes, a little shocked by it. About cooking dinner! In the Silverman's kitchen! It's absurd, that's what it is, that Jake can manage to wrest that out of him just by *standing* there, patting Sam's dog and looking pleased by the idea of eating.

Nothing to do but brazen it out, so he continues to guess celebrities as he toasts and sears and poaches. It's not a complicated dinner, but something he's made for himself many times before. Hollandaise sauce is fast enough to make, and Eileen's fresh Kaiser rolls are always around, and combined with thinly sliced pastrami, they become something greater than the sum of their parts. It's not exactly eggs Benedict, because eggs Benedict is on an English muffin with ham, not pastrami, and served open-faced instead of as a closed sandwich. But it hits in a similar strike zone, and honestly Sam thinks his version tastes better than the standard, which is why he's been making it for years.

The celebrity guessing winds up being a fruitful line of conversation: Sam doesn't land on the right one, but Jake has, separately, met a number of the ones he mentions, and those stories carry them through Sam poaching the eggs, toasting the buns, searing off the pastrami, and finishing the hollandaise with a pinch of cayenne pepper.

He has a moment of panic as he's plating. Should he ask Jake to join him out in the dining room? Pull down two of the chairs from where Sam put them, twenty minutes ago, on top of their table for the night, and sit down to properly eat together? Like a—

"Here," Sam says, shoving the plate awkwardly towards Jake, who blinks and takes it, looking slightly baffled.

But he just says, "Thanks," and then repeats it when Sam

passes him a napkin, now looking a little amused. But then he takes a bite, and his whole face changes; his eyes go wide, stay wide as he chews, swallows, takes another bite. "*Dude.*"

"Oh, come on."

"Okay, listen, I know I say this about six times a week, but I'm *really serious* this time, Sam: You have to put this on the *menu*," Jake says. "Oh my God, it should be the special *tomorrow*—why am I eating it; I should be photographing it."

"Oh, come *on*," Sam repeats, sure he's blushing. "It's just an egg sandwich with pastrami, basically! No, not *you*," he adds to Pastrami, who gives him a slightly woebegone look in response, as though he's taken her name in vain, before turning back to Jake. "It's not like it's anything special."

"It is, though." Jake takes another bite and, nodding to himself, says, "Crispiness from the hard roll! And sweetness from the poppy seeds, and richness and acidity from the sauce—and it's a really nice hollandaise, too, which is impressive, because the deli doesn't serve anything with that, right? Anyway, it doesn't matter except that it's well-seasoned on its *own*, and then the smoky pastrami and the creamy yolk from the poached egg... God. It's *really* good, Sam. I'm not just saying that! I—" He pauses, and his expression twists for the barest second into something closed-off and wretched that Sam doesn't entirely understand before it smooths out again and he finishes, "Wouldn't just say it. I don't. As a rule."

"Well," Sam says, smiling at him, "if it's a rule, I guess I have to accept the compliment, don't I? Thanks." He takes a bite of his own. It tastes how it always tastes, which is of course good, because Sam wouldn't keep making something if it tasted bad. Still, he doesn't see what all the fuss is about.

"Seriously, *why* don't you put this kind of stuff on the menu?" Jake asks. It's not the first time—he's asked after a number of the family meals Sam has cooked, and Sam's always given him half an answer, or one that was only partially true, or, most often, dodged the question entirely.

But abruptly, full of the warm glow of Jake's praise, Sam wants to be truthful. "Honestly? My aunt—this place—they saved my life. If I change things from the way they've always been, what kind of thanks is that?"

Jake stares at him.

Sam bears this with good enough grace, at first. After all, Jake does this semi-regularly, the dramatic incredulous look followed shortly by a series of questions; Sam is used to it.

Except this time, no questions appear to be forthcoming. Jake just... keeps staring at him. Eventually, Sam has no choice but to say, "Um. What?"

Jake blinks and seems to shake himself, reminding Sam briefly but fervently of Pastrami after a bath. He must remind Pastrami of this, too, because she mimics him, with a wide doggy grin like she thinks it's a game, before settling down in a crescent shape on the floor.

But Jake sounds completely serious when he says, "Sorry, I just genuinely need every brain cell I have to formulate a response to that. It's taking most of them to wrap my head around how you could even *begin* to think—and your aunt sounds so chill, I can't imagine she wants... No!" Jake is very clearly saying this final word to himself, since he picks up his last bite, adds, "Food first, it's too delicious and thus *distracting*; I need all my thinking power," and shoves it in his mouth.

There is a long pause, in which Jake's face goes on a long and arduous journey.

Trying not to laugh, Sam says, "Slightly too big a bite, then?" When Jake nods, pained, his mouth still visibly full, Sam half grins and says, "Betrayal's in the name, really. Since it isn't exactly eggs Benedict, I've always thought of it as... Pastrami Arnold."

Jake's eyes go wide and his chewing becomes frantic. After another few seconds he swallows, takes in a huge gasp of air and then, sounding crazed and almost furious: "Pastrami Arnold is genius! Your whole menu should be like this! This should be your

some sense that his fundamental nature was ill-suited to the adolescent experience, and he'd have to get creative if he wanted to fill in the gaps. No matter what he does or how hard he tries, at some point in any evening out, he always ends up here: a little bored, and a little unsure what people see in the experience, and wondering whether he's made enough of an appearance to leave without being seen as an asshole.

He's just decided he's past that critical point when Jake approaches him again, this time holding two shot glasses, and says, "Hey. Do you want to dance?"

"Oh," Sam says, startled. He hadn't been anticipating this, mostly because: "I feel like I told you my position on dancing some years ago? 'Terrible at it, public humiliation, I'd rather die,' etcetera?"

"I thought maybe you'd grown and matured," Jake says, in a voice that strikes Sam as a little too innocent.

"Really?"

"No," Jake says, grinning at him, "that's what the shot's for. Here." He pushes it into Sam's hand, then clinks his own against it and says, "Cheers!" Sam has no choice but to toss it back; he realizes as he swallows that it's a Lemon Drop and makes an unhappy face at Jake, whose grin deepens. "Yes, yes, it's a disgusting shot, I know—but I thought in honor of my own twenty-first, and also because nothing seems as horrible after you drink a Lemon Drop, since at least that's over. Come on—I am a professional dance teacher these days, you know. It's on my resume and everything."

Sam's mouth twists, but his body betrays him, listing forward slightly towards the tempting thought of being pressed close to Jake.

Jake's smile shrinks but doesn't vanish, as his eyes flick up and down Sam's body. His voice is warm when he says, "Sam. It's only dancing."

"Easy for *you* to say," Sam starts, in the automatic patter of their old argument, and then snaps his mouth shut. The rest of his piece here would have involved detailing Jake's lifetime of dance training, all the ways in which he'd never have to worry about knowing how to move, what looked good and what stupid, where his feet and hands were supposed to go.

But that argument doesn't hold water anymore. Jake would have had to relearn all that—the process all the more grueling, probably, for how absolute and effortless his physicality had been before—in the aftermath of the accident.

"Is it?" is all Jake says now, the corners of his mouth quirking as though it's a joke.

But a shadow passes over his face all the same, and it's that, more than anything, that makes Sam say, "God, you know what? Fine. You're right. It can't be worse than the Lemon Drop."

Jake beams at him, and takes his hand, and drags him out to the dance floor, where Sam intends to stay for exactly one song. One song is enough to be a good sport, but hopefully not quite long enough for any of his staff to notice him embarrassing himself and take videos on their phones. He's stiff and nervous as he follows Jake to a gap in the crowd, and Jake must notice, because he laughs and says, "Relax. There's no firing squad." He uses the hand that's not on his cane to position Sam, little taps and touches directing him. When Jake leans close and murmurs, "Seriously, loosen your muscles, for the love of God. You can't move if you're doing an impression of a wooden board," his breath is hot against the shell of Sam's ear. It makes Sam shiver, some of the tension seeming to escape with the motion, because after a second Jake runs a hand over Sam's arm and says, "Good, that's better. Now try to stop thinking about it; just move with me. Your body knows how to do this, you know. You *are* a human being." And then—

—well, somewhere in the sweating, sliding, subsuming haze of the next hour, Sam has a thought. It's just about the only real thought he has while Jake's grinding against him, or guiding him through a particular motion with expressive, clever hands, or pressed so close to him they might as well just get naked and have done with it. Most of what's filtering through his brain are filthy images, filthier images, images so filthy Sam's surprised at himself for even thinking them, and single-word assessments of the situation such as "mmm," and "good," and "hot." Normally, in a situation like this, he'd be awkward, worried about how he looked or whether he was taking too many liberties, misreading the signals, or otherwise making the other person uncomfortable. But somehow, with Jake's breath hot in his ear under the strobe lights, none of that seems to matter anymore.

And through it all, the one piece of higher-level thinking that manages to hold on is: *Oh my God, is this how it's supposed to feel?* Sam almost can't believe it, although the minute it occurs to him, he's sure that it's true. No wonder people love to go to clubs, to dance all night, to push themselves to their physical limits in pursuit of more time out, if this is how it feels for them—this feels *good*. This feels so good that Sam abruptly can't remember how he lived without it.

Jake must be feeling good, too; he still moves like a dancer, but he's looser now than he was when they were teenagers, when he was in regular practice for classical ballet. As in seemingly every other arena of his life, he moves with and around the cane as though it's an extension of himself, balancing his weight on it more or less as he needs to, occasionally using it to nudge someone stepping too close out of their space. The songs slide from one to another and Jake slides closer to him as they do, and as the time passes Sam notices that occasionally he, too, is bearing some of Jake's weight, that Jake is sometimes leaning against him or using his shoulders as a balance point. He doesn't look or seem tired, and, just as when they were younger, he's still much more controlled and intentional in his movements than Sam, on and off the dance floor.

Jake could step away, finagle an end to this encounter if he wanted. It becomes clearer and clearer that he *doesn't* want to, until it's so obvious that absolutely no one could be confused. By the time they reach the end of the hour, they're more or less fused together, panting and laughing and nearly spent; Jake's hard against him, impressively and also entirely unmissably, and Sam's sure Jake can tell he is, too. There's something almost funny about it, in a dangerous, unsettlingly hot way—this is how they might have behaved together at high school dances, if either one of them had been willing to have the difficult conversation they were avoiding then.

Jake turns and smiles up at him, eyes half-closed, his face lit in the blue and red strobe of the lights. It occurs to Sam, a little late, to consider the difficult conversation they're avoiding this time around, and what this one might be costing them.

"Aaaaand that's a set break," the DJ announces from the stage. "Back in ten. Use the bathroom! Get a drink! Call your mother, some of you, and ask her to remind you to respect yourself! Not you, though. Yeah, you there, in the—yeah. You need to respect yourself *less*, my dude; you're freaking me out."

As the DJ continues to argue with the young man wearing only a Speedo and a cowboy hat and gyrating so wildly he has upended several drinks, the music switches over to what's clearly someone's personal playlist. Sam and Jake, in mutual entertained agreement, duck off the dance floor while everyone is distracted by the absurdity, and slip out the doors before they can be separated by the crowd.

FOURTEEN
NOW: JUNE

Not for the first time in his life, Sam reflects that being neighbors with someone you're desperately hoping to bring home with you has real benefits. You don't have to ask if they want you to walk them to their place, or if they want to come back to yours; either way you're heading to basically the same destination and will have time to work out what to do once you arrive.

He and Jake amble their way back slowly, neither of them talking very much. It's a warm night and slightly hazy, the humidity of summer having just started to swell in the last few days, but the breeze is cool. Sam is grateful. He hasn't danced like that in years, if he's *ever* danced like that, and his body's making sure he knows it. There are trails of sweat still drying on the side of his neck; he can see a damp spot in the middle of Jake's back.

They're not drunk, or at least Sam isn't drunk, and Jake doesn't seem drunk. It's possible Sam's misreading things, that the silence coming from Jake is the sound of someone semi-wasted focusing all their energy on walking in a straight line, but he doubts it. He's almost certain Jake's proceeding quiet and slow up the road for the same reason Sam is: The energy vibrating between them is thick and unmistakable and entirely physical, beyond the need for words at all.

Or, at least, beyond the need for most of them. There's a little part of Sam that knows there are things they need to talk about, but roughly twelve seconds after he started dancing with Jake, that part of him was gathered up, gagged, and hog-tied. So all he's left with is the question: Why shouldn't he? The olive branch Jake had been kind enough to stretch between them has felt more like a twig these last few months, creaking and cracking, desperate for the comfortable peace between them to fall away to something more passionate, less controlled. Why shouldn't Sam lean on it that last crucial inch and snap it? What's the worst that could happen if he does?

Instead of the answer to that question, Sam's mind supplies him with the response to a slightly different one: He can see suddenly what will happen if he *doesn't* snap the twig, if he lets things carry on the way they've been going. The simplicity and horror of it almost makes him want to laugh. God, of course, of *course*, if Sam does that, it'll just play out exactly the same way it did before. Or, well, maybe not exactly the same way—hopefully featuring a lot less in the way of vehicular mishaps and grueling personal injury, for one thing—but the pattern, at least, would be the same. They'd circle around and around each other, like they did in high school, and avoid talking about the growing tension between them, like they did in high school, and then when they did eventually give in to temptation, they'd *still* be circling and avoiding things in the ways that mattered, like they did in high school.

But Sam, as he thanks his lucky stars for every beautiful day of his adult life, is not in high school. Neither one of them will ever be in high school again.

"Did you mean it," Sam asks, as they stop, automatically, on the street in front of Silverman's, "when you said people shouldn't keep doing things just because it's the way they've always done them?"

"Did I *mean it*?" Jake looks equal parts shocked and outraged. "Did I mean it, he asks! Why would I have spent so long arguing my case if I *didn't* mean it, Sam; what kind of psychopath..."

But he stops talking for once, his eyes going wide, as Sam steps into his space and lifts a hand to palm Jake's jaw. It's a question more than anything else, a request for permission Jake probably shouldn't grant, and which Sam certainly has no right to ask for; he leaves his hand there anyway, trying to memorize the feeling of Jake's soft stubbly beard, waiting for a response.

After a beat, Jake says, voice cracking on it, "*Seriously?* You want to do this right now? You don't want to, I don't know, spend another year or two thinking it about it, but not actually doing anything, while I also think about it and don't actually do anything, and we try to date other people and they can totally tell something is weird and—maybe you didn't do that, when we were in high school, I never—look, never mind! Just. Are you sure you wouldn't rather, um. Give yourself a little more time to consider, or to refamiliarize yourself with my less endearing qualities, or just, you know—"

"Yes," Sam says, as certain as he's ever been about anything. "I'm sure."

"Ah," Jake says, and blinks up at him, and swallows. He looks, to Sam, to be wrestling with something internal for a moment, but then his expression clears, and he smiles, pleased and uncertain. "Well. I mean. Okay, then. But you should know, I haven't been on the dating scene in years, and I'm probably rusty, and—"

Feeling as though he's returning to his own home after years away, Sam shuts Jake up by kissing him.

Jake had known how to kiss, in the broadest sense of the word, when they were teenagers. So had Sam; at its most basic level, the process is fairly straightforward. But neither of them had been particularly experienced, naturally talented, or, not to put too fine a point on it, *good* at kissing at the time. It hadn't mattered because each had been desperately interested in the other and at a similar level of skill. Back then, Sam would have rated them both as excellent in all aspects of hooking up, and been almost entirely wrong. He'd learned a lot in the ensuing years that colors the memories in retrospect, and he cringes a little these days to think of some of his own less advisable moves and techniques. But he's always been grateful that at least they'd both had fun and cared about one another, no matter how awkward it sometimes was, or how badly it all wound up ending.

Jake... does not kiss like a teenager anymore. Jake kisses like he's the most erudite, sophisticated man at the world's most erudite, sophisticated gathering, and Sam is a glass of punishingly expensive wine he's making a show of enjoying. He is slow and pointed and thorough, kissing Sam with such focused ferocity that he forgets entirely that he was in the lead here just moments ago. His hand falls from Jake's cheek to his hip as Jake reaches up to press just his fingertips against the sensitive skin of Sam's throat, stroking featherlight and then moving an inch or two to repeat the process, over and over. Sam hisses into Jake's mouth and feels him smile—puts a hand on the small of Jake's back to pull him closer—

A shriek interrupts them, making them both jump, though not enough to let go of each other. They turn, Jake's hand tight around Sam's jacket, to a mortified-looking Amber Baumbach holding the hand of Claudia, her oldest daughter. Claudia, roughly six years old and according to her mother allergic to only the exterior pastrami spices, seems to be in rapturous agonies as she looks back and forth between them and cries, "Mom! It's the deli man and my dance teacher! And they were *kissing*!"

"Hi, Claudia," Jake says, only slightly wearily. "Good eyes you've got there; you must eat a lot of carrots."

"I do," Claudia says somberly, nodding at him.

"I'm so sorry." Amber looks mortified; in spite of himself, Sam can't help but be amused. "She's not quite old enough to understand, uh, when not to... interrupt. We wouldn't usually be out here this late, though; my ex took her to a movie, and I'm just taking her home. So you don't have to worry about this in, um. In the future." Hastily, she adds, "Not that there has to be a future or anything! None of my business at all, obviously. We're just... going to go home now. So sorry. Have a good night!"

"Bye, Deli Man! Bye, Jake! I'll tell everyone in our dance group

I saw you kissing!" Claudia's tone suggests this is a favor, sparing them the trouble of doing it themselves. The last thing they hear before Amber manages to drag her around the corner is Claudia cackle to herself and add, "Kissing is *disgusting*."

"Ah, and here again we see the defining note of my life: dignity," Jake says, in a voice equally amused and despairing. "Always dignity."

"I think you came out of that with more dignity than I did; at least she knows your name." Sam rests his forehead briefly against Jake's. "Might feel more dignified inside? Fewer onlookers, for one thing. If, you know, you wanna come in."

"I think I've made my interest in doing that painfully clear," Jake says, and Sam grins, steps away to unlock the deli's front door.

The minute he's locked it behind them, they're pressed together again, Sam unsure which of them moved first and not actually caring. He's pushing Jake up against the glass—Jake's sliding a hand into his hair—Sam's halfway to undoing Jake's fly when he remembers that they don't want to make a total display of themselves here in the Silverman's front window. Joanie would probably film it, for one thing.

"My office?" he suggests, low and heady, in Jake's ear. "It's closer, and we'll have to deal with Pastrami if we go upstairs and wake her."

"All for that plan," Jake agrees breathlessly, and as Sam, regretfully, moves away enough for them both to start walking back there, he slaps his cane lightly. "This thing *will* get me up those stairs, but not quickly, and I feel time is of the essence here, don't you?"

He says it lightly, even wickedly, giving Sam a look that's hungry, anticipatory, eager—in short, it's an expression that's anything but shaming. Still, as Sam follows Jake back through the deli to his own office, he's swamped with the same regret that's dogged his heels, kept him from making a move, every time he's thought about approaching his feelings for Jake these last few months. Despite his own frank desperation to lay his hands on every part of the man, the memory of the ways in which Sam's choices damaged Jake's life pours a bucket of cold water on his libido.

This does not, however, completely extinguish the flame, which seems to burn too hot to ever entirely go out. So Sam says nothing, ignoring the hammering of his heart and the sudden clamminess of his palms, and steps into the office after Jake, shutting the door behind him.

Jake smiles at him, all bright flirtatious confidence, and says, "Where were we?"

"Here," Sam says, low, and pulls Jake back into his arms.

For a few minutes, Sam is again able to keep the elephant in the room out of his direct line of sight, and thus uneasily pretend that it isn't there. Jake is, in a word, distracting, and so Sam tries like hell to shut off his brain, let his body run the show. This works while Jake is licking into his mouth; it works while they're fumbling together towards, and then bumping into, Sam's desk. It *really* works when Jake tugs up Sam's shirt high enough to reveal his full torso and then, when Sam strips it the rest of the way off and tosses it aside, works his way up said torso, kissing and sucking and gently biting. Sam realizes dizzily that he's going to end up with a hickey, and then is hit with a wave of surreal, confused pleasure when he realizes Jake's the first person who ever gave him one. The reason he even likes them.

A surge of passion overrules Sam's higher thinking at this point; he reaches out an arm without looking to sweep the contents of his desk to the floor, and thus make room on the surface for Jake. The regret hits him a second later, as he's lifting Jake up to sit on its surface—God, he's going to have to clean all that *up*, why did he *do* it, nobody ever shows the *mess* in the movies—and then fades when Jake smirks, spreads his legs, hooks his left one around Sam's waist, and pulls him in. Then Jake is everywhere, touching Sam with his hands, his mouth, his thighs, moving from one thing to the next so quickly Sam can hardly breathe, let alone keep up. Not that he's complaining. Who could complain, about something so thrilling, so hot, so totally unprecedented even in their previous encounters?

But it's here that Sam's brain betrays him. Because when he calls to mind the hazy, sun-soaked memories of their youthful trysts, the time they'd managed to spend together before it all fell apart, he can't place the... Well, frenetic is the only word for the energy currently thrumming through Jake, underscoring everything he's doing. It's possible that this is just his vibe now, and everyone he hooks up with walks away feeling like they've encountered a really sexy tornado while they just stood there amazed at his power and speed, but Sam doubts it. He thinks Jake is probably doing exactly what Sam's doing: trying with increasing desperation to avoid seeing the damn elephant.

Sometimes life is about looking the pachyderm in the face. Sam sighs, and pulls away, and puts both hands on Jake's shoulders to still him as he says, "God, Jake, sorry, just—hold on. Are we really not going to talk about it?"

To Sam's surprise, the expression on Jake's face isn't one of resignation or even disappointment; it looks, to Sam, like full-bore terror. It sounds like it, too, when he says, his voice gone reedy, "Talk about what?"

Sam winces, wishing with all his Midwestern heart that he could swallow down this uncomfortable topic, never acknowledge or discuss it, and be perfectly fine with that, in the grand old tradition of many previous generations of Adelsons. However, his own fundamental nature, never a good fit in that particular area of the family structure, forces him to press on. "The... accident? The fact that we never *talked* again, the fact that I *ruined* your *life*—"

"What?" If Jake looked terrified before, now he looks as though Sam has just grown fourteen arms, burst into flames, and started singing the unforgivably bad Horseshoe Heights High fight song. "*What?* You didn't ruin my life! I ruined *your* life!"

"*What?*" Abruptly, Sam wishes he still had his shirt on, but he doesn't think it would be the height of dignity or tact to fish it out from where he tossed it behind the filing cabinet. He settles for crossing his arms over his chest. "You... What are you *talking* about?"

Suddenly they're both talking over each other:

"You dropped out of school—"

"School?! Jake! The bottom of your *leg* was crushed—"

"—and I couldn't talk my parents out of *pressing charges*—"

"—and your whole life was about your *dance career*—"

"—so you ended up with a criminal record and—"

"—and if I'd just stalled an extra few minutes before leaving—"

"—it wasn't even your idea to take the car—"

"—or done the smart thing right when you showed up and took your keys—"

"—and you took the blame and I was too much of a *coward* to—"

"—or called someone! Your dad, even! And anyway he *told* me, that day he came by, he told me about all the surgeries and how you couldn't go to Juilliard and how I'd, as I said, *ruined* your *life*—"

"*What?*" This time the fury on the word, and blazing in Jake's blue eyes, dams up the flow of words from Sam's mouth. "My father did *what*? When?"

"The day after," Sam says, hollow and sick all over again at the memory, the crawling shame down the back of his spine as fresh as it was that morning. God, he wishes he had his shirt. "He came over to the house screaming about it; I thought he was going to hit me. After he left my mother put me in the car and brought me... here." He gives Jake, who looks like maybe he's about to explode into a million enraged pieces, an uncomfortable half smile. "It's okay, really. I think he was just, you know. Upset because his son was in the hospital, and God knows I deserved it."

"No you *didn't*." Jake says this so loudly that Sam jumps a little. "No you didn't! It wasn't *your* fault that idiot didn't know how to drive, or to tell time, or what a stop sign was! It wasn't your fault my freaked-out teen brain decided the solution to parental rejection was copious drinking and *grand theft auto*! You were trying to help me, and in exchange I cost you everything. Everything! I couldn't even stand up to my stupid parents for you! And you think you *deserved* it, I—" He cuts himself off, his throat catching, and runs a hand over his face. "You deserved better, is what you deserved. A lot better. I'm sorry."

For a long beat Sam just stares at him. Then, entirely against his will, a choked-off half laugh escapes him as he says, "Come *on*. You're not serious!"

"I am as serious," Jake says, meeting his eyes with level, unyielding certainty, "as a heart attack. I'm so serious it might *give* me a heart attack, which would be a problem. If I die, how will I *murder my father*?" He pauses, thoughtful, and adds, "Although I suppose I could haunt him. He'd hate that."

"You don't have to haunt anyone," Sam says, "and I'd prefer you remain alive if at all possible, but... I don't understand. You never talked to me again—"

"*You* never talked to *me* again," Jake cries, looking genuinely aghast now. "Which I never questioned, because cutting ties is what you *should* do! When you try to help someone out and in exchange their parents try to get you *jail time*! That's categorically a relationship ender!" He runs a hand over his face, peering at Sam through spread fingers. "But you're telling me that all this time— God, Sam, for all these *years*—you've thought that *I* stopped talking to *you*? That I blamed you?"

"I mean," Sam says, with a wincing little shrug. "...Yeah?"

"Oh, I'm going to go submerge myself in the deep fryer," Jake mutters, clearly as much for himself as for Sam. "I'm going to lock myself in the walk-in 'til I'm a Jakesicle. Listen, I know you don't serve alcohol down here, but do you have booze upstairs? Because, I mean, not trying to suggest I learned nothing from my teenage mistakes, but: I could *really* use a drink. I know we agreed the office was our move, but..."

"Yeah, that was then," Sam, who could use both a drink and a shirt, agrees. They proceed up the stairs without talking, only the thud of Jake's cane hitting the wood—and, eventually, the gleeful bark of Pastrami—breaking the silence.

Once Sam's shown Jake his (admittedly paltry) liquor selection and acquired a fresh T-shirt, he takes Pastrami out for a quick potty run. Feeling like an idiot, he briefly outlines the situation to her as they go and asks her to be chill when they get inside. Logically, he knows that likelier than not the only part of this hasty, one-sided discussion she understood was her own name, but when they get inside she does, unusually for her, go straight to her pillow and lie down. She is—small mercies—asleep again in moments.

And in additional mercies, Jake has produced two drinks, one of which he is sipping, and the other of which is sitting and sweating invitingly on Sam's counter.

"It's a Paloma. Well, a half-assed Paloma," Jake says, gesturing at the glass to indicate Sam should take it. "I hope you weren't saving that can of grapefruit juice in the back of the cupboard for anything."

"Honestly? I thought it was expired," Sam admits, but bravely takes a sip anyway.

It tastes fine—good, actually—and Sam makes a pleased noise as Jake smiles and says, "It almost was. Good 'til next month; I checked."

"The industry's rubbing off on you," Sam says, grinning at him, but Jake's smile shrinks down until it's barely a sliver.

"Something like that," he says, looking down into his own glass. He swirls the contents for a moment and then, setting it down, firmly says, "Look. Sam. I can't do this with you—hell, I can't *live* with myself—if you're going to carry on thinking that you... that I —" He cuts himself off, shakes his head, tries again. More quietly, he says, "I'm not saying it was great, you know, or that I loved it, but it wasn't your fault, and it didn't ruin my life. Changed it, sure; but things are always doing that. I'm not interested in letting it take away anything else, not from either of us." He meets Sam's eyes, his own frank and pleading. "Can we just... wipe the slate? Start again? Agree that it was a horrible freak thing that should never have happened and... let it go?"

"You're asking *me*?" Sam blinks at him, stunned, his brain

scrambling to catch up and meet the moment. "But *you're* the one who should get to—" Sam pauses, takes a breath, realizes he's arguing against something he desperately wants, and tries again: "I mean. Yes? Obviously, *I'd* be fine with that. Are *you* fine with that?"

"Be pretty weird of me to suggest it if I wasn't," Jake says, with a slightly crooked smile. More quietly, he adds, "You know, I never blamed you, Sam. Not even back then. You were only trying to help; you were the one person who was only trying to help. That's how I remember it, and I kept a lot of journals at that point on the advice of one of the seven therapists my parents sent me to see, so. It's on the record and everything. I can prove it."

Somewhere in the back of Sam's mind, a door opens. It's a familiar door, covered in band posters that slightly embarrass him now, a handwritten sign on paper torn out of a notebook insisting, *EVERYONE KEEP OUT!!!!* The version of Sam it belonged to, seventeen and stuck all these years on the very last night it belonged to him, steps out, and grins, and walks away whistling. So relieved to be free that what had trapped him there in the first place hardly hurts at all.

And all Sam's inhibitions seem to walk out with him, leaving him only a man, and Jake nothing more or less than someone he's never stopped wanting.

Suddenly, it's all very simple.

"I need you to know," Sam says, realizing the truth of it even as it hits the air, "that if what you want right now is anything—and I mean *anything*—other than to spend the rest of the night in my bedroom making up for lost time, you should leave. Go home. Right now."

For a second Sam thinks he sees a flicker of hesitation in Jake's eyes, but before his heart can fall, the moment's past. Sam probably just imagined it, nerves or something; there's no doubt at all in the look on Jake's face as he drains his glass, sets it down, and smirks at Sam. He sounds blissfully, invitingly certain as he says. "Do you know what? Wildly enough, I think I'm good right where I am."

Sam rounds the counter in three steps; this time when they kiss there's no question of who's leading who. There's a moment where Jake tries to direct things, but it's only a moment. Sam, sure of his footing now, pushes Jake gently back into the counter by the hips, cradles the back of Jake's head in one hand, and lets the other one roam as he kisses him with all the unwieldy, overbearing tenderness he's been containing for months. Jake makes a soft, surprised noise into his mouth and then all but comes apart in Sam's hands, all his earlier frenetic energy drained away. He's languid and boneless against Sam, tipping his head back easily when Sam wants access to his neck, raising his arms obligingly for Sam to peel his shirt off. When Sam leans away to get a look at him, meaning to lift him up and put him on the counter, Jake's eyes are wide and starry, his pupils blown.

"God, Sam," he says, his cheeks flushed crimson. Sam's whole nervous system lights up, thrilled, to hear just how hard he's breathing. "You, ah. You've become. Very good at that."

In the warm glow of this praise, Sam decides there's nothing the counter can provide for him that the bed wouldn't do better. But he lifts Jake up anyway as he says, "Well, you know, I've had a lot of time to practice," his body seeming to decide to go forward with his original plan regardless.

Or maybe it's just talking to Jake's body, on the deep, physical level more powerful even than speech that Jake used to talk about, way back, when he was talking about why he loved dance. Certainly, the second Sam lifts him, without even touching the counter, Jake wraps both legs around Sam and puts his hands on Sam's shoulders, balancing himself. In a breathless moment of desire Sam realizes Jake's *only* using his hands for balance, and only barely—the grip of his thighs is powerful enough that Sam could probably let go of his weight entirely without his actually falling. A little dizzily, he realizes Jake must keep himself in much the same condition he had when he was in dance classes and rehearsal five times a week, just modified the exercises around his new parameters.

It's so surprisingly hot—it makes Sam so unbearably fond of him—that he feels briefly and fervently that he might burst from it, pop like an overfilled balloon. He kisses Jake as he carries them both to the bedroom on slightly unsteady legs, overwhelmed by the situation more than by Jake's weight. It's that or say something that's far too much and... well. Either far too soon or far too late, depending on which way you look at it.

Sam doesn't look at it. He looks at Jake, the way Jake's responsive and pliable under his hands, his mouth; the way Jake looks and touches him like he's not sure Sam's totally real, that this isn't some impossible, fantastic dream. He looks at Jake until he can't remember ever wanting to do anything else.

It's a good night, maybe the best Sam's ever had. If, once or twice, he thinks he sees that flicker of worry in Jake's eyes, it's probably only paranoia, just a remnant from years of misplaced shame. Nothing he needs to worry about.

FIFTEEN
NOW: JUNE

The next morning, despite the fact that it dawns as painfully early as ever, begins with what is easily one of the best awakenings of Sam's life. Although he's usually one of those people who finds waking up a series of little agonies, today it's soft, lazy, his whole body feeling loose and relaxed. He's comfortable in a way he isn't entirely familiar with, and rubs his head lightly against his pillow, sleepily confused by the way it feels different against his cheek than usual.

It's only when the pillow huffs out half a laugh and sinks fingers into his hair that Sam realizes fuzzily that it's Jake, and blinks his eyes open. He must have fallen asleep with his head on Jake's chest; when he lifts it, Jake lets the hand in his hair slide down to his neck and says, "Hi."

"Hi," Sam breathes, half-certain he's still asleep. Did that all really *happen* last night? The bar, and the dancing, and the conversation, and the *sex*. God, that thing Jake did with his—

"I turned off your alarm," Jake says, derailing Sam's train of thought. "Sorry. I only let you sleep a couple extra minutes, and I wouldn't have normally. I just think it's cruel and unusual self-punishment that you start your day with an air-raid siren."

"'S the only way I'll wake up," Sam protests, yawning on it in the middle. "Sleep right through everything else. Should be getting up even earlier, honestly, but, ugh. I can't bear to." Sitting up properly, he takes a brief self-assessment and winces at Jake. "Speaking of what a person can bear: I'd kiss you right now, but I think my morning breath might be kind of gnarly."

"That is decidedly mutual," Jake says, with a little grimace, and then grins at him. "Let's risk it."

They do. As a result—and for the first time in years—Sam is late unlocking the deli's front door for the staff, and comes downstairs to see, on the other side, the glaring faces of Alphonse and Eileen.

Al pulls him into a brief and surprising hug when Sam opens the door, then pulls away and snaps, "We thought you were dead, man!" as he pushes past him to the kitchen.

Eileen, even more surprisingly, seems almost amused. "He thought you were dead," she confides, sotto voce, when Alphonse is out of earshot. "But *I* heard you copy my drink order. Hit you harder than you thought it would, eh, kid?" She cackles as she heads into the back, and Sam decides not to tell her that he gave the drink to Jake after one overwhelming sip. She seems so pleased with herself.

It was worth it, in any case, even if Alphonse does spend the next hour occasionally glaring at Sam and saying he's glad he's alive. As the streaky dawn light brightens into a warm June morning, Sam thinks almost anything would be worth it for a few more minutes in bed with Jake. And he thinks, too, that today he could face any irate customer, any grim daily total, any stupid, poisonous review. The knowledge that Jake is upstairs, snoozing comfortably while Sam starts the day, is like a balm to all the petty wounds of working life.

As they get closer to opening, the rest of the morning shift shuffles in for their slightly later call times. Joey's late, grinning and sheepish, waving Sam off again when he offers to let them just take the day. They need the money, apparently, to help defray the cost of some mysterious afternoon plans. This element of the unknown draws the attention of the rest of the staff, who, as they finish their opening tasks, all drift towards the front to observe or participate in the ongoing attempt to get them to divulge the details.

This is why, when Jake comes down five minutes before the deli opens, everyone on shift is loosely grouped in front of the stairwell. Even if it weren't for the hour, or the loose, unkempt state of Jake's hair, it's obvious in a glance what's happened between them: Jake is wearing one of Sam's favorite T-shirts and a pair of his boxers, that latter of which fit him like regular shorts but very visibly are not.

Jake sees the assembled at the same moment they see him, when he's about halfway down the stairs. He freezes, instantly turning the unhappy gray color of overcooked meat; the staff freezes, although some of them only after their mouths have dropped open; everyone stares, aghast, at everyone. Jake's eyes meet Sam's, panicked and too wide, and he squeaks, as though speaking only to Sam, "Oh, God. I... forgot."

Sound erupts from the room, everyone seeming to decide to speak at once.

"I KNEW IT," Joey shrieks, pumping their fist in the air. "Luce owes me twenty dollars; I *knew* the two of you would have to get over yourselves eventually and bone!"

"I should've *guessed* that's why you were down late for the door this morning," Alphonse says, grinning at Sam and shaking his head. "I bet even death wouldn't have stopped you, you'd just have floated down and unlocked it as a ghost, but if it was him distracting you? Completely checks out."

"How long has this been going on?" Eileen demands, and, fixing Sam with a gimlet eye, adds, "Joanie's going to be very displeased to be hearing about it from *me*, you know. *Very* displeased."

"You don't have to tell her," Sam says to Eileen. He hasn't glanced away from Jake, who is starting to look less panicked and more grimly resigned to his fate; there's even a faint glimmer of amusement in his eyes.

Sam should quit smiling, probably. It's just that he hasn't been able to stop since he woke up this morning.

And then Jake's smiling, too, and running an embarrassed hand over his face, and laughing the strained, slightly desperate laugh of those in situations where there's nothing to do *but* laugh. After a beat Sam starts laughing, too, and then they're all laughing, and shaking their heads, and getting back to work. Someone calls out, "About time, you crazy kids!" While Sam knows logically that it *must* have been Eileen, he can't quite convince himself that's possible.

Jake, with a look at Sam that says quite clearly, *I am playing it cool but have died ten thousand deaths inside*, turns around and proceeds back upstairs at a rather quicker pace than he descended. He's gone for a few minutes and then, seemingly having decided he has no choice but to brazen it out, re-emerges wearing the same stolen T-shirt, but also a stolen pair of Sam's sweatpants.

"I don't remember saying you could borrow my clothes," Sam teases, not meaning it at all, when Jake joins him at the far counter. If anything, he finds Jake's casual appropriation of his wardrobe a promising sign, not to mention upsettingly sexy.

"Yeah, well, you didn't say I could announce that we hooked up last night to the entire staff in the most personally embarrassing way possible, and I did that anyway, so." Jake shrugs, his smile not quite reaching his eyes. "Might be best to assume I'm a bit of a wild card."

Mindful of the fact that they have an audience, however occupied everyone might seem, Sam bumps his shoulder against Jake's. "You're not really worried about that, are you? Because I promise you, it's fine. They like you! Nobody's going to be weird about it."

Again, Jake's smile looks slightly hollow; he never did, Sam remembers, like to be seen by a group with anything else than perfect control of himself. "Thanks, that... helps. Look, can we go to dinner tonight, maybe? Somewhere less, uh, here? Not that here isn't great, it's just attached to your apartment, and I want to actually talk to you, not, um." He glances up at Sam, his cheeks flushing and his smile abruptly looking a lot more genuine, and finishes, "Not get too distracted to talk to you."

Sam beams at him, delighted by this idea. "Absolutely. Johnny's? After close? They're just around the corner, and the food's great."

"Great," Jake echoes. He glances around, looking hunted, before confiding in low tones, "I feel like a zoo animal. I'm going to go to work now, where no one's ever seen me in my underwear *or* yours."

"Do you not count those leotards you used to wear as underwear?" Sam smirks when Jake blushes. "Wait, do you *still* wear them? Because if so, I'd like to see—"

"Bye, Sam!" Jake says with finality. But he pauses, blush deepening, and then leans in and quickly kisses Sam before hurrying off.

They don't end up making it to Johnny's. Around 3 p.m., Jake walks back into the diner with his hair askew and his eyes wild. The wild eyes aren't surprising—Jake looks like that a few times a day, most days, and often over such minor horrors as "Someone on television used an idiom wrong," or, "The burritos at a nearby restaurant are slightly different than they were fifteen years ago." But the hair is downright alarming, from Jake.

"Uh," Sam says. "You good?"

"Not really," Jake admits. "I'm kind of in a bit of a... situation." He runs a hand through his hair, pulling it straight up as he does so, which at least answers the question of how he came to look like he's about to be struck by lightning. "Weird question, but how much do you know about, like, catering?"

Sam gives him a flat look, not sure if this is a joke or not. When Jake just stares imposingly back at him, he gestures at the deli around them, and then at the delivery van visible through the open window.

Jake's face collapses into a comical little scrunch of regret, and then he says, "God, right, sorry, I'm an idiot, terrible phrasing, of course you know about catering, sorry, I wasn't like—"

Sam, abruptly remembering he can, steps into Jake's space, kisses him silent, and then runs a hand through his wild hair a few times, taming it back down. Jake seems to deflate slightly, sagging forward to rest his head on Sam's shoulder. So quietly Sam can't be entirely sure he heard it right, Jake murmurs, "Christ. I'd forgotten how nice it is when you do that." Then he straightens up, and offers Sam a rueful smile, and says: "Hi, first of all, should have started there, and sorry again, and: I meant, like, the legal side? Of catering? Contracts or whatever?"

"Oh, sure," Sam says. "I know a little. Why?"

"Well, you know the recital coming up? On Friday?"

Jake looks very relieved when Sam nods, as though he was expecting Sam to have forgotten the assorted conversations they've had about it over the last several weeks. "Yeah, of course. You're afraid Jared S. is going to break his ankle and ruin your fledgling reputation as an instructor."

"Jared S. is the least of my worries!" A long, involved tale follows this, although Jake insists Sam not interrupt his work and so trails Sam around the restaurant to tell it. When he steps into the kitchen he reaches into the bin of hairnets by the door and puts one on, undoing Sam's work to smooth his flyaways down, without even breaking flow. There are a lot of personal grudges at play between people Jake only half-knows, so Sam doesn't quite follow all of it. The gist seems to be: The event's long-time caterer has pulled out at the last minute, and claims that the studio owes them not only the money they would have paid for the meal, but also a cancellation fee.

"But they're the ones who canceled?" Sam's puzzlement creases his brow so deeply that he can almost hear his mother telling him it'll stick that way.

"I know!" Jake cries. "I know! But they say a cancellation fee if in case *anyone* has to cancel."

"Well, that's ridiculous."

"That's what I said! But they say we'll have to pay, and we'll have to pay someone else extra to do it last minute, and—"

"Oh, don't worry about that," Sam says, waving a hand. "I'll do it. Or, rather, we will."

Jake's mouth snaps closed; his eyes widen. "What? No you won't; it's in three days! You need at least a week's notice—"

"I mean, we *say* that." Sam offers Jake a slightly sheepish smile. "But exceptions are kind of the rule there. We do a lot of funerals and stuff like that, and there isn't usually a ton of lead time. Besides, a dance recital is, what, fifty people? Seventy-five?"

Jake bites his lip. "Around that, yeah, between students and parents."

Sam shrugs. "Right, so: no big deal. A couple of deli trays, a veggie platter or two, and—hold on." Raising his voice so she'll hear him from her alcove of the kitchen, where the mixer and deck oven live, Sam calls, "Eileen!"

"Yeah?" As expected, she doesn't bother coming into the main kitchen, just hollers back unseen.

"You think you could muster the will to do a couple of dessert trays for Friday? The nice ones, with the lemon squares and brownies? Maybe the mini coconut bars?"

"*This* Friday? Go fuck yourself."

Jake's eyes go wide with horror. He waves his hands frantically at Sam, making an entreating face, but Sam grins at him and shakes his head, mouthing, "Relax, she's fine." To Eileen, he calls back, "What if I told you it was for a dance recital at Jake's studio? Little kids and their parents? Also, their normal guy screwed them last minute, so if you don't do it, there'll be no dessert for anyone."

There's a weighted pause, during which Jake looks like he's considering the fastest exit strategy, but every visible member of staff starts to snicker or smirk. Then Eileen calls, "Okay, Sammy, you can eighty-six my last request. I'll even do the mini cupcakes; kids always like those."

Sam rolls his eyes, but cheerfully enough. "Thanks, Eileen. You're a peach."

"Don't make me hurt you," Eileen warns him, and then immediately turns on the mixer, its loud thunking and thwacking both unmistakable and impossible to shout over.

"Sam," Jake says, his eyes still wide, "you can't just... I need a quote, for one thing, to make sure we can even—"

"Nope, stop, it's on the house," Sam says. "Obviously. Least I can do for all the free labor you've given me."

"It wasn't free! You've already paid me in food!"

"Not what I owe you," Sam says firmly. "Not by half. Anyway, seriously, do you really want to argue with the easiest solve for this problem?" He waggles his eyebrows suggestively, lowering his voice. "Think of all the better things we could do with the time you'd spend hunting down another last-minute caterer."

Jake meets his eyes, flushing slightly, and hesitates. But then, slowly, he nods. "If you're... sure?"

"Very sure," Sam says. He reaches out and squeezes Jake's shoulder, his interest and his pulse both spiking when Jake sighs and leans into the touch. "I can start the prep tonight, and do most of the work myself. You can even help, if you want to. It'll be fun."

"Sometimes I wonder if you've ever understood what fun means," Jake says. "Like, even one time, in your whole life." Then, lower and more sincere, he adds, "*Thank* you, Sam."

"It's nothing," Sam says, and he means it, at the time.

But, as it turns out, it's not nothing.

That's not to say that doing the work is a problem; far from it. Everything comes together, and Sam enjoys preparing it immensely. It just... isn't a couple of deli trays and a veggie platter, and ends up meaning more to Sam than all of his previous catering jobs combined.

Jake does help him prep that first night, which is really the deciding factor, the one variable that changes all the others. Because when Jake once again starts talking about how Sam should do his *own* thing, should make what *he* wants to make, the kind of food he makes for family meal, Sam finds, for the first time, that he has no excuse not to. It's not a paid or contracted job; it's not like he's changing the catering menu, or the deli's menu. It's a one-off. Why not?

They end up blowing off dinner at Johnny's that night. Instead, Sam makes a variety of test dishes for the recital after the deli closes, which they eat in lieu of a proper meal. Jake's delighted by every bite, at one point bursting into actual applause, and this time when Sam pulls him back to the office, nothing interrupts them.

The next two days are much the same: Jake slipping over to his own apartment in the morning to change for work and then ending up at Sam's again that night, flush against Sam's chest, saying filthy things against the shell of Sam's ear. Sam thinks he could get used to it, this languid, relaxed new cast to his movements, his mood. Being Jake's friend was wonderful, but being *with* Jake is so much better that Sam laughs whenever he thinks about it. It blows everything else—even the time he spent with Jake in high school—out of the water.

Jake insists they reschedule their Johnny's date for as soon as things calm down, the night after the recital. Sam agrees readily enough. He assumes Jake wants to discuss what they're doing here, what they are to one another, to avoid making the same mistake they did when they were teenagers. He's fine with that. If anything, he's looking forward to it. He's never felt so entirely on the same page with anyone.

The night of the recital, Sam loads the catering van and drives the ten minutes to Jake's studio. It's an unassuming building next to the Cuyahoga River, which feeds up into the lake; the area was heavily industrial for generations, and Sam double-checks his GPS to make sure he has the right address. But as he pulls closer, he sees a variety of children in outfits that remind him of Jake back in the day, trailed by resigned-looking parents. He grins, and parks.

It would be silly for it to be one of the greatest nights of Sam's life. It is anyway; he'll just have to live with that.

Jake, first of all, is astonishing. Sam didn't know what to expect. He's never been to a dance recital before, and Jake's always talked about this job as though he was barely hired and is seconds away from being canned at every moment, holding on by the skin of his teeth. Sam thought there was a real chance he wouldn't see Jake at all, at least until after the show was over. But instead, as Sam leans against the back wall of the large classroom space that's serving as tonight's auditorium, he's delighted to see Jake take the stage with a microphone and serve as the evening's MC. He announces each group of students and what they'll be performing with gusto, and with enough detail that everyone—or, at least, Sam—can tell he's built a personal connection even with the classes he isn't teaching. And Madame Louisa, looking on from the sidelines, is positively *beaming* at Jake. She looks so proud of him she might burst.

Sam can understand the feeling. His chest aches watching Jake sparkle with a more grounded version of his old panache. To see him make eye contact with a nervous eight-year-old and mouth, "You got this, Jared!"—Sam can't bear it, has to duck out of the room and start preparing the food for the post-show reception. He probably should have started doing that a while ago anyway, so it's a win overall.

And the way the food goes over with the crowd... that, in Sam's opinion, is more than just a win. It's *proof*: that Jake was right, that the food Sam likes cooking is good enough to deserve a place on Silverman's menu. His savory green onion blintzes, which were inspired by one of his favorite snacks from the bakeries in Asia-Town, make one parent so happy she insists on taking his number to start placing wholesale orders. When Sam tells her Silverman's doesn't really do that, she just shrugs and says, "Well, you're going to have to!" Sam's not sure if that bodes well or ill for his own happiness, but he's positive he'll find out soon enough.

Some of the exchanges genuinely *do* bode well, however. He gets three future catering orders off the chicken schnitzel sliders alone, and two more on the strength of his miniaturized Pastrami Arnolds, which is gratifying. Eileen's dessert trays net them three more requests, and at least a dozen people promise to stop by in the near future, impressed by the food.

There is one strange moment. Sam could swear, just for a second, that he sees Marty in the crowd. A former regular, Sam hasn't laid eyes on the man in months, and he's been a little concerned. At first he assumed the Kiss of Death review got to him, but as customers have trickled back in without an appearance from such a consistent visitor, Sam's started to fear the worst. It couldn't be good for a man's heart to eat as much corned beef as Marty did before that damn review came out; what if something had happened to him?

But the guy who makes startled, guilty-looking eye contact with Sam for half a second before disappearing into the crowd... it *has* to be Marty, doesn't it? Sure, he's across the room, and wearing a hat, and Sam's eyes could be playing tricks on him. But wouldn't that be a weird trick for them to play? He's been concerned about Marty, sure, but not so concerned as to hallucinate him.

But then Jake is next to him, vibrating with the energy of the night, the release of all those built-up nerves. Sam crushes him into a hug and congratulates him, makes him eat a slider, feels himself flush with pleasure when Jake doesn't move away from him, loops his arm around Sam's back instead. He must talk to fifteen of the parents like that, unbothered by the image they present, the fact that those people will assume they met Jake's partner—

—which, Sam realizes with a huge grin, is what they will have done, so. No harm there at all.

They go back to Sam's place that night without having to talk about it, and Jake gives Sam such a profound and thorough thank-you that Sam sees stars, nearly blacks out. He falls asleep with Jake curled against him, Pastrami snoring happily at the foot of the bed, and thinks that maybe somehow he's done it, and found everything he wanted.

SIXTEEN

NOW: JUNE

The next morning Sam unlocks the door for Alphonse and then, for the first time in years, goes back to bed. He doesn't sleep, of course—his body is too used to being awake and cooking at this hour—and after about twenty minutes of fruitlessly listening to Jake breathe, he gives up and makes them both breakfast in bed.

It's worth it, though, for the way Jake looks at him when he brings it in, sleep-mussed and barely awake. Sam thinks almost anything would be.

There *is* a slightly strange moment just before they go downstairs together; Sam comes out of the bedroom and finds Jake standing rigid, staring down at the table by the front door. Sam glances at it, bewildered—all that's on it is a couple pieces of junk mail and his house keys—but he says, "Table haunted, then? You look like you've seen a ghost."

It's a joke, but for a second, when Jake turns to look at him, Sam almost thinks it's true. Jake's face looks ashen, drawn thick with misery. But then he smiles and brightens and says, "Sorry, all good, just having a flashback to going downstairs in your underwear. I'm wearing pants, right? You see them, too?" So Sam laughs, and assures Jake the pants are indeed there, and forgets about it. It's easy to let go of, especially when Jake catches him against the doorframe, kisses him thoroughly, and insists they follow through on their postponed dinner at Johnny's tonight after close.

He sails through the morning, in the best mood he has been in in years. He sings along with the songs on the radio. He laughs with customers who normally drive him up the wall. When Pastrami jumps up and puts her paws on his chest, he dances with her like she's a person, to her obvious delight. He feels a singing new gratitude for every chime of the bell when the front door opens, having learned not to take it for granted; he feels a singing new gratitude for Jake, smiling at him from what's become his usual table when he stops in for lunch.

So when Marty steps into the deli, Sam's first thought is to be grateful. Proof at last that he hasn't committed nitrate-related manslaughter; everything's going his way. And he's smiling when Marty, holding his briefcase in front of his chest like a shield, cries, "I'm sorry I was weird last night! Have mercy on an awkward soul! Don't cast me back out into the grim, corned-beefless wilds!"

"Nobody cast you out in the first place, Marty. You cast yourself out—it's not *my* fault if you believed that stupid review."

Sam glances into the dining room again as Marty makes a series of hesitant hedging noises, obviously struggling for the right words. To his surprise, he notices that Jake has taken on a pallor and looks like he's been replaced with a version of himself who died a few centuries ago. When Sam manages to catch his eye, Jake stares back at him with an expression of such utter, panicked despair that Sam decides he's going to have to cut the conversation with Marty short. He becomes even more convinced of this when Jake immediately glances away, like he can't bear to look at Sam a moment more.

"Listen, it's fine," Sam says, even though he'd like to be obnoxious about the gap in patronage for a few more minutes. If nothing else, he thinks it's what Deb would do. But he's still watching Jake over Marty's shoulder, and increasingly certain something is badly wrong; it's all he can do to continue the conversation at all. "Honestly, I'm kind of touched to hear you couldn't find better corned beef... Actually, sorry, one second. Jake? Are you leaving?"

It's a rhetorical question; Jake obviously *is* leaving, because he's throwing his stuff into his bag so quickly Sam's a little afraid he'll chuck his laptop to the ground by mistake. But he looks up at the sound of his name, eyes wide and frantic, gaze flicking from Sam to Marty, who has half turned to see who Sam's talking to—

"Oh, hey," Marty says, sounding confused. "I thought you were working this morning." His face creases as Jake's falls; after a second, he turns back to Sam. "Rich of you to be giving me crap for keeping my distance, since the whole thing is his fault, and you don't seem to have any issue with *him*. But I *am* glad you two have connected and buried the hatchet; that's nice to see."

"What?" Sam says, baffled. "What are you talking about?"

"Oh, God, don't say *that*," Marty says, his eyes darting from Sam to Jake and back again, the color draining from his face. "Months I haven't come in here! Months! In order to avoid doing this exact—but, wait. You're pulling my leg or something, right? You have to be. He must have told you. You already know he *wrote* that review, and this is all... a joke..."

Marty keeps talking. Sam sees his lips move, but doesn't hear a word. His ears have filled with static; his mouth has been stuffed with ash. As he watches Jake collapse back into his chair like his strings have been cut and drop his head into his hands, Sam knows with chilling certainty that it *must* be true, that it has to be. If it wasn't, Jake would be putting up some sort of protest, not looking as though someone just told him he only has twenty-four hours to live.

"Sorry," Sam says, interrupting whatever Marty was talking about. His voice sounds strange in his own ears. "Jake... did... what?"

There is a long pause, in which Marty looks from Sam to Jake and back again, and then, into the sudden, ringing silence, says, "Oh, God."

Out of the corner of his eye, Sam sees several heads pop up on the other side of the service window to watch the show.

Another long pause. Then Marty tries, in doomed tones, "Seriously, any chance that in five minutes you're going to say, 'Ha ha, Marty, we really had you going, you thought you'd made things so *unbelievably* awkward, but in fact—'"

"Marty," Sam says through gritted teeth, only giving him this much on the strength of his many years of loyal patronage, "either order your goddamn sandwich, or get out."

To his questionable credit, Marty has the audacity to immediately reply, "Corned beef and Swiss on rye, extra juicy, hold the mustard," and hold out his credit card beseechingly.

Woodenly, Sam takes the card. He punches a random number into the register—certainly not the price of the sandwich, which Sam cannot currently remember despite setting it himself, but less than twenty dollars, anyway. Marty doesn't complain, just takes his card back and, as Sam begins making his sandwich, steps smartly to one side of the counter. Everything about him suggests he will be revisiting this whole encounter for some years in those awkward moments just before sleep, when the human brain will sometimes decide to pull up a cruel highlight reel of personal worsts. Though it's not kind, he hopes Marty *does* have to relive this moment over and over. God knows Sam's going to.

"Sam," Joey says, in an urgent tone of voice. "I think you should let me make that sandwich, and you should take a fifteen."

"I'm not due for a fifteen," Sam says. He's not looking at the counter, but then, he doesn't have to look to correctly assemble a corned beef and Swiss cheese sandwich. He's perfectly free to continue to stare at Jake, who is still slumped over the table with his head in his hands, as though literally frozen in horror.

"I think you should *take one anyway*." Joey's tone is so concerned now that it pulls Sam's gaze to their face, and then, curious about what they're looking at in such obvious horror, to his own hand. He realizes, startled, that he's holding a piece of Swiss cheese—or something that was one a piece of cheese, anyway.

Without noticing, Sam seems to have closed his fist tightly around it. When he opens his hand, little broken crumbles rain down onto the floor.

They remain there for several seconds before, relying on the sixth sense for dropped food which is possessed by all dogs, Pastrami bursts excitedly into the room and gobbles it up. Normally, such an event would be followed by a victory dance, and then perhaps a series of tricks intended to elicit more exciting floor cheese to rain from on high. Today she looks up at Sam, whines from low in the back of her throat, and butts her head against his leg. When he doesn't move, she walks over to her dining room pillow, curls up on top of it, and puts a paw over her eyes as though she can't bear to watch.

"Fifteen," Sam repeats, staring at his own palm, the cheesy film across it. "Right." He turns on his heel without saying another word—not to Jake, not to anyone—and walks out, letting the back door slam behind him.

For the first five minutes, Sam is alone in the alley between Silverman's and Jake's building. This is for the best; it's an interval in which he more or less loses the power of speech, at least for anything beyond muttering incoherently to himself. He paces in a long, tight, furious oval from one end of the alley to the other, occasionally mumbling fragmented, unhelpful things like, "This whole time!" or "Not a word!" or "We *slept* together!"

It can't be true, it *can't* be... But even as Sam thinks that, he knows it's denial. Of course it's true. Of course Jake wrote that stupid review, the one which almost destroyed Sam's business. Of course he did! It's a concept that, if anything, makes everything make *more* sense, not less. *That's* why Jake was so horrified when he realized this was Sam's deli, and *that's* why he wouldn't accept any payment for his work, and *that's* why he's been doing the work at all! It wasn't out of the kindness of his heart or, as Sam had allowed himself to think in his sappiest moments—and, as it turns out, his most *foolish* ones—because Jake wanted the excuse to spend time with him.

But no! Of course not! Jake wanted the excuse not to feel like a terrible person, and Sam's an idiot, a perfect idiot, for letting himself imagine otherwise.

It is at this point, naturally, that Jake comes outside. He looks... bad. He's shaking, a distant part of Sam notes, sure that's something he would normally care about; he doesn't. All he can see when he looks at Jake is all the opportunities he's had, over the last few months, to *say something* to Sam, to own up to that damn review. All the time they'd spent alone together, comfortable and easy, talking with no pressure or stakes like they were still just kids, and Jake hadn't said anything at all.

Sam, too angry to summon a single word of greeting, nods and then walks right past him, continuing along his pacing route as though he didn't see Jake step outside.

"Please, Sam," Jake says. His voice is small. He looks small, all at once, in a way he never has to Sam, even though Sam's always been the taller of the two of them, broadly built where Jake was limber and lithe. "I'm so sorry."

"For what, Jake?" Sam demands, stopping without turning around and throwing his hands in the air. "Or should I say *Norman?* What are you sorry for? For writing it in the first place, or for lying to me about it?"

"Technically," Jake starts, in wheedling tones, "I never actually—"

"Oh, absolutely not," Sam snarls, rounding on him. "*Absolutely* I'm not doing that, what do you take me for, are you kidding? If you're going to come at me with 'technically' right now, you should just go, man. Forget it. I'm not going ten rounds just to get you to admit you know what a goddamn lie of omission is."

"Okay," Jake says, looking ashamed of himself, holding his hands in the air. "Okay, you're right. I'm sorry, I shouldn't be coming at it like that, and I *know* I should have told you, I just... I really *didn't* know it was your place when I reviewed it, and the situation with Kiss of Death was... is... It's all pretty complicated, okay? And a really long, messy story, and once I realized what I'd done, I was afraid you might react, well." He looks at Sam and winces. "Like this? And there was all the stuff about the accident and we hadn't talked about that *either* and then it was all happening so fast, and I—dinner!" he cries, interrupting himself and jabbing an index finger in Sam's direction in excitement. "Johnny's! Tonight! That's why I *asked*, because I was going to *tell* you, and then if you got this mad about what I'd written, at least we'd have until dessert to—"

"You think I'm angry," Sam says, molasses-slow with fury, "about what you wrote in the article?"

"I mean," Jake says, and grimaces. "Aren't you?"

"Of course I am!" Sam nearly shouts this; it's so loud that a few nearby pigeons, normally implacable, scurry hastily away from him, although they aren't quite frightened enough to go to the trouble of flying off. "You were horrible! You nearly killed my family's restaurant! You suggested we were infested with *vermin* when I know for a *fact* you'd never set foot inside! You said you couldn't imagine why the place had stayed alive so long, and that whatever it was that *had* kept it around, we must have semi-recently taken it out back and *shot* it! You said—God, no, wait." Sam gets a grip on himself, reins it back in, because: "This isn't the point. I *am* angry about that, of course I am, who wouldn't be? But if it had just been that, if you'd just come to me *before* all of this and said, 'Sam, listen, I'm sorry, but a few months ago I decided to tear down your family business for kicks, and—'"

"It wasn't for kicks!" Jake both sounds and looks near tears of frustration. "I really needed the money, okay? And I didn't know it was your place, and it really sounded like—look, I'm not saying I didn't make some really bad decisions, I did, but I was misinformed! I didn't know what I was talking about, and I wouldn't have written it if I did, and I'm sorry. I know that I should have told you. I *wanted* to tell you, but—"

"Oh, what?" Sam snaps, abruptly disgusted with Jake, with this whole conversation. "What was it that stopped you? Was I too generous in feeding you, is that it? Too willing to pick things up where we got cut off? Is it *my* fault that you *kept* this from me, that you *slept* with me without *saying anything*, because I said you shouldn't *move out* that very first day you—"

"I'm a coward, Sam!" This bursts out of Jake at a volume that, if the pigeons had not already scuttled away, might have startled them into actual wing usage. "Okay? Is that what you want? I'm just a coward. I couldn't get over myself and ask you out like a normal person in high school; I couldn't tell my parents the truth about the accident; I couldn't bring myself to make you hate me! Over an article I didn't even want to write in the first place! I was *scared*!"

"Then you should have done it scared." Sam's not yelling now. His voice is quiet and cold, and the flat, unamused laugh that slips out of his mouth is even colder. "What do you think we're even *doing* here? This"—he gestures around himself in a broad, encompassing way—"is your life, Jake! And my life, not that *that* seems to matter to you one way or the other, but it's still life! Real life! It's all for *keeps*; you don't get to wake up one day and decide you're off the hook for your choices just because you're *scared*, or you're *sad*, or you'd rather they didn't *count*. It all counts!"

Hell, Sam's eyes are swimming suddenly, but his voice doesn't betray him; it stays even and razor-edged as he snaps, "And sometimes, Jake, do you know what? Sometimes you try your best to do the right thing, you do the very best you can do with whatever you've got, and you *still* get it wrong. You get it wrong, and you have to live with that, and without whatever it's cost you. A mistake—a mean review—I could have forgiven that, if you'd tried to do the right thing." He forces himself to look Jake dead in the eyes, even though he knows his own are glittering with held-back tears. "But you didn't even try, Jake. You didn't even *try* to tell me. Not once."

"Tonight," Jake tries, sounding desperate in a way that, just an hour ago, would have twisted Sam's heart in his chest. "I said—dinner! I was going to tell you at—"

"Sorry," Sam says, bitterly sarcastic, "but all I have to go on there is your word, and it turns out that's mud, so."

Jake reels back half a step, looking as though Sam's struck him. For a second Sam thinks he's going to... to do *something*. To start screaming, or burst into tears, or, if previous times Sam's seen this expression on Jake's face are anything to go by, get drunk and steal an expensive automobile.

Sam finds, to his detached amazement, that he almost wishes Jake would. This has already gone too far—Sam has already said a dozen things that he will regret saying later, no matter how deeply Jake's hurt him—and yet he's almost hungry for an escalation, for the tension to reach such a devastating snapping point that it tears them both in two. It might feel good, Sam thinks, in the way there are certain things that only can feel good when you feel very, very bad. A root canal, for example, is something nobody wants, right up until the minute they need one—then it's the thing they desire most in the world, to be rid of that ruined, agonized nerve.

But on the other hand, maybe escalation isn't necessary. After all, Sam feels in pieces already, every bit as crumbled inside as the slice of Swiss he crushed. He can't fathom what Jake's thinking—what a fool he's been, to ever imagine he could—but the man certainly looks less whole than he did in Sam's bed just this morning.

Jake sounds it, too, when, blankly, he says, "Oh. Mud. Right."

Whether it's Jake's hollow tone or the thought of this morning, and the associated cognitive dissonance of realizing that was mere *hours* ago, all the fight drains out of Sam. He's exhausted, suddenly; he feels almost sick, as though expending so much emotion at once has burned out some critical internal engine, and nothing can run without it.

"Just... go," Sam says, putting a hand over his eyes and gesturing towards Jake's building. "I don't want to see you right now. Please just leave." Then, all but snarling it in his abrupt anger at remembering it's necessary, he adds, "You can send Joey our social passwords, by the way. Thanks for all the *help*."

"Sam," Jake says. It's the smallest voice Sam's ever heard him use, and for a second Sam wavers, wanting to fix things. Wanting to make this okay for Jake somehow, except... except, Sam remembers, resolve washing over him again, it's not his job to make things okay for other people. Especially when those people have made things far, far less than okay for him.

"Fine," Sam says, tight. "*I'll* go, then."

He turns around and walks into the deli without looking back.

SEVENTEEN
NOW: JUNE

Sam gets exactly twenty-four hours to be furious. Without entirely meaning to, he spends nearly all of them cleaning.

More specifically, he spends them cleaning the deli, giving it the sort of deep, multi-step scrub-down even health inspectors don't call for. The drains, the ovens, the deep fryers—even the grease trap, which is such a disgusting job that Sam usually hires someone in to do it. Not today! Today he stomps upstairs, hearing each of his footfalls ring through the building, and puts on the clothes and shoes he wears for really nasty work before stomping back down again. He's pretty sure he hears a collective sigh of relief when he steps out the back door to access the grease trap from the exterior panel, which Sam can't blame anyone for. He doesn't want to be around himself right now, either.

A few months ago, the algorithm that controls Sam's digital life fed him a video of some food celebrity; Sam doesn't remember who he was now, only the concept he laid out. He called it the Restaurant Rancidity Index: a system by which one could rate the energy in any given eatery. There were a variety of tiers of rancidity, along with guidelines for identification of said tiers, and suggestions for each one as to whether or not it's worth eating there. And there was also a long segue about how one single person could tip a whole place into a bad energy, which involved a lot of emphatic hand gesturing and, eventually, an off-screen man laughing and saying, "Dude, you gotta chill, or people will think you're talking about someone specific."

Sam's own personal Rancidity Index rating is currently the highest it's ever been, off the charts to a degree that his mind is still struggling to map. And so, for all he knows he should be containing them—for all he tries to force them into cleaning, which is at least productive, something with a tangible *result*—his feelings seep out into the restaurant anyway, poisoning everyone's mood.

Or maybe the poison would have been there regardless, and isn't entirely Sam's fault. Maybe they're angry, too, or hurt, or regretful about growing attached to this person who turns out to have betrayed them all. It wouldn't surprise him, but he doesn't know, because for the rest of the day nobody really talks to him. That's probably because from the time Sam returns to the deli until the last closer leaves for the night, there are essentially no moments in which he is not grunting, groaning, or grumbling to himself while he disassembles and scrubs every piece of equipment that isn't actively in use. This is on purpose: Sam doesn't want to talk, not to them, not to anyone, and is relieved when they leave him alone.

Instead they try to talk to each other, not that it goes well. Alphonse ends up snapping at Eileen, who turns around and snaps at Joey, who storms out fifteen minutes before the end of their shift exclaiming, "I don't need this! It's still technically my *birthday week*," as though the honoring of a "birthday week" is a holy writ the entire staff has violated. Sam watches them go without saying anything, cold and empty, as though his rage has burned through everything inside of him and left nothing behind but charred earth.

Then he disassembles the dish room faucets, one at a time to make sure the staff can still work, and cleans each piece so thoroughly that each one looks, upon reassembly, like he just picked it up from the store. It should be satisfying. It isn't.

He growls low under his breath and moves on to the next project.

Sam should sleep. He doesn't. Or, at least, he mostly doesn't. Around four in the morning, he passes out on his living room couch in the middle of trying to fish one of Pastrami's toys out from underneath it, and wakes up to the piercing scream of his alarm only an hour or so later.

As he shuts it off, a jolt of such agonized heartbreak shoots through Sam that it shocks him. He had forgotten, under the anger and emptiness, that he was capable of other emotions, and he can't even place what's caused this one for a second. He just lies on the couch, reeling with the intensity, for a long moment until it comes back to him: Jake—God, it was only *yesterday*—smiling up at him and sliding a hand into his hair, saying maybe there was something to these restaurant hours after all.

For all this last week was, in the grand scheme of Sam's life, the space between one breath and the next, for a minute there it had felt like... God, Sam can hardly bear, now, to even think it. It felt like maybe, for *once*, it wasn't just going to be him looking after everyone else. Like maybe this one time it was going to be *mutual*.

But Jake, Sam reminds himself harshly, isn't the person he seemed to be, so. Any conclusions he might have drawn were based on false information, and are thus useless to work from.

A little part of Sam, one which has been out cold since Jake's secret was revealed, stirs slightly at this point. It asks in a querulous voice whether Sam thinks that's entirely fair. He's known Jake a long time, hasn't he? And he knows, if mostly by inference, that Jake's had a difficult year. Isn't he, Sam, intimately familiar with what it is to be so unhappy you lose track of yourself, that you can't be honest even when you know, deep down, you should be?

He crushes the voice into silence and goes back down to the deli, where he glowers at roughly everyone and everything in his eyeline.

At least, he glowers until just before 10 a.m., which is when Luce bursts, sobbing, through the front door.

. . .

It takes Sam nearly forty minutes, and a copious amount of snacks, to calm Luce down enough to tell him what happened. For a while, all he can get out of her is tears; then there's a few minutes where all she'll say is, "I'm not a triplet anymore, Sam, all right? You'll back me up with Mom and Dad? They can be *twins* like they've always really *wanted* and I can be an emancipated sibling!" Then, to Sam's sympathy, but also increasing frustration, tears again. This does, at least, clue him in to the general area of the problem, but leaves him at sea in terms of specifics. The triplets have always fought amongst themselves, but it's contained and insular, all three of them closing ranks if anyone else tries to get involved.

Luce has apparently let this allegiance go, because when she finally runs out of tears, she tells Sam everything. It takes her a while.

Some of it is stuff Sam already knew, either by witnessing or inferring it over the years. Daisy and Iris are closer with each other than with Luce. Daisy and Iris have never quite understood Luce (and, though Luce doesn't say this and Sam suspects she doesn't know it, vice versa). Daisy and Iris are a matched set, and signal in a lot of subtle ways that Luce should consider herself lucky to be along for the ride.

Sam also already knows the broad strokes of the old fight Luce fills in as backstory: how angry Daisy and Iris had been a few years back, when Luce first said she wanted to go to art school. He lets her tell him anyway because it's so obvious she needs to, but he could hardly have forgotten. It had been the Adelson Family Bone to Pick for the better part of a year, David and Mara pushing for a more "traditional degree" while Daisy and Iris insisted that they were triplets and meant to do things together. Sam had not been in attendance for more than a handful of the conversations about it. That was when his sisters were in high school, and the uneasy détente he'd reached with his parents at that point extended to birthdays, holiday dinners, and the occasional weekend cookout.

He'd never had much to contribute to the general discussion, beyond the never well-received, "I think Luce's art is really good, and it's her life, so. Maybe she should just do what she wants."

She had done what she wanted in the end—or, at least, she'd gone to art school. But she'd stayed in Cleveland, turning down an offered spot at a prestigious program in Rhode Island to do so, and lived in off-campus housing with Daisy and Iris. She'd said at the time that she'd thought about it, that staying local was what she wanted, but Sam's not surprised to hear now that she had desperately wanted to accept the Rhode Island offer.

None of it's a surprise, really, until she gets to the bit about the job and the apartment.

"Okay, so," she says, dropping her voice low, "don't tell anybody this—well, you can tell Joey. They already know."

"Thank you," Sam says solemnly, holding back, out of brotherly duty, *If I find myself wanting to discuss my little sister's relational issues with one of my barely-over-teenaged employees, especially one who I'm ninety-five percent sure is dating you, I think probably my best move is to go get checked for head trauma.*

"Well... I kind of got. Uh. I guess you could call it a job offer?" Luce says, almost whispering now. "For next year? One of my professors is... you won't know her, probably, but she's a really famous sculptor. She runs an artists' retreat down in the Cuyahoga Valley, about an hour from here? And every few years, she picks a graduating student, and, um." Luce flushes, and, looking like she's both uncomfortable and trying not to smile, mumbles, "I mean, they do kind of say she picks the most promising... Look, whatever, I'm not trying to brag, but she picks someone and makes them artist-in-residence? And they live at the retreat, and keep an eye on the place, and check guests in and whatever. And get paid, obviously, which is great. But the rest of the time they're able to just. Work? And, um." So quietly Sam almost doesn't hear her, but excitement audibly thrumming through her voice, she says, "A lot... a lot of the people who have done it before have gone on to have pretty big careers, Sam. Like, *big* big."

"Luce, *wow*," Sam says, thrilled enough for her that even the deep, dark pits of his Jake-related unhappiness don't dim his smile. "That's huge! Or, I mean, what do I know about art? But it sounds huge. Congratulations!"

"Thanks," Luce says, sounding upsettingly grateful to hear what's surely the only appropriate response to such news. For a second a brief, bright grin slashes across her face, before she sighs and drops it. Her voice turns bitter as she says, "But, you know, Daisy and Iris want to stay here. *They* like the idea of getting an apartment downtown, where *they're* hoping to work, and where a lot of *their* friends are planning to live. In fact, they like that idea so much that yesterday, while I was hanging out with Joey, and without even *talking* to me, they went and... and.... rented one!"

"What," Sam says, blinking at her, "like, just for the two of them?"

"Ha! I wish!" Luce narrows her eyes, drumming her fingers on the tabletop of the booth in the back corner Sam led her to when she came in crying. "That would be fine, honestly. I don't know what they want me hanging around for anyway! They couldn't make it more obvious that I don't fit, but they can't just let me *go*, either, I don't—ugh, but it doesn't matter. No, Sam, not just for them. Three bedrooms! One for each of us!" Snorting down at her hands, Luce adds, "They hoped I'd be cool with taking the small one, because they found it."

"So, wait," Sam says, slow as he processes, in growing annoyance, what she's saying, "they just found an apartment, liked it, *assumed* you would live with them, and signed a lease?"

"A lease they can't afford," Luce says, giving him a slightly wild-eyed look, "without me paying 'my share'! And when I said, 'I can't do that, I'm not staying in Cleveland, I've got this incredible opportunity,' they said I was being selfish. That *I* was! They never even *asked* me, Sam. But I'm the selfish one!"

Luce seems to be on the edge of tears again, though this time tears of rage; after yesterday, Sam can relate. He says the most comforting things he can think of and then, falling back on his natural instincts, offers to make her something to eat, which she gloomily accepts.

He makes her a plate of salami and eggs, because it had been her favorite when he was a teenager, when he was watching the triplets and making them dinner at least two or three nights a week.

Luce looks for a second like she might cry again after all when he sets the dish down in front of her, but she just mutters, "Aw, Sam," and gives him a one-armed hug before devouring it.

She tells him about the actual fight that drove her here today while she eats; it sounds, as Deb would say, like a real humdinger. Much was said that should not have been said, and a fair amount of the things that *did* need to be said probably would have been better shared another time, another way. Daisy and Iris had called Luce stubborn, difficult, flaky; Luce had called Daisy and Iris self-involved, exclusionary, cold.

Sam attempts, as best he can, to provide some comfort. But it quickly becomes clear that Luce doesn't want comforting—she wants a place to stay that she doesn't have to share with her sisters. That seems only fair to Sam, so he takes her upstairs and gets her set up in the room that was his when he first moved here, the room he vacated when Deb left. Luce thanks him, hugs him, but is mostly subdued; she doesn't even make a joke about the awful band posters that still adorn the walls, even though she'd usually die before passing up a chance to rib Sam about his terrible teenage taste.

He leaves her to get settled, intending to think over the problem and find a way to approach it while he works through the rest of the morning. He's expecting a fairly light day. Jake's social media work has definitely driven traffic back up, but not quite to the levels it was before the mass exodus that was, as it turns out, also a direct result of Jake's work. During the weekdays they're nearly back to standard play, and even exceeding it sometimes, but that's running on foot traffic from nearby office buildings. It's always been comparatively dead on the weekends, when the various suburbanites who work nearby have no interest in coming back downtown just for a bite. That's been even more true since the Kiss of Death—so, Jake—tanked all their traffic. For the last few months, Sam's been lucky to see three or four customers, total, in the whole run of a Sunday. He'd even been semi-considering closing the deli on the weekends, and had held off only because the lost hours would cause issues for his staff.

All in all, Sam should have plenty of time to think through a plan of attack for dealing with the triplets. He's even intending to send Joey upstairs to cheer Luce up when they arrive for their shift at eleven. But to his surprise, when Joey does step through the door, a customer comes in behind them. Then another. Then another, and another, and another. Two of them, Sam realizes with surprise, are people he recognizes from the recital the other night.

By 11:30 a.m., they're fully in the weeds, Sam hollering orders over his shoulder from the register so Joey can scoop salads and slice lunch meat. The volume of humanity inside the space quickly becomes oppressive, taking the space from Sunday-morning dead to a fever pitch Sam associates with the High Holy Days, large nearby sporting events, and the nightmare that is Labor Day Weekend, when seemingly everyone in Ohio descends on downtown for the annual Cleveland National Air Show. It's not that he's complaining; it's great to have a rush like this, and Sam can tell within the first hour that today's take will go a ways towards covering the gaps Kiss of Death directly caused. It's just...

"Do *you* have any idea why this is happening?!" Sam asks Joey, after they've been at it about an hour with no signs of traffic slowing. Some of the traffic is people he recognizes, but most of it is obvious strangers and new customers, many of whom seem to be taking pictures of themselves in front of the counter. "Not that it's not great and all, but where are they all *coming* from?"

Instead of answering, Joey pulls out their phone and starts scrolling. This annoys Sam so deeply that he almost breaks one of his cardinal managerial rules—better to be curious and make genuine asks of his employees than to be harsh or demanding—and snaps at them about being too busy to text right now. He doesn't, if only barely, and is rewarded for his forbearance, in a way. After a second of scrolling, Joey makes a pleased sound, passes their phone to Sam, and groans, "All right, all *right*, I'm getting there," when the person they're currently serving insists they put their phone down and focus on scooping potato salad.

Normally, hearing a comment like that would make Sam feel a little frisson of validation vis-à-vis his own methods of management: Anybody who talks to anyone else with that kind of insistent, demanding condescension comes off looking like a huge asshole.

But he's not paying enough attention to get even the inconsequential hit of self-satisfaction he would have received if he'd fully noticed the conversation. Instead, he's looking at a post on their socials from a few weeks ago, the one Jake had filmed of Sam talking about the deli's history. His heart wrenches in his chest to see it. The version of Sam captured within looks so happy and hopeful, and keeps glancing besottedly just off-screen to where Jake was filming him.

The Sam of today feels, for the Sam in the video, something between pity and embarrassment. It couldn't be clearer from the footage, even with the sound off, that the poor guy has no idea what he's in for.

But, also: "I don't get it?" Sam says, glancing back at Joey, who has moved on from potato salad to macaroni. "Jake posted it *weeks* ago; why would it be bringing people in *now*?"

"For God's sake, Sam, look at the *numbers* on it," Joey says, in the weary tones of the young talking to the ancient about technology. Sam, at thirty, resents this in the extreme, but he doesn't mention this as he glances at...

"Holy crap!" Sam says, staring at the tiny, stylized numerals as though they might scurry off if he were to glance away. "When did this blow up this much? I scrolled through a few days ago and everything looked relatively chill!"

Joey shrugs with one shoulder. "A couple of big-time celebrities reposted it this morning." There's an awkward pause in which Sam can tell they're both thinking the same thing, so he's not surprised

—unhappy, but not surprised—when Joey says, cautiously, "I kinda think that. Well. I don't know how much you've talked about there, or worked out, or whatever? But we *do* know someone who knows a lot of folks in this kind of space. I think maybe Jake—"

"You know what?" Sam says, too loud, handing the phone back to them. "Who knows why this happened? Don't look a gift horse in the mouth, that's what I say."

Joey looks, for a second, like they're going to say something else, push back. Then they sigh. "All right, Sam. You're the boss."

The rush runs for several hours before it finally peters out to a slow trickle of customers. At some point in the middle Luce comes downstairs and, seeing they need it, starts helping; Sam's able to train her up quickly, leave her on the register, and go into the back to help the prep crew. That night he teaches her how to do several of the closing tasks, and has her fill out some paperwork so he can pay her for her time. She's grateful, excited, and agrees to help out as needed while she's staying upstairs.

It's at this point that the phone calls start.

For the next week, Daisy and Iris call the deli every day, multiple times a day. They're calling Sam's cell, too, and presumably Luce's; he always answers but tells them they'll have to talk to Luce if they want answers to questions about her. They say Luce isn't speaking to them, and Sam says he's aware of that, and Daisy and Iris demand that he fix it, make it all right between them.

But Sam can't do that, can't begin to work out how. This isn't like when they were children and fighting over the same toy or video game; Sam can't break out a schedule to share things between them, or talk to them in a low voice until they all feel a little less wound up. They are, all three of them, fully grown adult women, and it's up to Luce to decide how she wants to move forward. At least for now, the answer to that question seems to be, "Here at the deli, without them."

And it's pathetic, but Sam's *glad* this is what Luce wants. He's glad she's here, even if he does keep catching her making out with Joey in the walk-in. He's glad to have her company at work and even more so at home; it keeps him from spiraling into the dark pit of Jake-centered despair that he would otherwise, by now, be living entirely within. He doesn't come up with anything to help the situation between the triplets, and he's guiltily afraid it's because he doesn't really want to.

He can't keep Luce here forever, of course. She has that job offer for next year, and, anyway, insisting that she stay wouldn't be so different from what their sisters have done here. Sam doesn't want his to become another voice in Luce's head telling her she needs to be small, do what keeps the peace, just for something as inconsequential as his comfort.

But he still feels his stomach sink when, the following Friday afternoon, Daisy and Iris walk through the restaurant's front door with stormy expressions, their faces identical in more ways than one.

EIGHTEEN

NOW: JUNE

"Daisy," Sam says, blinking at the two of them. "Iris. Uh. Was I expecting you?"

"We decided it was time to drop by and sort things out," Daisy says in sunny tones. "We understand that Lucy was upset, but enough is enough, don't you think?"

At the same moment, raising one eyebrow, Iris demands, "Sorry—do we need to make an appointment? Does *Lucy* have to make an appointment when *she* wants to come by? Because it seems like *she's* here a lot."

Sam doesn't feel good about it—it isn't brotherly of him—but he's always hated it when they do this, the simultaneous-speaking, twin-telepathy thing. They're *not* twins, first of all, Luce's claims of being an emancipated sibling aside. And, secondly, because their personalities are essentially diametrically opposed to one another, the tonal shift is brutal, and it always gives him a headache trying to figure out which of them to answer first.

He decides to tackle Iris's questions now, since she actually asked him something. "No, you don't need to set an appointment, and neither does Luce. You're all welcome here whenever, you know that. I just didn't realize you'd be coming by today. If I'd known, I might have—" Sam manages to choke back, "Steeled myself emotionally for the fight you're about to have in the middle of my business, and maybe also looked into soundproofing the walk-in so you don't put everyone off their food," but only by the skin of his teeth. He finishes, instead, with, "Prepped you... some lunch?"

"We ate," Iris says, flat.

"It's four in the afternoon," Daisy adds brightly. "So lunch would be a little weird, no?"

"Sure," Sam says, pinching the bridge of his nose. He can feel the headache building already, especially when they cast him identical impatient looks. God, he's too old to be in the middle of this—they're *all* too old for him to be in the middle of this—and he feels abruptly ancient and wizened, as though he'll crumble to dust in the next heavy breeze. "I'll... just go get Luce, then?"

"Thanks!" Daisy sings out, as Iris mutters, "Whatever."

Sam goes to the back, telling himself as he does that he is not fleeing from the specter of his younger sisters. Luce isn't in the kitchen or Sam's office, but he finds her out back sitting with Joey, looking at something on their phone and laughing. He hates to do it to her when she looks so happy, but:

"I regret to inform you that our sisters are here," Sam says, and winces when all the blood visibly drains from Luce's face. "Or, uh, my sisters, I guess, since you've decided you don't want to—"

"What right do they have to come here?" Luce demands. Her voice is shaking. "Kick them out! Tell them they're not welcome!"

Joey, Sam notes, is glaring at him now, even though they're usually chill and mild-mannered. It's all Sam can do not to glare back; it's not like it's *his* fault the two of them showed up.

Still: "It's. You know. A business? Open to the public? And also... the *family* business? So, not that I agree with what they've done, at all, you know that, but. I don't know that kicking them out would be—"

"Oh, what good are you," Luce snarls, and jumps up, stalking into the restaurant without another word. The door slams behind her.

Sam takes a moment to breathe deeply, remind himself that she didn't mean that. He knows she didn't mean it. She's just hurt and upset and scared and young, this is a lot for her, he can't possibly expect her to—

Joey interrupts his train of thought, their voice sharper than he's ever heard it. "*Seriously*, Sam? You couldn't just tell those little cu—"

"Whatever you're about to say about my baby sisters," Sam snaps, his tone harsher than he means it to be, "*don't*, all right? I understand that you're only interested in one of them, and I think, honestly, that I've been pretty chill these last few months! As you romanced her before my eyes! But if you finish that sentence, Joey, I swear to God I will come down on you like a ton of bricks for all the 'fifteens' that are really twenty-fives because you're out here with your tongue down my sister's throat—"

"Jesus," Joey mutters, cutting him off and standing abruptly. "I wish Jake hadn't written that *stupid* review. I liked you a lot better with him around." And then they, too, stalk into the restaurant, leaving Sam, once again, to try to remind himself to take it easy, to see their side.

It's difficult, just now. Perhaps that's because of the inherent stress of the moment. As Sam hears, from outside, voices rising from within Silverman's, he thinks grimly of the Restaurant Rancidity Index, and wonders if he'll need to track that chef from the video down and let him know they've broken his scale.

It's difficult to give Joey the benefit of the doubt here because what they said cut deep, struck right at the heart of his own churning, swirling thoughts. He, too, wishes Jake had not written that *stupid* review, and not just because it hurt the business, and hurt Sam, and ended things between them before they could even really start up. If Jake hadn't written that review, he would still *be here*, in the deli, right now, and Jake is the sort of person who would know how to handle this situation with the triplets. Jake would raise his eyebrows and say something cool and collected that would draw the fighting to a halt. Jake would assess everyone's positions and come up with a compromise. Jake would, if nothing else, have it in him to crack a series of jokes, or start humming a cheerful tune while somehow managing to sound sarcastic, or otherwise bleed the tension out of the room. He wouldn't be the way Sam always is in situations like this: hopelessly trying to balance everyone's feelings like a towering stack of dirty dishes, and inevitably sending them all crashing to the floor. He'd be competent. Confident. *Helpful.*

Abruptly, Sam misses him so much it feels genuinely life-threatening. He's not sure if he hates himself or Jake more for that, just that it stings and smarts even after he's pushed past the initial shock of agony and gone back into the deli himself.

The raised voices he could barely hear from outside are, unsurprisingly, quite a bit louder from within. They are, also unsurprisingly, having more or less exactly the same argument Luce described to him the other day: Daisy and Iris can't understand what Luce's problem is, why she won't just move in with them, and Luce, having stewed with rage for days, is nearly incoherent. She keeps shouting things like, "Personal autonomy!" and "Didn't even ask!" without any of the surrounding context, as though the other parts of her sentences have flounced off in a huff. Occasionally someone—Sam is almost certain it's Joey—is throwing in a supportive "Yeah!" or "That's right!" after she speaks, though is generally immediately drowned out by the other two.

Taking a deep breath and trying not to think about Jake or how much easier this would be with him to hand, Sam steps into the dining room. He's not surprised to see it's hemorrhaging customers; he wouldn't want to continue eating somewhere where this was happening, either.

The three of them are positioned as though preparing for battle. Luce is on the employees-only side of the deli counter, running a furious hand through her short, dark, and currently partially purple hair over and over again. Across from her, Daisy and Iris's faces are twisted into matching expressions of icy fury. The two of them have their lighter hair pulled back today, smoothed down and twisted into the sleek knotted buns they've both favored since high school, and which Luce, whose hair has their father's curlier texture, has never been able to pull off. Sam wonders if they did it on purpose, to make Luce feel the differences between them more acutely, and then feels uncharitable for even considering it.

They're all standing the same way: arms crossed, shoulders thrown back, feet planted slightly apart, and holding so much tension in their respective necks that Sam thinks he could probably play them like guitar strings. It's a familiar position: Mara, Sam remembers in a dizzying wave, had always stood like that when she was furious. He can practically conjure the image now, even though it's been years since he's seen his mother angry. The last time, barring the accident, was during the Great Yom Kippur Schism, while she and Deb were sniping back and forth at one another about seemingly every grudge they'd ever carried.

Sam's often wondered if it might have been easier for the two of them, him and his mother, if either one of them was more like Deb, and preferred just fighting things out to avoiding them. He's fairly certain that's why it's been so long since he's seen Mara get mad. He's had the sense for some time now that she feels too guilty about what happened after the accident *to* get angry with him, or even in front of him, not that she's ever managed to admit as much. Some days he feels good about that, vindicated in his lingering sadness and hurt. Some days it depresses him so much he can hardly stand to think about it.

Today, watching her posture sketched over his sisters' shoulders, it makes him want to cry.

"Girls," he starts, instead of telling them this. It's how he would have approached an argument between them when they were children, and it's a mistake; they all turn to glare at him. Wearily, he thinks at least it's stopped them glaring at each other.

Only briefly, because: "We're *women*," all three of them snap, and then, looking horrified to have been caught doing the same thing in the same moment, turn back to one another and resume fighting.

"Of course you are," Sam says, not that they're listening to him anymore. "I just meant—I was hoping—for God's sake, would you just *listen* for a second?"

All three of them fall silent, which alerts Sam to the fact that he delivered that last bit more than a little too loudly. The last remaining customers in the deli glance up at the volume and then scurry out, leaving the place as dead and empty as it was at the peak of the aftermath of *Jake's* Kiss of Death review. Would any of this even have happened if not for that stupid review? If Luce hadn't had the excuse of wanting to help out at the deli? If Sam hadn't been so wrapped in everything, been paying more attention to what was really going on?

"What?" Iris snaps. "You think you can fix this, Sam? *You?* You're not even part of this! What do you know about—"

"I *know*," Sam returns, his voice dropping into a low, dangerous register, "how easy it is to lose your *family*, Iris, all right? I know! The three of you are acting like—"

"The *three* of us?" Luce demands, throwing Sam a glare that makes him wince. "I'm not *acting* like anything; *they're* the ones who don't even think of me as a—"

"*We* were just trying look out for your *future*," Daisy cries. "We've never lived apart, and you're the one we always had to carry, you know! Never making your own friends, or—"

"I make my own friends!" Luce looks and sounds near tears of rage now. "I have plenty of friends! And a partner! And a job lined up, which is more than either one of you has got! Just because I wasn't invited to as many birthday parties as you when we were *seven*—"

"The *three* of you," Sam bellows, drowning them out, "are acting like there aren't any consequences to this! Like you can just stand here and be horrible to one another and then let it all pass under the bridge, because you're family and that's what happens. But sometimes it *isn't* what happens! Sometimes you *break* something, and you can't ever take it back or put it right again, and then you have to carry it—"

"Oh my God," Iris says, rolling her eyes, "not everything is about *your* trauma, Sam, okay? You don't know what the hell you're talking about, and—"

"Actually," a soft, female voice says from somewhere behind Sam, "in my experience, he's got that one dead right."

All four siblings spin, mouths dropping open, to see Deb standing in the doorway.

Once he's over the shock of seeing her—and with no small amount of relief—Sam lets Deb take over. He's grateful when she instructs him to go to his office and wait for her; he's even more grateful when, a few minutes later, the shouting dies down, and she saunters in sans triplets, looking pleased with herself.

"I sent them over to Joanie," Deb explains, sitting down in the chair across from the desk and smiling at Sam. "You'd never believe it based on how in touch she, uh, *really* isn't with her *own* feelings, but she's great with this kind of thing for other people. She'll make them all sit in a circle and agree that they can only talk when they're the one holding some weird crystal or amulet or whatever else from that junk pit of a shop, and shut them up when they go too far." When Sam makes a doubtful face, she laughs. "I'm serious, you know. I've seen her do it. How do you think your mother and I get through funerals and bat mitzvahs without making fools of ourselves?" When Sam blinks in surprise, she winks and adds, "What? I don't tell you everything, you know. Anyway, it'll be easier for Joanie than you. You're too close to be objective."

"Well, that's... probably right," Sam admits, and slumps down slightly onto his hands. After a second, feeling the oddness of their positions acutely, he adds, "Do you want to switch seats? It's weird being on this side, when it's, uh, technically your office."

"Nah," Deb says, and, grinning at him, kicks her feet up onto the desk. "Kinda like the view from this side, honestly. Much less to worry about over here."

"That's *definitely* right," Sam mutters, and sighs, and then smiles back at her, helpless not to. "It's good to see you. Thanks for coming."

"Oh, sure," Deb says, waving a hand as though it's nothing. "Talya's off presenting a paper at some academics-only conference this week, and it seemed like a good time to stop in, see how it's all going. If I'd realized it was going to be World War III when I showed up, I might have picked a different week, but maybe it's for the best that it worked out like this. You don't, sorry to say it, really have my expertise in sister-on-sister crime."

Sam grimaces, thinking of some of the fights he witnessed between Deb and Mara before the Great Yom Kippur Schism, after which communications between them largely ceased. He hates to even think it—it makes him so sad for the triplets he can hardly bear it—but: "Is that how you and my mom were, then? At their age?"

Deb laughs, a bright, bell-like peal. "Me and Mara? God, no. Of course not. We were *much* worse." In the tones of a fond reminiscence, she adds, "We did have a couple of humdingers like that here at Silverman's, I'll grant you. She threw about half a tub of whitefish salad at me once, you should have *heard* my mother go on about the cost and the mess. You missed meeting your grandma Sandy, but she could really blow her top when she was mad enough."

"Yeah," Sam says, the corner of his mouth lifting. "I've got the sense that's a family trait. The three of them are certainly giving one another a run for their money."

"Oh, stop, that'll work itself out in the end." Deb waves a hand. "Part of the reason you *have* sisters is to fight with them. It's how you grow. I would've kept fighting with Mara 'til the day one of us died if she hadn't bowed out, and I still would now, if she ever showed up ready to go a few rounds. Sometimes I even wish she would. It wouldn't be fun, but." She shrugs. "A lot of what's worth doing isn't any fun. That doesn't mean you shouldn't do it."

"I'm not sure if I should take comfort in that," Sam admits, "but I do, a little."

"Good, Sammy," Deb says, offering him a smaller, sadder smile. "That's good. It hasn't been much fun here these past few months, has it?"

Sam sighs heavily, slumping forward to put his head in his hands. "No," he says, and then, rather more honestly, "Well... yes *and* no," and then, so honestly he feels like it might peel his skin off, "It's kind of been the most fun I've ever had and the least all at once? I think maybe the best way to describe it is like..." He pauses for a moment thinking, and then, on another heavy sigh: "Imagine... finding a winning lottery ticket at the exact moment you're struck by lightning, thinking it's for ten million dollars, recovering from being struck by lightning, going to cash in the ticket, and discovering it's only worth five dollars and, also, somehow, you owe them an additional twenty."

Deb makes a face at Sam. It's a familiar face, but the familiarity is not, in this case, very comforting, since Sam is used to seeing it directed at customers who have said something like, "Can you tell me—is the salmon here grass-fed?" or, indeed, "Please cut all the pastrami seasoning off of the pastrami." He makes one back, which he intends to communicate that he knows he doesn't sound like he's doing amazing, but which, based on Deb's raised eyebrows, mostly communicates that he feels like crawling under the desk and never emerging again. In fairness to her, that *is* more or less how he feels.

"That bad, huh?" Deb says finally. "I thought the numbers had been looking better?"

"Oh, it's not the *numbers*," Sam says. "Or it *is* the numbers, sort of, but not directly. They have been doing better! It's just the reason they were bad in the first place that's getting to me."

"Sammy, *tell* me you're not still hung up on that stupid

review!" Deb sounds mildly appalled now. "You can't let these things *get* to you like this; it's been months."

"It's not the review I'm hung up on," Sam says, hearing the note of bitterness creep into his voice and not caring enough to fight it back, "so much as the reviewer, actually."

Deb raises her eyebrows again, so high this time that they nearly meet her curly, salt-and-pepper bob. "Sorry... what?" Lowering her voice, she adds, "Not that I'm judging, but isn't Norman Endicott a little old for you?"

So Sam tells her about Jake, wishing he could pretend even to himself that he didn't want to—that he wasn't, to a genuinely painful degree, desperate to talk about the whole thing with some-one. He's been so desperate to do so that he's been considering going to Joanie, but he's glad it worked out like this. Deb's a good listener, asking occasional clarifying questions like, "Wait, the guy from the car? Back when you were in high school?" and "Wait, he waited *how* long to tell you?" and, at the end, "Listen: Do you want me to have him killed? Because I know a lot of archeologists, and while I wouldn't call any of them likely to be excellent hitmen, I can promise they'll know where to bury a body."

This last makes Sam laugh, which is at least a relief. It occurs to him as he does that it's the first time in days, as though Jake took all the mirth with him when Sam told him to go. "I don't think having Jake assassinated—"

"That little shit isn't important enough to assassinate," Deb corrects, as though the point is quite critical to her. "It would be a straightforward murder, and it would serve him right."

"I think we can skip it," Sam says, rolling his eyes, but a little pleased in spite of himself. "After all, it's not like I didn't nearly get him killed in—"

"Oh, what happened when you were teenagers was his fault," Deb snaps, sounding as annoyed as she always has whenever this comes up. It occurs to Sam, for the first time in thirteen years, that maybe she was annoyed *for* him—not, as he'd assumed at the time, upset that it had happened at all, and all but forced her to take him in. "He said as much to you himself, didn't he? It was on him and that idiot in the other car, and *you* took the collateral damage. I really *could* kill him, you know, for that more than for any of the rest of it. For a while there I was sure you'd never get over it."

"I'm not sure I ever did," Sam admits, letting out a shaky breath. "Sometimes it feels like I'm still that kid, you know?"

"Nah," Deb says, and throws him a smile, so sudden and bright and proud that Sam has to blink abruptly stinging eyes. "You're not. I know you're not. It's what I'm doing here, actually, if you want to get down to brass tacks."

"What do you mean?"

"There's only one thing you really could have done differently," Deb says, with a little shrug. "Back then, I mean. One choice you could have made that might—and only might—have changed the way things played out. You could have asked for help. You could have called your parents, or me, or the cops."

"I *know*," Sam groans, the old shame washing over him again. "I know, I know, I've thought about it a hundred times—"

Deb cuts him off by holding up an imperious hand. "I was speaking, Samuel, and I'd rather die than let a man talk over me, even you." Eyeballing him and apparently finding him suitably chastened, she continues: "I'm not trying to rub your nose in it, kid. I'm saying, that's what you could have done, and you didn't do it, because you were a child and you didn't know any better, and also because that's your gap."

Sam's brow furrows. "My what?"

"Your gap." Deb's expression goes soft, and she glances at the photo of her wife on the desk. "This is one of Talya's pet theories: Everybody has at least one big, loadbearing gap, a place where something important is supposed to be but isn't. Hers, for example, is tact: She's going to tell you the facts even if doing that is horribly, breathtakingly rude. Me? I don't have anything where my middle gears are supposed to go—I'm cool or I'm furious, but there's nothing in between. And you, Sam: You don't ask for help. Even when you really need it. *Especially* when you really need it."

"I... don't, do I." It's not a question; Sam realizes it's true, horribly, undeniably true, even as he says it. "I don't ask for help. God. I *never* ask for help."

"Nope!" Deb's voice is bright again, a cheer in it that Sam can't quite parse. "It was my biggest concern about letting you take over this place, in fact: Sometimes, everyone needs a little help, especially in this industry. No faster road to ruin than refusing to admit no deli is an island, and I couldn't bear to watch you drive the place into the ground over something small and stupid, something that would be fixable if you could just reach out. Too sad; too wasteful."

"But," Sam says, his own tone filling up with despair, "but if that's my gap, then we should just give the whole thing up, right? You take it all back over? Because—"

"Hush. We're not going to do that," Deb says. Her smile now is so happy; Sam doesn't understand at all. "Because do you know what you did, Sammy, when business got bad? You talked to Joanie; you asked around for advice; you let that little turd help you, even though it was his fault to begin with. You *called me.* It's hard, you know, to close a gap, but you cared about this place enough to get over yourself, and that's worth more to me than any numbers. My mom would have told you the same." She puts her feet down at last, leans across the desk, and takes his hand. "That's why it's *your* place now, kid. Not probationary: yours. I've seen what I needed to see. That's why I came to town, to let you know, and get the paperwork started."

Sam stares at her for a long time. Then, ashamed by the way his voice cracks on it, he demands, *"Really?"*

Deb nods, looking desperately pleased with herself. "Retirement suits me, and responsibility suits you. It's time." She glances around, her nose wrinkling, and adds, "I'll tell you what—you better let me take some of this stuff with me. It's creepy, you sitting here all day staring at a picture of my wife."

Sam thinks for a second that he's going to cry; instead he nods, and then bursts out laughing. All this time trying to preserve the place in amber, to ensure he never made a wrong step. He never, he realizes as he calms down, really believed this would happen. He'd kept it all as it was, afraid of changing a single thing, so it would be ready when Deb asked for it back, and kindly but firmly told him he'd failed.

He didn't fail. He *didn't fail*. The truth of it settles into his bones as he thanks Deb and hugs her and stares a minute too long at the + *Sam Adelson!* Post-it on his door.

And as it does, little plans he never even let himself notice he was making begin to unfold, one by one, from a previously locked drawer in the back of his mind.

NINETEEN

NOW: AUGUST

It takes Sam a few weeks to stop waiting for the other shoe to drop.

Things don't usually work out for him, that's all. If his life has taught him anything, it's not to put too much faith in any stroke of good fortune. Too often, Sam's found that good luck is, in fact, ruinous luck in a cheap costume, dressed up to lure him into a false sense of security before sweeping his legs out from under him. It makes him nervous when things are going too well, especially with the Jake disaster so freshly behind him. He can't help but tense up, determined to be prepared for it all to go wrong.

But this time, amazingly, it doesn't go wrong.

He thought Deb would change her mind with a few days to hang around, observe, and be convinced to turn against him by the thick summer humidity that always used to sour her mood. He was sure that she would determine upon reflection that he's not fit to take over after all. She doesn't. Instead, she seems more relaxed inside the walls of Silverman's than he's ever seen her, joking with the staff and regular customers, doctoring a nametag so it reads, DEB SILVERMAN: EMERITUS PROPRIETOR. Most of the people who see it don't even register it as a joke, but when Talya arrives three days after Deb does, free from her dig for a few weeks due to some unfortunate flooding, she laughs like it's the funniest thing in the world.

It hurts, honestly, that laugh. Seeing the way their shared humor crackles between them throws Sam back into too many conversations with Jake, how easy it all felt until it became so devastatingly hard. But it's good to see Talya, who had made a special effort with Sam from the moment she and Deb first met, a few years into Sam's time at Silverman's. She's kind for all she's blunt, and Sam can tell Deb's filled her in on his romantic agonies. Talya handles him with the sort of care he imagines she brings to fossils she's excavating, telling him stories about terrible breakups in her academic circle and insisting he join her and Deb for dinner most nights, even when he can tell Deb herself would have accepted his half-hearted excuses, left him to determine his own fate.

Sam's not sure if it's that, or the way the staff throw him a surprise congratulations party at which no one lets him cook anything, or the fact that Eileen bakes him a Black Forest cake; maybe it's just the bubble of helpless, overwrought pride that swells in his chest as he watches Deb's name get scraped off the back office door and replaced with his own. But whatever it is, as one week unwinds into a second, and then a third, Sam finds himself ready not to determine his own fate, but to embrace the one the world has already presented to him.

He said it to Dani at the West Side Market, didn't he? Just before Jake turned up and everything kicked off? Silverman's is Sam's one true love, written in huge, bold letters across the ventricles of his heart. Jake confused things for him for a minute there, made him think that perhaps there was room in his life for another kind of love, but Sam was kidding himself. The lesson of his teen years, which he'd learned thoroughly and well, was that he was the kind of person who couldn't be trusted with another person's heart. Now he knows that whether that's true or not, trusting another person with *his* leads to ruin and anguish and abject humiliation, and isn't worth the trouble.

But Silverman's... Silverman's is worth the trouble. Silverman's can't go behind his back, or lie to him about what it wants, what it's done, who it is. Silverman's can't hurt him, not the way Jake hurt him, and Sam's even starting to believe that *he* can be trusted not to hurt it. He *knows* Silverman's, what it needs and what it's likely to ask of him, where its weak spots are, how to help it when it's struggling. He feels, inside its familiar, beloved walls, not only like he's part of something, but like that something is worth being part of.

That's enough. Silverman's is enough; of course it's enough. Sam's pretty sure if he keeps telling himself that, one of these days he'll even start believing that it's true.

In service of this goal, Sam does what he's always done when his personal life is a shambles: He puts his head down and works through the disquieting sense that he's lost an essential organ. He clears Deb's stuff out of her office and replaces it with his own; he reorganizes the entire dining room, as well as the apartment upstairs. Trying to believe it has nothing to do with what Jake said, he puts the Pastrami Arnold and the green onion blintzes on the menu during the second week Deb's in town. She and Talya rave about both dishes, and the customers do, too, extensively enough that Sam drafts up a potential new menu and starts workshopping it during family meal. The staff are effusive about the results in a way that deeply gratifies him—true food people can't and won't fake it when it comes to deliciousness—and that makes him feel good, or close enough to good to get on with. He's not sure he'll ever feel properly good again, with this lingering sense of betrayal and despair biting at the back of his heels, but "close enough" is just fine.

This conclusion—that close enough is just fine—seems to be the one the triplets come to as well. Deb was right about Joanie and the power of her conflict-resolution skills; that first afternoon all three sisters slink back into the deli after several hours, looking drawn and chastened but, at least, speaking to each other. To Sam's amazement, they all willingly come back for several more chat sessions with Joanie playing referee, never discussing a word of what was said upon descending on the dining room for post-conversation sandwiches. By their last meetup, nearly a full three weeks after the initial blow-out, there's an easy energy between them that Sam's never seen before, even when they were small. Daisy and Iris have agreed to find a roommate, and even seem excited about Luce's job, and Luce makes it clear that she has abandoned all desire to emancipate herself from triplethood.

"Confidential," Luce tells him, smirking, when Sam asks her what the hell they talked about to manage that. "Sister stuff. Sorry —as a brother, you're simply not qualified."

But Joanie laughs when he asks her, and shakes her head, and says, "Oh, Sammy. Never could leave well enough alone, could you? You get that from your aunt, you know. I won't tell you what they said—it's their business—but they just got a little mixed up, that's all. Sometimes you get so attached to the idea of who someone is that it's hard to see the actual person right in front of you."

Sam knows how that is all too well, and is sure based on her expression that it must show in his face. He retreats back to the safety of Silverman's before she can ask him about it.

Unfortunately, the safety of Silverman's is somewhat conditional, that condition being the disposition of his aunt, his aunt's wife, and his aunt's best friend. In the circumstances, it takes Sam a few days too long to realize this, and, as such, he doesn't recognize the danger until it's already upon him.

It's a Wednesday morning in August when the three of them descend on him in what's obviously a coordinated attack.

They box him at the front counter like pack hunters in one of those nature documentaries Sam used to binge back in the day, when he first moved in upstairs. Deb's causally leaning against the doorway that leads to his office and the kitchen, blocking it off. Talya's got her elbows balanced against the flip-top section of the counter, preventing any exit that way. And Joanie's to his left, tucked up against the prep space where she's absolutely not supposed to be and keeping him from turning his focus away from them. They all have identical anticipatory expressions on their faces—a mixture of concern and resolve that spells nothing but trouble.

"Oh, God," says Sam.

Deb laughs. "For heaven's sake, don't look so scared. You're not in trouble."

"Too old," Talya agrees, and looks surprised when the other two give her identical horrified grimaces. "What? Is that rude? He is! An adult can't be in trouble with another adult, not *really*. Not in the way you mean, anyway."

"My love," Deb says, in the fondly exasperated tones of the happily married, "it's not that that's not a fine point well made, but a bit rude, yes. Comments about someone's age—"

"Almost always are," Talya finishes, sounding as though she's remembering it as she does. "Right, right. Sorry, Sam."

Sam grins at her, shaking his head. "Not to drive home the wrong point or anything, but I liked it, actually."

"Too *young*," Joanie groans, and everyone laughs, even—if looking slightly confused about it—Talya.

And then, when Sam's guard is down, they strike: Joanie gives Deb a Look with a decidedly capital "L," and Deb clears her throat and says, "Speaking of being young, and old, and, uh—"

"You're moping, Sammy," Joanie says, cutting to the heart of the thing with a roll of her eyes. "And we've all seen you mope like this once before—only *once* before—"

"Deb didn't even *know* Talya then!" Sam doesn't bother saying, *What are you talking about?* on the theory that it would be a pointless waste of breath. "She couldn't have seen me! Foul!"

"Oh no," Deb says, very dry, "whatever will we do? Kid, come on. You know that's not the point."

"What *is* the point?" Sam is very afraid of the answer, because he's so sure it's going to be—

"We want you," Talya says, in bright if slightly fatalistic tones, "to let us set you up!"

Sam groans. It's just as he feared; it's worse, even, because it's all three of them together. Over the years, Sam has gone on many dates with many men found for him by each of these three women. They have been... interesting. Some of the guys have been perfectly lovely, if not entirely thrilling to Sam; some of them have not been his cup of tea but have entertained him deeply in terms of what they said about the matchmakers' respective tastes; some of them have been, genuinely, train wrecks. One of them had been a *literal* train wreck: He and Pierre, who had turned out to be both a close-up magician and an aspiring improv actor, had been trapped for hours on the way to dinner behind a train-versus-unfortunate-fallen-rock situation. Things had thankfully started to move again eventually, but part of Sam died in that car. When, afterwards, he asked Joanie where she'd even found the guy, she'd shrugged and said she met him in line at the post office.

But he's never once been subjected to a man chosen by all three of them *together*. Even the idea chills his blood a little, for all he loves each one of them and knows they mean well.

Luckily, before he has to work out a way to express this that will *not* end in his having dinner out of guilt with someone who, for another example, scoops a dollop of baked beans off Sam's plate with his hand halfway through the meal, Sam is saved by the bell.

He turns, delighted by the cheerful sound of the front door dinging open, and his grin dims only a half watt when he realizes it's Marty. Marty, Sam reminds himself, is the landlord of the building behind them, and a long-standing regular who has been eating here for years; Marty isn't the one who organized or signed off on the Kiss of Death review; it's not Marty's fault Jake wrote it, or that Jake slept with Sam without bothering to bring it up. Marty, if he did anything, did Sam a favor by accidentally spilling the beans. At least Sam found out before things got any further entangled. Given how much it's hurt already, he kind of can't imagine the horror of making that discovery any later than he did.

There's an expression of nervous anticipation on Marty's face, which makes Sam groan for the second time in ten minutes. "Holy crap, not you too. Tell me they didn't rope you into this setup thing?"

"What?" Marty says, looking wrongfooted and genuinely baffled, as Deb, behind Sam, snorts. "God help me, I haven't come back in weeks; have I somehow put my foot into something *again?* I'm sorry. It's physiological and can't be helped."

"It's all right, you're innocent. He's trying to accuse you of colluding with us." To Sam's surprise, Joanie's tone of voice is one Sam usually sees her pull out exclusively around men whose vibes scream, "I am a monstrous asshole." When he glances at her, she's giving Marty a lingering once-over. "In our dastardly plot to find him love and happiness. Rude of him, really. I don't believe we've ever even met before."

"We haven't. If we had," Marty says, a slow smile breaking over his face, "I'd remember. I'm Marty."

"Joanie," Joanie says, dimpling at him. "Can we get you something, Marty? Cold beverage? Something to nibble on? It's on the house, since Sam went and insulted you like that."

"You don't work here," Sam and Deb point out together. Joanie ignores them both, and so misses the look of excitement they flash at one another, quick as lightning. If Sam's excitement is partially selfish—he would love the focus to turn, just now, towards Joanie's romantic prospects instead of his own—it's not like he has to say so.

"Since you're kind enough to offer, I sure wouldn't say no to a corned beef sandwich with Swiss and a glass of iced tea." Marty says this as though it's just occurred to him, as opposed to the same lunch he's been ordering for years. He still hasn't looked away from Joanie, or so much as said hello to Deb, who Sam knows for a fact he went to high school with.

"Coming right up." Joanie's practically purring. "Sam'll put it together for you himself, won't you, Sammy? Go on, don't keep the nice man waiting."

Sam opens his mouth to point out, again, that she *does not work here,* and also that he not only works here but is, in fact, the boss. But Deb catches his eye and makes an entreating face, and, more importantly, steps away from the doorframe, clearing the path to the kitchens. Realizing he shouldn't look a gift horse in the mouth, he flees with a nod and, feeling a little silly about it, satisfies his pride by taking his sweet time about preparing the dish. He also sneaks Pastrami a couple of bites, ensuring Marty's sandwich will come out ever so slightly light on meat. Is it a little petty? Sure. But Sam thinks he's earned a little pettiness, all things considered.

By the time he returns with the order all boxed up and bagged, Joanie has made her way around to the front of the counter, where she's leaning against the deli case in a way obviously intended to accentuate her curves and laughing uproariously at nearly everything Marty says.

Joanie has done this sort of thing in front of Sam before; her method of flirting is bold, assertive, unmistakable, and fairly singular. Its results, as far as Sam can tell, are... mixed. Men usually either shrink back and away from the onslaught of attention or act bored by it, unsurprised, as though they think it's their due.

But Marty looks deeply and genuinely delighted by her, and there's a bright, satisfied gleam in Deb's eye. When Sam walks past her with Marty's bag in hand, she leans over and whispers in his ear, "I can't believe I never thought of introducing them! He's been moping around that building ever since he got divorced a few years ago, and his ex is a *nightmare*; she made sure she got all the friends in the split. He told me last Thanksgiving that he's been making friends with his tenants for people to talk to!" She slaps him lightly on the arm and hisses, "Don't *spoil* it, oh my God, just give him the bag and back away slowly." Sam has to choke back his laughter—the urgency in her voice suggests life-or-death stakes—but he does as he's told and makes his escape.

He tries to make his escape, anyway. Before he can slip out back to take a fifteen and, hopefully, allow enough time to pass that Joanie, Talya, and Deb forget about setting him up entirely, Marty finally turns away from Joanie and says, "Sam! Wait! Where are you going?"

"On... break?" Sam says, confused.

"Where?" Marty pushes, his expression suddenly nervous again. "Is your break, like, something you could do here? In the dining room? Where I can see you?"

"Am I under surveillance?" Sam says this jokingly, but the expression it produces on Marty's face isn't exactly a comfort. "What's going on, man? Why do you need to be able to see me?"

"Oh, uh... no reason," Marty says, slightly wildly. He glances at Joanie, and, too quickly, says, "The shop next door, right? I'll come see you... I should just go, quickly, because... Right. Yes. I am leaving. Nice to meet you! Sorry! Goodbye!"

Baffled, Sam stares at him as he turns on his heel and starts hastily walking towards the door. Joanie, he notices, is doing the same thing, but with a lovelorn look that seems only to have been intensified by this bizarre behavior.

But when Marty reaches the door, he pauses, two fingers resting on the handle. It's a long moment that he stands there—such a long moment that Sam starts to wonder if he's entirely all right—before Marty swears, shakes his head, says, "You know what? I can't do this," and stalks back up to the front.

"Right," Marty says, planting one hand palm down on the counter and rooting around in his bag with the other. "So, the thing is, I promised him I wasn't going to do this. I promised him! I like the kid; he's my friend. He laid out the whole thing for me and said the least I could do was go along with things his way, distract you like he wanted, keep my mouth shut if he didn't want me to tell you. That seemed fair enough to me, after I blew up his spot the other week. But I just think—I mean, I'd want to know, if I was you. And I think he *does* want you to know; why else would he tell me about it, right? It's not like my track record with his secrets is so great."

"What the hell are you talking about?" Sam's heart is hammering in his chest for all he has no idea what's about to happen; his body feels slightly ahead of his brain, somehow. "Who—"

"Just hold *on*," Marty says, "it's stuck under my... There!" And he pulls out, with a flourish, a slightly crumpled issue of *Hearth* that Sam has never seen before. In fact:

"Jesus Christ, is that a *print* issue of *Hearth*?" Is Sam trying to avoid the impact of what he suspects that magazine contains? Sure, but still: "I didn't even know *Hearth* still did those. I thought they were phased out alongside VCRs and landlines, back when Al Gore invented the internet."

"Who?" Joey asks innocently, before Marty can reply, which makes him, Joanie, and Deb laugh, and Sam scowl.

When Marty stops laughing, he says, "If you know a better place than *Hearth*'s print issue for the discerning divorcee to find punishing crossword puzzles, I'm all ears." Sam says nothing, and the anticipation overmasters his nerves; his eyes flick back to the magazine, and Marty smirks. "Also, print subscribers get the issue a few days before the stories come out online, and landlines are better in an emergency. The internet isn't everything." Glancing at Joanie, he adds, "Just to cycle back to that divorce comment for a second—it's not like a recent divorce or anything. I'm all healed and therapized and ready to get back out on the—"

"Marty!" Sam's voice is maybe *slightly* strangled. "Could this maybe wait!"

"Right," Marty says, and sighs. "Right." He passes over the magazine, and then, talking too quickly as Sam stares down at the cover, says, "I want you to know that I tried to get him to tell you about a hundred times. We've gotten to know each other pretty well since he's been living in my building—he teaches my kids' dance classes, too—and I know he didn't mean to hurt anyone. He just made a mistake, and then..." Marty sighs, looking uncomfortable. "I don't want to speak out of turn, and it's not any of my business, but I think that jackass back in Los Angeles really messed him up. He was so afraid of how you'd take it, and even though I tried to point out that the reactions he was afraid of didn't sound like you—"

"Marty," Sam says quietly. "Please stop talking."

On the cover of the magazine, in the small font sidebar that teases the articles within, are printed the words, KISS OF DEATH'S KISS OF DEATH, BY JAKE THOMPSON (AKA NORMAN ENDICOTT).

"Oh, shit," Deb breathes, which is when Sam realizes she's hovering over one of his shoulders. He steps away from her, wanting some space, as he rips the magazine open and starts rifling through, dismissing feature stories and glossy photos and advertisements and—

there.

When I was in high school, I was in love with this guy who lied all the time.

I could never understand why he did that. He was so great already, exactly the way he was. Why lie? Lying, as I understood it, was something a person did in order to cover up shortcomings, and as far as I was concerned, he didn't have any.

I didn't know, then, the mechanics of falsehood. I'd never sat in on a doomed celebrity wardrobe fitting and watched a roomful of people smoothly insist that no, really, the outfit looked great. I'd never attended the opening of a highly anticipated new restaurant and pretended, with a commitment that was probably more theatrical than necessary, to be a regular patron instead of a reviewer. I'd never had the chance to get used to lying, and then *so* used to lying that I could do it easily, without even noticing. What did it matter, after all? Who could it hurt?

But that's the thing about making a liar of yourself: Eventually, it always matters. What starts as a tiny, inconsequential lie can begin to bear weight, and then more weight, and then so much weight you'd do *anything* to keep it from breaking, or to get to spend just one day more pretending it is true. And when, finally, it does break, you have no choice but to realize how much damage you've done—which was, in my case, a considerable amount.

At least one of the apologies I owe I don't deserve the opportunity to deliver, and I won't add insult to injury by airing his business in public. But to the rest of you I owe, at very least, the truth.

I have held many jobs over the past ten years, but, among other things, I've been a restaurant critic. It is strange, lonely work, or at least it has been the way that I've done it. I have written only for *Hearth*, and only under the pseudonym Norman Endicott, which was created to protect my anonymity. For years, I believed that decision—writing under a pseudonym—to be one of personal and journalistic integrity: I thought being unknown would help me feel safe to punch up, and take shots at the sort of pricey, overblown places Kiss of Death used to review.

Unfortunately, I have recently come to doubt my own integrity in the extreme, and suspect the only way to even hope to recover it is to return to a place of honesty, however uncomfortable or personally damaging that honesty might be.

Five months ago, I accepted a payoff to write a Kiss of Death column attacking Silverman's Deli, a beloved local restaurant in Cleveland, Ohio. I did not, for the record, know that's what I was doing, but it is, in all the ways that matter, what I did. The person who approached me with the idea for this particular column was someone close to me, who I trusted, and while what I've done is terrible, what I didn't do is even worse:

This person told me a series of lies about the conditions at Silverman's—lies which I had an obligation to investigate before repeating them, and did not. They brought me a variety of unappetizing dishes that they claimed were from Silverman's—a claim which I had an obligation to verify before reporting on the food, and did not. They offered me a meaningful sum to do what they insisted was a public good and rip Silverman's apart—to help "defray the opportunity cost of work to help the community," is how they phrased it. However, regardless of how the offer was phrased, I had an obligation to refuse it. I did not.{EDITOR'S NOTE: We are saddened and horrified by the unscrupulous behavior of this contributor. This will be Mr. Thompson's last piece with *Hearth*.}

In my defense, I very badly needed the money. I was freshly out of a toxic relationship with a wealthy man in Los Angeles; by the time he cut me loose, he'd isolated me from my friends and family and controlled my finances for the bulk of my adult life. It also took me longer than it should have to realize I was being used by the source of my "information" regarding Silverman's. When I finally got around to doing the digging I should have done in the first place, I discovered that the person pushing the negative story had a significant financial incentive for wanting Silverman's to fail.

But that's about all I can say in my defense. Did I think about the livelihoods of the restauranters, the staff? No. Did I think about journalistic integrity or ethics? No. Did I think about the community surrounding each place, the effort that goes in, every day, to keeping things going? No.

I didn't think about any of that until I had the opportunity to spend some time hanging out at Silverman's Deli, a place I had not actually visited when my previous review was published. I would like to say here, as emphatically as possible, that I could not have been more wrong. The food at Silverman's is some of the best in this city, and the staff and proprietor surely the best anywhere. Anyone would be lucky to get to enjoy a meal there, and I consider myself entirely unlucky—a classic, tragic fool—to have closed their doors so firmly behind myself.

Silverman's never deserved the Kiss of Death, but this column does. Thanks for reading, and I'm so sorry. If, someday, someone out there takes up the mantle of lampooning the restaurants that *do* need humbling, a word of advice from your old pal Norman: Your due diligence matters, and you need to do every last inch of it before you move forward. If, and only if, it turns out they deserve it, then I hope you give 'em hell.

TWENTY
NOW: AUGUST

If there was any justice in the world, the deli would have gone dead quiet as Sam read. Quiet, Sam imagines, might have been nice.

But this is Silverman's, and discounting the weeks it was dead because Jake killed it—although, Sam remembers, discomfited to realize he's been ignoring this fact for weeks now, Jake did then more or less bring it *back* from... Hell, Sam's so confused he's losing track of his *thoughts*. It is not quiet, that's the point: Joey is still taking orders, and diners are still sitting at tables talking amongst themselves, and the ever-present background racket of the sanitizing machine in the dish room ka-chunks on, the same as it ever was.

There is a distinctly ominous silence emanating out from around Sam, extending in front of him to Marty and, more worryingly, back into the kitchen. Steeling himself, he turns—

—or, at least, he tries to turn. He realizes by way of running into her that Deb has resumed leaning over his left shoulder, and that Talya has hooked her chin over his right one. Joanie, Sam notes, is leaning over Marty's shoulder, looking at something on his phone; amused in spite of everything, Sam has to hope it's a photo of the article.

"Can I," he starts to say, and has to pause to clear off the frog that has suddenly appeared in his throat. He tries again. "Can I maybe get some space, please?"

"Mm," says Deb, clearly not really listening. She reaches out and grabs one side of the magazine.

"Still reading," Talya agrees absently, gripping the other side.

Wearily, Sam sighs and drops down into a crouch, limboing underneath the bar of their arms; they don't seem to notice, just step together to close the space he'd occupied.

When he turns, Alphonse and Eileen are both staring at him through the service window, along with—Sam swallows—every other member of staff on shift today. The minute Sam looks at them, some internal dam seems to burst, and they all start talking at once:

"Come on, let me see—"

"What does it *say*?"

"Did Jake write it? Is that what he—"

"Oh, someone go and snatch it off them, it's been—"

"Sam." Sam turns again; it's Joanie, who has disentangled from Marty after all, and is standing right in front of him. "How do you feel?"

A squabble breaks out behind them, presumably over the magazine; Sam ignores the squawks and low-level crashes. "Honestly? I have no idea."

"Really?" Joanie is smiling at him, small and kind. "Are you sure?"

Sam opens his mouth to say he *is* sure, he really *doesn't*, but can't quite find the right words. He was so angry—he'd been *right* to be so angry—*had* he been right to be so angry? He doesn't know anymore; abruptly, he can't remember why the whole thing mattered so much in the first place. Surely, in the scheme of all he and Jake have weathered together, not to mention the things they've had to manage alone, one stupid review is small potatoes. Maybe if he'd just let Jake explain that horrible afternoon... Well, okay, Sam probably still wouldn't have *loved* it, but he thinks he would have understood.

Honestly, and horribly, the violation of journalistic ethics is a salve to his wounded pride. He's embarrassed to admit it even to himself, but the thought that Jake had been concealing a desperate hatred for Silverman's, and thus for the part of Sam that *is* Silverman's, had been the hardest pill to swallow. It had been so... so *wonderful*, so new, to share this work and this place that meant so much to him with Jake, to feel seen and encouraged and celebrated. To realize it must have all been a lie had cut him so close to the bone that Sam thought he would never recover, but in this new light, the wound is shallower than he thought.

A thought, clear like a bell, cuts through the noise of the deli and the whirling dervish of Sam's thoughts: *Man, you have been in love with this guy since* high school. *Are you seriously going to let one stupid magazine column ruin the rest of your life?*

"God," Sam says, "I have to talk to him."

"Are you sure?" That's Deb, who has stepped up to put a hand on his shoulder; she's giving both him and Joanie a doubtful look. "Because from where I'm sitting, this kid has messed you up one time too many."

"Oh, stop," Joanie says, flapping a hand at her. "You haven't met him, at least not as an adult; *we* all hung out with him. He's fine. He's better than Al Fiskar, that's for sure, and you were fine with *that* as a setup."

"Al, our pickle guy?!" Sam demands, briefly but entirely distracted. "Deb! He's like seventy!"

"He's... fifty-one," Deb counters, wincing slightly. "After everything, we thought you might, uh, enjoy a more mature—"

"Oh my God, Marty, tell me you know where he *is*," Sam says, turning away from this madness before it can engulf him again.

"I... do," Marty says carefully. "I do know that. But, well, what are your, uh, intentions? Because I really *wasn't* supposed to say anything, and if you're planning to, I don't know, give him an earful, then I think I'd rather not—"

"I don't want to fight with him," Sam says, low and urgent, not looking away from Marty. "At all. I won't do anything... I don't know, bad or crazy or... or anything! I just want to talk to him. I promise."

Marty hesitates, but then he sighs and says, "Ah, well. He's, uh. In the alley outside, actually. Moving out." Reaching up a hand to rub at the back of his neck, he adds, "I may or may not have promised to distract you until... let me see here... seventeen minutes from now? So he should still be back—"

But Sam's already dashing through the restaurant, ignoring the cheers that follow him.

When he gets outside, Pastrami panting and excited at his heels, Sam looks around wildly. He realizes that he is, foolishly, half expecting to see Jake just standing in the center of the alley staring back at him, and decides maybe it's for the best he takes a moment to catch his breath.

But then Jake—or, at least, a pair of legs, one arm, and the end of a be-stickered cane, which Sam assumes is Jake—*does* appear in the alley. The person these appendages belong to is mostly obscured by a tower of small, precariously balanced items, which is being carried by the arm that isn't holding the cane. That arm looks to be nearly at its limit, and Sam moves forward without so much as thinking, let alone catching his breath, as he calls, "Hey, can I help you with those?"

"God, yes, thank you," says Jake—because, on hearing his voice, Sam's assumption of his identity becomes a fact.

When Sam scoops the boxes out of his arms, revealing the face hidden behind them, Jake's smiling; the expression falls into one of horror when he realizes who he's looking at.

"Sam," he gasps, flailing to grab the boxes back and managing only to knock several to the ground; Sam hears something shatter inside one of them and winces. "Shit, I'm so sorry, you weren't supposed to have to see me or—Marty said he would—oh my God, wait, Pastrami! Stop! Don't! I can't pet you right now, it's—"

"Jake! Calm down. It's okay," Sam says. "Although, Pastrami,

Jesus, get off him. Where are your manners? He's not going to have pocket pierogies every time you see him out here! Let it go."

Pastrami, up on her back legs with her paws balanced on Jake's chest, barks happily at Sam, licks the side of Jake's face, and then settles down to sit directly next to him instead of trotting back to Sam. She could not more clearly be communicating "I'm glad to see this guy; where has he been?" and Sam feels himself flush, suddenly embarrassed.

Jake is also flushed, although there's a certain eyes-bugging-out-of-his-head quality to it that Sam suspects he, himself, lacks. "Sorry, but when you say it's okay, what do you mean, exactly? 'It's okay that you're standing here?' 'It's okay that you accidentally let me do manual labor for you when I, justifiably, hate you?' 'It's okay if you pet my dog?'" Sounding like it's shaming him slightly to do so, he adds, "It is kind of killing me *not* to pet the dog."

"Of course you can pet her," Sam says, shaking his head. "Let me just—" He turns, sets what boxes he's still holding safely down on the curb, picks up the ones that were scattered, sets those down, too, and then holds out his arms entreatingly for the small stack Jake clawed back from him. Warily, Jake hands them back, and in turning to add them to the curb Sam notices for the first time the car parked in the mouth of the alley, just a few feet away.

Sam finds himself oddly emotional at the sight of Jake's old green Jetta, many years worse for wear. It's clear it changed hands at some point, unless Jake never mentioned being incredibly into a specific sorority or the Kent State football team, but there's no doubt it's the same car Sam used to peek through his backyard fence looking for.

The trunk is open. Sam, thinking it might send the wrong impression to load anything into the car, gently shuts it, and sets the boxes down on top.

Then he takes a deep breath, turns around, and says, "I read the article."

Jake does him the courtesy of not playing dumb; his eyes, which had been starting to look a bit calmer, bug out again. He says, "How? It doesn't even come out until—" and then, darkly, "*Marty*. What else did he tell you? About how I made a fool of myself begging for his help, I bet, *and* that I'm moving in with my sister, who currently forty percent hates me, because I inadvertently destroyed her relationship! And now you feel like you have to help me, but you don't, Sam! You don't! I didn't want him to tell you because I'm not—I didn't do this to make you—to *obligate* you—"

"Jake," Sam says, quiet, calm. He smiles. "Can I talk for a minute? Please?"

Jake opens his mouth and then, looking relieved, closes it. He takes a breath. He nods.

"I read the article," Sam says again. "And I talked to Marty, and I think—what I think is—is I don't want to waste any more time. I mean, what, am I going to wait *another* thirteen years, and then bump into you at some gas station, and gear up to spend the rest of my life with you only for some insane circumstance to throw us off course again? I'm tired of *almost*, Jake. I'm tired of wanting you and not having you; I'm tired of waiting for anything else to come close. I don't want to be as old as *Al Fiskar* and staring at you from across the room at someone else's wedding, realizing I wasted whole decades just wanting! I refuse."

Jake's mouth has fallen open. He stares at Sam with it hanging like that a few beats too long, before, sounding dazed, he says, "Who the—sorry, this isn't important, but who the hell is Al Fiskar?"

"Our pickle guy," Sam says. Slightly ruefully, he adds, "Apparently, he's what the people in my life consider a fitting romantic option for me, which, I'll admit, may have helped me find my forgiving spirit."

"Did you read the *whole* article?" Jake demands, sounding almost angry now. "The part about me basically taking a *bribe*? Letting my sister's stupid fiancé trick me into tanking your review without ever setting foot inside? I'm a disgrace to the profession,

Sam! To the whole point of critics! You're not supposed to forgive me!"

Sam shrugs. "So?"

"What do you mean, so?"

"So," Sam says, taking a step closer to him, "what? I get that I'm not *supposed* to forgive you; what happens if I do anyway?" More quietly, holding Jake's gaze, he says, "It's not like I don't know how it goes. I'm sorry, for what that's worth. It sounds like it's been... hard." He pauses, and adds, "Wait, what do you mean your sister's fiancé—"

Jake's face screws up in irritation, and he practically spits. "*Brian*. Full name Brian Matthewson; might ring a bell?"

"Wait," Sam says. "Like the Matthewson Restaurant Group? The place that keeps trying to convince us to sell the building?"

"That's the one." Jake runs a hand through his hair; Sam's not sure if the disgust on his face is for Brian or himself. "Not that it's any excuse, but he's the one who told me Silverman's was infested with rats and roaches. He also brought me some truly nasty takeout that I think, now, must have been from somewhere else? And he had four different people text me their food poisoning stories. That was convincing, until I did some digging and realized they all worked for him." Scowling, Jake adds, "That makes me sound like I deserve credit for researching things—I *really* don't. I didn't work it out until I saw the letter from his firm at your place that last morning."

"Shit," Sam says, his heart clenching as he realizes just how awful these last few months must have been for Jake. "I'm sorry, man. To use you that way—I mean, I wouldn't be able to civil with someone after something like that. I kind of want to find this guy and yell at him on your behalf. It sucks that your sister's marrying him; bound to make family holidays kind of awkward."

"Oh, she's not." Jake's smile looks more like a grimace. "I told her about it, and she got really mad and called him. And she said, 'Brian, how could you do something so sneaky and underhanded?' and he said, 'Calm down, Lila, it was just the one time and only second base, I swear,' so. Wedding's off." Jake takes a breath, and then, before Sam can reply, adds, "Also, are you *insane*? You should want to yell at Brian on your own behalf! You should want to yell at *me* on your own behalf—"

"But I don't." Sam shrugs, and adds, with a wince, "Given all the givens, I wish I could undo the yelling I already did, or at least redistribute it where it belongs."

"You're serious," Jake says after a beat. "You read the article, and you—you know what I did, and you're—it's just—okay? Just like that?"

"I mean," Sam says, with a small smile, a little shrug, "maybe try to curb the urge to give me star ratings on anything for a while? Unless it's five stars, obviously. In that case, I want it in writing."

Jake's mouth compresses in a thin line; then a small sound escapes him; a second later, clearly against his will, he's cackling, one hand pressed against his mouth to hold the sound in. He reels forward—Sam meets him, catches him—Jake puts his head down against Sam's shoulder and laughs so hard he might as well be crying.

Surprise, relief, joy; whatever it is, it takes Jake a few minutes to calm down. Sam spends those minutes thinking, rather blissfully, of nothing beyond how good it feels to share space with Jake again after all these weeks apart. Maybe it's down to the ways they grew up together, or maybe Sam's going to have to radically readjust his personal belief system towards a concept like soul mates, but even his body feels comfortable with Jake's in a way it never has with anyone else's.

That's probably why, when Jake's finally caught his breath, Sam realizes he's wrapped Jake up in his arms without even noticing he was doing so. Jake seems to be suffering from a similar lack of self-awareness, because he has twined himself tightly into Sam's grip, both hands fisted in the back of Sam's T-shirt. Sam moves back the barest fraction of an inch and then they're kissing, and then...

...well, if he's honest, then Sam loses track of things for a bit.

They kiss for a long time, he knows that; he knows there's a heat to it, a hunger, that's somehow deeper and richer than it was the last time they did this. That was only a few weeks ago, but Sam feels like he's a different person now than he was then; a different person than he was at seventeen; a different person than he was at sixteen, the day Jake's well of personal gravity drew Sam down from the light booth. And Jake—God, Sam thinks he could kiss Jake every day for the rest of his life and find under his lips, every time, both a completely different person and exactly the same one.

It's a good kiss, that's the point, and things are right on the edge of becoming indecent when Sam becomes aware of the hollering.

He ignores it, at first. What could it possibly matter? It doesn't sound like anyone's in agony—Sam didn't hear anything explode—they're all excited about something, whoever they are. Good for them. Honestly, it's probably just the staff—

—who all watched him run out here after reading the article—

"Oh, God," Sam says, pulling away just enough to let the words out and slightly afraid to open his eyes. He's remembered, too late, that the spot where he and Jake are standing is just below the large window that sits against the far wall of the deli's kitchen. The window starts at a height of roughly Sam's shoulders, which means: "Here's a horrible question for you: Is, uh…"

"Is the entire staff of Silverman's," Jake says faintly, "including a woman who I assume to be your aunt, staring at us through the kitchen window? *Yes*, Sam. Yes they are."

"Didn't really need to ask, I guess," Sam mutters, laughing on it slightly. "It's not like I can't tell that's Eileen saying we should get a room." The word "room" reminds him, and, his eyes slamming open, he adds, "Hey, oh my God, don't *move out of your apartment*; is it too late? For you not to move? I mean, I guess probably it must be, right? Hell."

"Uh," Jake says, flushing. "I mean, no, because I didn't want to break my lease and I couldn't afford to get another place and Marty felt *really* bad, so. I was just going to leave all my furniture here and sleep at my sister's, honestly. We were going to crash out together, but I bet she'd be relieved to change that plan. And Marty's been begging me not to go anyway, so. I think he'll be chill." Glancing at the window full of onlookers, which Sam has not yet been able to bring himself to face, he adds, "I'd say we could just go back to mine, but I wouldn't call the condition it's in right now... good. Currently, it's more a series of trip hazards than an apartment."

"And accessing my apartment requires entering the deli, which I may never be able to do again." Deciding he has to face the music, Sam gives Jake one last swift kiss before he breaks away and turns around to look toward the window.

Sam was expecting to be mortified, but instead he's oddly touched by the row of smiling faces, family whether by blood or bond. Ever since he was young, he's thought of himself as a loner, the sort of soul doomed to singularity, but looking up at all these people so clearly happy for him, it's hard to hold onto the lie. Sam's made mistakes; he's had to figure things out on his own—he's been alone, time and again, of that there's no doubt. But that doesn't have to mean alone is how he's supposed to be. Like anyone else, all he really needed was the right people.

"I'm taking the afternoon off!" Sam calls up to his crew, to another round of cheers. "But call me if you need anything, and if someone can come down and grab the dog—"

"Yeah, yeah, kid, I'll keep an eye on the place and the mutt," Deb says, rolling her eyes. "Have some fun for once in your life."

"Go already, you idiots!" Eileen snaps, and Sam beams up at her, at all of them, before he takes Jake's hand and starts leading him towards the mouth of the alley.

"Wait!" Joanie sticks her head out of the back door, and flaps a hand at Sam when, wearily, he opens his mouth. "I know, I know, I'm not supposed to use this door, but first of all—Pastrami! Get in here!" She waits while Pastrami streaks inside, waving off Sam's grateful nod with a hand. Then, lowering her voice, although not enough not to be perfectly audible, she says, "Jake. You know Marty pretty well, right? So—while you're here and everything—is he a *nice* guy, do you think? I just want to get a sense of him."

Out of Joanie's range of vision, Sam shakes his head violently; he sees Jake's glance flick, amused, to the window above, where Deb is doing the same.

"He's a perfect bastard, since you ask," Jake says with remarkable conviction, "and you should absolutely avoid dating him at all costs."

"Thank you *very* much," Joanie says, beaming like she'll never stop, "that's all, have fun," and she vanishes back into the deli.

Sam, shaking his head, resumes walking. "They'll keep watching until we go away," he explains, not that Jake seems to be putting up any resistance to being led. "Can you leave your car here for a minute?"

"For another hour at least," Jake says, sounding a little breathless. "But Jesus, I mean, I thought they'd all hate me! I thought *you* would hate me! Forever! I thought—"

Sam shrugs, still walking. He hasn't let go of Jake's hand. "People make mistakes, you know? They get that. God knows they've made plenty; God knows I have. Anyway, come on. I want to show you something."

They walk in easy silence, holding hands, up the two blocks of East Ninth Street that stand between the deli and looking Lake Erie in the eye. The road doesn't take them all the way to the shores; it dead-ends at the top of an incline, at the bottom of which sits industrial warehouses, machinery, and the shallowest of the Great Lakes.

Sam's pleased, as they approach it, to find luck is on his side. Below them, as he hoped it would, the longest, ugliest rooftop of the longest, ugliest warehouse appears, in spite of being gray, almost white.

"They're seagulls," Sam explains, his voice low, when they've stopped. "They all gather here during the day, and then, if you catch them at the right moment, or something makes a loud enough—"

He's interrupted by a resonant boom below them, a sound like a forklift hitting a pole. It's enough. The entire rooftop of birds takes flight at once, painting the whole sky briefly in dazzling, dizzying white.

"They do that," Sam says, satisfied, as Jake gapes up at them.

"Holy shit," Jake breathes. "It's... beautiful."

Sam agrees, although he's not looking at the birds. He's looking at Jake, all the versions of Jake he's known and loved, the one he lost, the one he found again. He has no idea what's going to happen from here, but for once in his life, he's glad not to know. Deb was right. It's about time he had some fun.

As if hearing this thought, Jake's eyes slide to his, wide and still slightly disbelieving. Laughing on it a little, he says, "So, uh. Since we're not going to go through with the traditional thirteen years of radio silence... what happens now?"

Sam smiles, and then he laughs, and then he shrugs. "Honestly, I don't have the faintest idea. I was hoping maybe we could figure it out together?"

Jake's answering smile is better than any natural wonder. "Deal."

EPILOGUE

A FEW YEARS LATER...

Sam had been disappointed the first time he visited the Arcade as a child, a fact that he chalks up to the name. He had been expecting a low-ceilinged room full of Skee-Ball and video games, not a long, multi-story indoor shopping center with enormous, vaulted windows where there would, typically, be a roof. If it had been called "The Big Bright Hallway" or, indeed, "A Place Where You Will Be Allowed to Run Around Freely While Your Parents Study in the Tiny Food Court," he might have taken to it more immediately.

Even so, after only a few minutes, his sense of loss wore off, and from that point on it had been one of Sam's favorite childhood places. He'd spent hours exploring it, popping in and out of various shops, getting to know the owners—often elderly, at least back then, and settled in their old family businesses. Deb used to take him sometimes, too, the deli being only a few blocks away, and talk shop with the owners in the way only two proprietors of an old family business can.

It's almost a shame, Sam thinks, that the place is closed today for the wedding, for all the decorations have made it sparkle and shine. He'd like to have some of those conversations for himself, now that he, too, has earned a place in those highly selective ranks. He resolves to come back another day and, setting down a stack of covered hotel pans, reaches up to straighten his bow tie—

"Stop!" Jake lets this bellow out like a war cry, descending on Sam as if from nowhere and gripping each of his wrists in one hand. "Don't *touch* that, Sam, oh my God!"

Sam, used to this sort of thing by now, raises an eyebrow. "Is there a bomb wired to it, then? Or was it just soaked in deadly neurotoxins?"

"*You*," Jake says, looking accusingly from one of Sam's hands to the other, "are soaked in deadly *fabric* toxins, actually." This, while dramatic, is not exactly untrue. Sam looks down and winces to see that his hands are indeed lightly coated with oil, which must have dripped down the side of one of the pans he was carrying. "Have a heart. Think of the—well, I guess there isn't any way to make 'think of the children' apply to fabric, is there? Think of the *smaller fibers*, Sam!" Making his eyes round, he adds, "Think of how *sad* everyone will be if this wedding is *ruined* by a well-oiled bow tie—"

"I really don't think anyone would notice or care," Sam argues, although he doesn't resist, just smiles, as Jake grabs a kitchen towel off the nearest counter and begins wiping Sam's hands clean. "Especially not at this wedding. I mean, remember that pool party last summer? This is basically the same guest list, and I can't imagine there was anyone there who didn't see today's bride and groom—"

"La la la," Jake says loudly, "I'm not listening; I'm not remembering that! I saw nothing!" Fixing Sam with a stern look, he adds, "It's our duty as Joanie's best men to have seen nothing. And it's your duty as my boyfriend to support me in my delusions."

Sam grins. "That doesn't seem right."

"So long as they are within reason and for the overall health and sanity of all," Jake finishes smoothly, setting the cloth down and releasing Sam's hands. "Which, I promise you, this is. My brain is feeble and riddled with holes and will collapse under the weight of those memories; they're too horrible. No one saw anything and nothing happened! We can all agree!"

"All right," Sam says, amused, and puts a hand on Jake's back. "We can all agree." He looks Jake up and down, taking in the perfectly tailored fit of his tuxedo, which, despite complaining for weeks about having to wear a "penguin suit," he looks much better in than Sam does. Speculatively, he says, "How much time do we have before the ceremony? I should really be letting the staff do this anyway."

"Something I've said ten times already this morning."

"I mean, I *am* in the wedding, and it *would* be stupid to mess up my clothes." Sam affects his most innocent expression.

Jake meets it with a roll of his eyes. "Again, I think I was probably saying that in my sleep last night, but sure."

"And so if we have an extra twenty minutes, we could—"

"Not that I don't appreciate the spirit of that offer," Jake says, his grin a sudden, sharp slash across his face, "and not that I don't *very* much intend to take you up on it later, but: We don't have twenty minutes, Sam. We have six."

"Six?!" Woebegone, Sam tries and, for obvious reasons, fails to look down at his own bow tie. "God, I was going to try to fix it properly before the ceremony; I'll *never* manage it in six minutes."

"Oh, here," Jake says. He rolls his eyes, but fondly, as he reaches up, undoes Sam's tie in one quick movement, and begins re-tying it from scratch. "You could have just asked me, you know. I'm practically a professional bow-tiest."

"Is that a profession?"

"Obviously should be," Jake says. He's standing, Sam is pleased to note, rather closer than he thinks is entirely necessary for securing the tie in place, his arms against Sam's chest. "You're proving there's a market for it literally right now."

Sam opens his mouth to say something frankly filthy about what he's *really* in the market for just at this moment, but he's interrupted by Deb approaching them at speed. In a purple dress and spiky heels, she somehow looks more terrifying than she does in her usual ensemble these days, which typically involves at least one frightening gardening tool hooked to her person. Jake steps back, not seeing her, and pats Sam twice on the chest as if pleased with his own work, only for his face to fall in comic shock when Deb grabs him by a sleeve and starts dragging him away, barking, "You too, Sammy!" over her shoulder.

"Do you think," Jake says, his cane thumping ringingly against the floor in a way Sam's almost certain is done on purpose and to make a point, "maybe the wedding planning has gone to your head, Deb? Just a bit?"

"I think I told you two to leave the catering to *your staff*," Deb says, glaring at Sam, "and to meet us up front *fifteen minutes ago*," but she does, at least, let go of Jake and slow down to a strolling pace.

"They're not *my* staff," Jake says, too innocent, while Sam makes an apologetic face at Deb, who shakes her head, looking more amused than angry. "I'm in an entirely different business! Just because that business happens to have offices upstairs—"

"Oh, save it," Deb says with a laugh. "I have a dozen friends I want to introduce to you tonight; you can do the pitch for them. I've heard it, frankly, enough for one lifetime. Do an old woman a kindness in her twilight years—"

"You're sixty-one." Sam rolls his eyes, more entertained than he wants to let on. Deb and Jake's half-joking argumentative vibe isn't the sort of thing he wants to encourage, even if he does find it funny, and think they both must be getting something out of it. "So I think 'twilight years' is pushing it."

"This doesn't concern you, kid." Deb says this breezily, even though this conversation started with an argument about the Silverman's staff, and, as such, technically *only* concerns Sam, of the three of them. Deb might still pop in occasionally with her EMERITUS PROPRIETOR nametag on, but she'd realized quickly that retirement bored her, and so most of the time, these days, she's either running her farmstand on the west side of town or off on a dig site somewhere with Talya.

And Jake, of course, doesn't work for Silverman's at all. It's true enough that they turned the old apartment above the deli into an office after Jake insisted, as a condition of moving in with Sam, that they find a place that would allow Sam to develop even an iota of work-life balance. The location of his office does, certainly, mean that Jake is *at* Silverman's much of the time, often drifting downstairs with his laptop or to take a lunch meeting in the dining room. And yes, if pressed, they would both have to admit that Jake does still make a number of the social posts, and regularly discusses strategy with Sam, and sometimes jumps in to help at the counter if they're really in the weeds.

But Jake's real job, the one he turns out to be so good at that Sam's fairly certain it was his true calling all along, is teaching dance, and guiding young dancers looking to work in the space. He's basically taken over for Madame Louisa at the dance studio and will be stepping up into her role officially when she retires in the fall, but the offices above Silverman's aren't for teaching. Up there, Jake holds career counseling sessions for older students, and seminars about boundary setting and healthy versus unhealthy standards in the professional dance world, and stage-safety clinics so comprehensive he's started to get bookings with local theater programs and school districts. He also offers free sessions for dancers experiencing what he calls path-altering events—changes, whether through accident or illness or injury or mental health issues or whatever else, that affect a dancer's ability to perform. Sam's pretty sure that's Jake's favorite part of his job; certainly, it's the part that connects the most with others and has driven a large following on professional social media channels. His numbers rival Walt's these days, but for doing something good, not ghoulish. Sam knows Jake takes a slightly petty kind of pleasure in that, but he, himself, thinks it's kind of beautiful.

Regardless, what started for Jake as a one-man career-consulting firm that he largely set up as a side gig is now a three-person team—four, if you count Pastrami, who moonlights there using her training as a therapy dog. One of those people is Iris, who, to everyone's surprise, is quite good at it. If he'd had to guess, Sam would have said the whole thing was more in Daisy's line, or at least Luce's, since the two of them are generally better with people than Iris. But Daisy has been working in public relations for the mayor's office since shortly after graduation and seems happy, and Luce's art career has taken off to such a degree that she's in New York most of the year anyway. Regardless, Jake says Iris is good at the work, handling career counseling for students who conclude that they don't have the inclination or skill to try to make dance their profession. Apparently, her brand of blunt clarity and sarcasm really speaks to your average teenager, and she's also a lot better than Jake is at telling people no, which Sam can tell Jake deeply appreciates.

Sam could point all this out, but it would take a while, and he doesn't get the chance anyway. They reach their destination, an anteroom where the entire wedding party has gathered, and their little traveling group is broken apart immediately by greetings and instructions. Everyone is positioned and staged for a variety of photos and then chivvied off to their respective spots for the ceremony.

It is, Sam has to say, a *lovely* ceremony. Joanie is radiant and ecstatic in her flowing champagne-colored dress, and Marty looks even happier than he did the day Sam told him the Pastrami Arnold was going to stay on the menu for good. (This isn't a metric Sam would normally compare against someone's actual wedding, but Marty did say, at the time, that it was the best day of his life.) Their vows are short and sweet and heartfelt and slightly dirty, and when Joanie says, "I promise to love you when things are easy, and even more when they're not," Jake reaches back and grabs Sam's hand, squeezes hard, doesn't let go.

That's the first moment which almost makes Sam cry; the second is when he pauses, as Joanie and Marty walk beamingly down the aisle, and glances over the assembled guests. Luce and Joey in the front row, off again as far as Sam knows but looking like they might be on again by the end of the night. Iris and Daisy next to them, still identical but with very different styles these days. Talya beaming and dabbing her eyes; Eileen, freshly retired, and her boyfriend, who is perfectly lovely so long as you don't ask him anything about his years running a professional clown school. Alphonse and the rest of the full-time Silverman's staff, some of whom are working the event but all of whom Joanie insisted be in attendance to see her tie the knot. His parents and Jake's, sitting together in the back row, having made amends with each other after a series of peace-summit dinners that were, at least on Sam's end, a lot easier to both face and manage with Jake sitting beside him.

With a lump in his throat, he realizes that if he and Jake get married, a number of the people in this room will be in that one. It's a nice thought, heartwarming, even if it does make Sam blink hard against the threat of tears before they can actually fall.

Jake must be thinking it, too; the two of them have talked a little, just recently, about the idea of next steps and taking the plunge. They're both in favor as far as Sam can tell, but it's a new discussion still, and a bit awkward. He doesn't want to say anything that will tip things in the wrong direction or put pressure on the situation, but he smiles, relieved, when, as they're dancing together a few hours later, Jake says, "Listen, Sam, I'm sorry, but I have to say it: When we get married—"

"*When?*" Sam says, delighted. When Jake flushes, having clearly said more than he meant to, Sam takes pity, and downshifts into a joke: "If this is you proposing right now, you're being very subtle about it."

"I'm not proposing," Jake says, rolling his eyes but not totally able to suppress his smile. "I'm just saying—when, if, whatever. It doesn't matter for the purposes of this conversation: I just need you to promise me something."

"That is, to my understanding, what people do at weddings,"

Sam says mildly, and then, when Jake glares at him, laughs. "Okay, okay! What am I promising?"

Jake straightens a little in Sam's arms and clears his throat officiously. "On the date, should it occur, of our hypothetical nuptials, I need to *know*, okay, that you are not going to say anything—anything at all!—about the Kiss of Death review. It's not that I don't understand the importance of the review to our story, it's just that I believe there are *some* times in life that it's better not to say the words "Kiss of Death." That's a phrase that has no business being in a wedding vow, Samuel! It's like a sacrifice laid upon the altar of divorce!"

"Hmm," Sam says, considering. "It's not that I don't see your point, and I'm definitely not looking to lay anything upon the altar of divorce, but I'm just not sure I can commit to that at this juncture. Avoiding the phrase, yes, that's fine. Avoiding the review entirely? I don't know."

Jake pulls a face of comical despair. "*Really?* You can't, in the event of our hypothetical wedding, see your way to not bringing up my horrifying mess of a—"

"No," Sam interrupts, and catches Jake's gaze. "I can't, because I'm *glad* you wrote that review, Jake. I'm glad. We wouldn't be here if you hadn't, and I, for one, wouldn't be anywhere else."

"Oh," Jake says in a small voice, and smiles. "Well, I mean—me neither, obviously." Flushing slightly, but looking desperately pleased about it, he adds, "Thanks."

"Sure." Sam leans down and kisses him, letting his lips linger long enough to serve as a promise of what's to come later tonight. When he pulls away, he layers on the earnestness as thick as he can and says, "Although, after today's touching events, you might be able to convince me that I should write vows in the style of Joanie and Marty's toasts at dinner. Those really moved me. In fact, here's a first draft: 'Baby, you're the love of my life and I never want to be without you! But for some godforsaken reason, there's only one way I feel able to express that emotion, so everybody buckle up for my best rendition of a Creed song that's totally inappropriate for the situation, the lyrics to which I have *definitely* misunderstood. We've locked the doors and there's no escape—'"

Jake's laughter is loud and long, and he shakes his head, still beaming, as he calms down and looks up at Sam. "You know what, I might have some notes," he admits. "But we've got plenty of time to work something out."

A LETTER FROM THE AUTHOR

Dear reader,

Huge thanks for reading *Second Helpings*! I hope you enjoyed watching Sam and Jake face their pasts and find their future. If you'd like to join other readers in hearing all about my new releases and bonus content, you can summon those updates directly to your inbox:

www.stormpublishing.co/dylan-morrison

If you enjoyed this book and could spare a few moments to leave a review, that would be hugely appreciated. Even a short review can make all the difference in encouraging a reader to discover my books for the first time. Thank you so much!

I love stories about second chances, people who meet again after years spent apart. They fascinate me, because the nature of growth and change fascinates me—the way it's often incremental from within but monumental when seen from without. I think they capture something strange and cool about the human experience: To live a full life is to make a series of beautiful, complicated, intricate mistakes, and to find they've put you on unexpected paths that lead to surprising places. I wish you all the best in making yours.

Thanks again for being part of this amazing journey with me and I hope you'll stay in touch—I have so many more stories and ideas to entertain you with!

Dylan

KEEP IN TOUCH WITH THE AUTHOR

www.dylanmorrison.net

instagram.com/dylanthyme
facebook.com/dylanjstrand
tiktok.com/@dylanthyme
x.com/dylan_thyme
linkedin.com/in/dylan-strand-92aa43219

ACKNOWLEDGEMENTS

The last year of my life has been a wild one. As I sit here typing at the tail end of 2025, I'm not sure there's any arena left where things remain as they were when it started. The changes are almost entirely for the better, but they've still been complicated, difficult, sometimes exhausting. And because the nature of change is that it changes you, I find myself before you in one of those strange liminal spaces of self: not quite the person I'm becoming but not quite who I was before, either.

Writing acknowledgements from such a place is an interesting challenge. There are so many people I want to mention, people who have aided and guided and shaped me, but pinning down that gratitude in words while said shape is actively changing is... harder than I would have thought. So I'm going to keep it simple, and quickly thank those people whose impact on my life runs deeper than any internal shift could obscure: Hannah Bond, whose support, kindness, brilliance, and willingness to listen to me ramble improves my life every day; my family, whose warmth, generosity, and humor buoy me through a harsh world; my friends, who never stop teaching, amusing, and surprising me; Kathryn Taussig and the team at Storm, who make it possible for me get these stories into the hands of people who enjoy reading them; and, last but far from least, said readers, who have been so lovely and generous about my work, and who I hope to continue to entertain in the years to come.

In wineries, back in the days before modern air filtration systems were invented, fermenting grapes would cause dangerous levels of CO_2 to accumulate. To prevent staff asphyxiation, the buildings were designed with air currents in mind, constructed so that a single opened window could sweep fresh, clean air through the entire space. For many years of my life, and for a variety of reasons both in and out of my control, the noxious fumes of anxiety, self-loathing, and imposter syndrome grew so thick within me that I could barely breathe. The people above were kind enough to throw open my windows, and I will be forever grateful.

Finally: This is a book that is at least in part about being a teenager in a suburb of Cleveland, Ohio. As someone who was himself once such a teenager, I would be remiss if I didn't take this opportunity to thank a man I've never met, one who has sadly died and will never read this, but who nevertheless looms large over my own experience of adolescence. Sir Terry Pratchett's Discworld novels, introduced to me by the incomparable Anastasia Frank when we were both roughly twelve years old, taught me more about writing, human nature, belief, integrity, and the kind of person I wanted to become than, I am sorry to say, all of the reading I was actually assigned in school combined. This isn't a knock on that curriculum so much as it is a nod to Pratchett's absurdly deep well of talent, not to mention his profound wisdom. I am so sorry that I never got the chance to meet him, and so grateful to have walked a few decades in world where he walked, too. GNU Terry Pratchett. Thank you for your work, which came into my life when I sorely needed it and made me a far better person than I would have been otherwise.